ON POTATO MOUNTAIN

On Potato Mountain

A Chilcotin Mystery

Bruce Fraser

GRANVILLE ISLAND
PUBLISHING

Editors: David Stephens, Melva McLean
Copy Editors: Adriana Van Leeuwen, Neall Calvert
Cover and Text Designer: Jamie Fischer
Cover Painting: "The Raven" by Cori Creed
Chilcotin Map: Jamie Fischer
Author Photograph: David Hay

First printing 2010
Printed in Canada on recycled paper

Library and Archives Canada Cataloguing in Publication

Fraser, Bruce, 1937-
On Potato Mountain : a Chilcotin mystery / Bruce Fraser.

ISBN 978-1-894694-82-7

I. Title.
PS8611.R366O66 2010 C813'.6 C2010-905117-3

01 02 03 04 05 06 15 14 13 12 11 10

Granville Island Publishing
212 – 1656 Duranleau
Vancouver, BC, Canada V6H 3S4
Tel: (604) 688-0320 Toll free: 1-877-688-0320
www.GranvilleIslandPublishing.com

To Gail

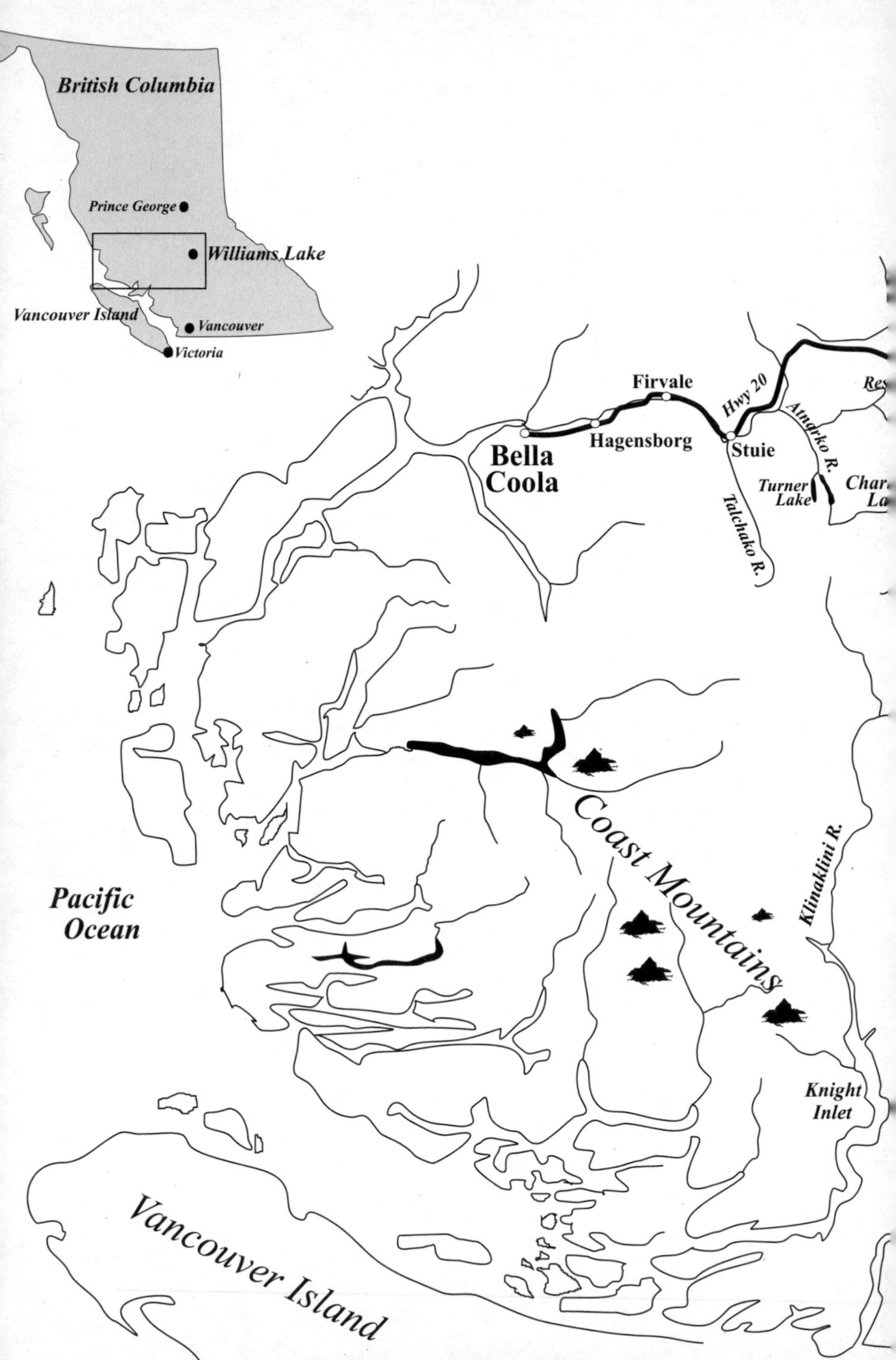

British Columbia
Prince George
Williams Lake
Vancouver Island
Vancouver
Victoria
Firvale
Hwy 20
Bella Coola
Hagensborg
Stuie
Atnarko R.
Turner Lake
Talchako R.
Coast Mountains
Klinaklini R.
Pacific Ocean
Knight Inlet
Vancouver Island

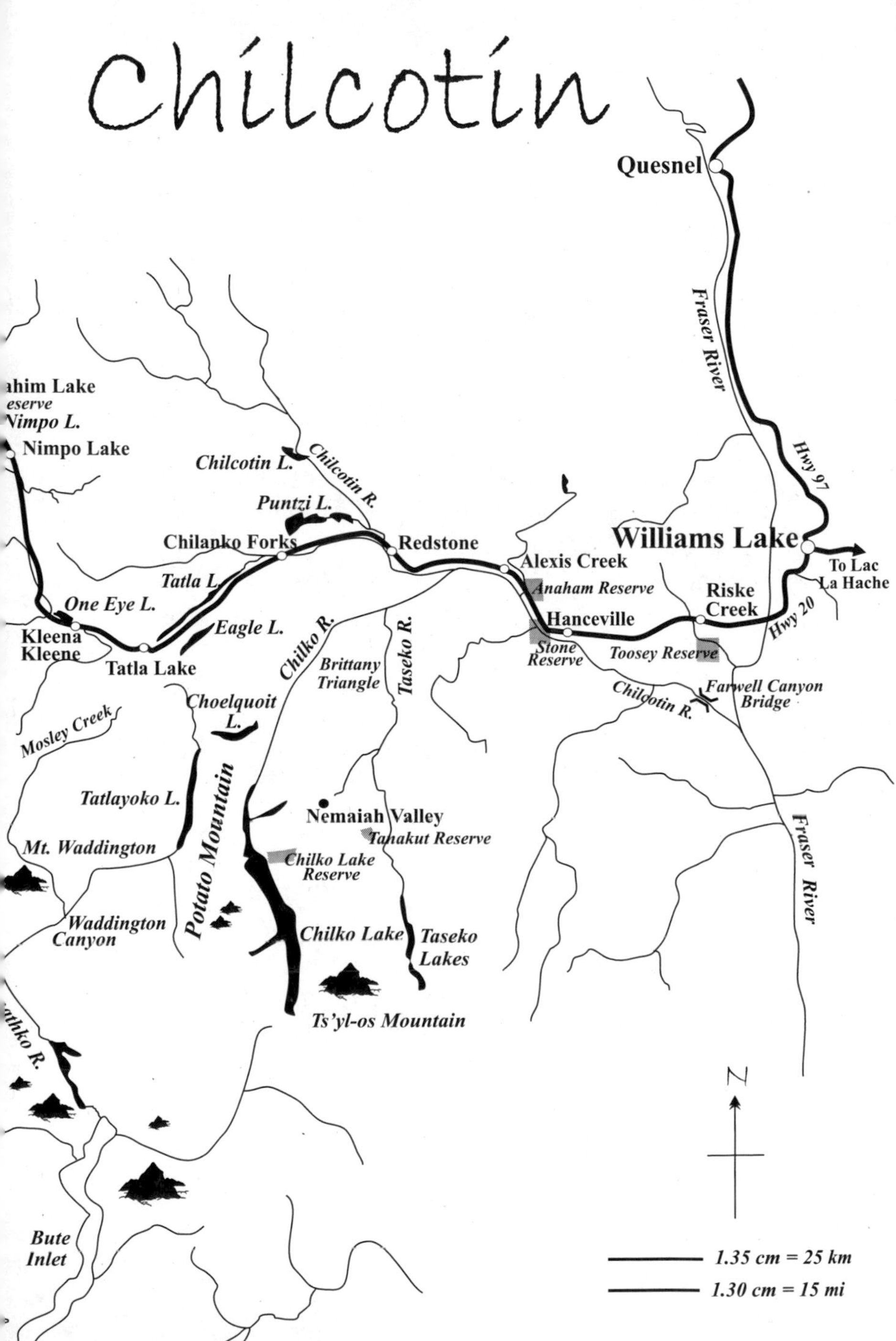
Chilcotin
Quesnel
Fraser River
Hwy 97
Williams Lake
To Lac La Hache
Riske Creek
Hwy 20
ahim Lake
eserve
Nimpo L.
Nimpo Lake
Chilcotin L.
Chilcotin R.
Puntzi L.
Chilanko Forks
Redstone
Alexis Creek
Anaham Reserve
Hanceville
Stone Reserve
Toosey Reserve
Tatla L.
One Eye L.
Eagle L.
Kleena Kleene
Tatla Lake
Chilko R.
Taseko R.
Brittany Triangle
Chilcotin R.
Farwell Canyon Bridge
Choelquoit L.
Mosley Creek
Tatlayoko L.
Potato Mountain
Nemaiah Valley
Tanakut Reserve
Mt. Waddington
Chilko Lake Reserve
Waddington Canyon
Chilko Lake
Taseko Lakes
Ts'yl-os Mountain
Fraser River
athko R.
N
Bute Inlet
1.35 cm = 25 km
1.30 cm = 15 mi

ACKNOWLEDGEMENTS

Special thanks to my daughter, Rebecca Fraser, and to all my constant readers: Nancy and David Hay, Wendy Muhic, Peter Granger, Sarah McAlpine, John McAlpine QC, David Roberts QC, Jennifer Fraser, Jeff Lowe, my son, Lauchlan Fraser, Julia Wells, Allie Drake, and my five fellow philosophers.

CONTENTS

PART 1

There is a tribe of Dene among them, who inhabit the banks of a large river which flows to the right; they call themselves Chilk-odins.

Simon Fraser's Journal, June 1, 1808

CHILCOTIN

The word *Chilcotin* defines the river, the land, and its people. The land, a high plateau, has broad valleys covered in tall grass and aspen groves. At higher elevations are pine, spruce, and fir forests. Crowning the plateau on its south and west flanks are the coastal mountain ranges. Protected and cradled by this stony barrier, the spring-green and autumn-gold grassy hills unfold, undulating two hundred miles all the way to the eastern boundary, the brown silt-laden Fraser River. The Chilcotin, one of the Fraser River's major tributaries, nourishes the plateau. Born in the coastal mountains and fed by a vast lake system, it enters the Fraser River from the west midway between the Rocky Mountains and the sea. Frozen for six months of the year, the Chilcotin wakes from its winter spell, then rushes to complete its annual life cycle in its allotted time. The land is the anvil on which nature's blows shape the souls of the people, captivated by its harsh charms, who choose to live their lives in its unremitting grasp.

The Fraser River's headwaters are the Rocky Mountains. Fed by melting snow and glaciers, the waterway heads northwest before turning at Prince George and then cutting a trench southward halfway between the Rocky Mountains and the Coast Range. It gathers strength from its tributaries until its surging waters break through the mountains at Hell's Gate—farther south of the Chilcotin—and eventually empty into the Strait of Georgia near Vancouver.

Long before recorded time, the first people—Dene, an Athapascan tribe—migrated from the north, but not before the land was made habitable by their mythical hero, *Lendix'tcux*. The savage story of how Lendix'tcux transformed the beasts into animals, birds, and fish—thereby preparing the land for the Dene—was passed down from generation to generation. It was imbedded in the memory of old Antoine, a shaman—or in their language, a *deyen*—by his grandfather.

The people who settled on the plateau called themselves Tsihlqot'in, and their river and their land was named Tsihlqot'in. To the people of the blue Chilko River, all that they walked on and paddled over was sacred. Antoine spoke of his ancestors' life on the land to all who would listen:

> *Before my time, before Reserves, our people survive on the land and waters. In summers, Tsihlqot'in fish salmon returning from sea to spawn in the streams and lakes: Chilko, Taseko, and Puntzi. They hunt deer, moose, and the caribou; pick sour berries and dig succulent roots on Potato Mountain. They travel in bands of big families*

throughout land depending on season and chance of fish and game. They live well when the salmon come up Great River from the sea. In the years salmon fail, people they starve. In the winters when land freeze, Tsihlqot'in survive in pit house on small game, dried salmon, and wild potatoes.

Beside fishing, hunting, and gathering, our people speak with same tongue, have same stories and customs, and defend our land. They beat off raids by other tribes and attack neighbours. On shadow side, where no mountains or big rivers, Carrier—another Dene tribe—speak with different tongue and have different customs and stories. Towards rising sun and Great River Plateau are Shuswap, and over mountains in midday sun Lillooet, neighbours of Salish coastal cousins at mouth of the Great River.

Yes. Two rivers flow from our land to the setting sun and coast. One slices through mountains at Waddington Canyon. It carved from rock by churning Homathko. Other past Anahim is swift Arnarko to Bella Coola. Tsihlqot'in trade with coast Natives of Bella Coola and Homathko. At times when winters on plateau too raw, number of bands and hunting parties move into coast valleys. Qiyus—*you call them horses—come to Tsihlqot'in even before white man. Raiding party go to Nicola and steal 'em. Qiyus better than canoe, faster than dog.*

Grandfather tell me first time Tsihlqot'in seen white man. He says to me, "As boy, I camp with family at mouth of Chilcotin River where meets Great River. I seen white man in canoes pass by on way to coast."

That was in June 1808, when Simon Fraser—a Hudson's Bay Company fur trader and explorer—discovered and named the Great River "the Fraser" on his journey south down it to the sea. Antoine's grandfather's stories of the beginning, of how the land was transformed by their mythical hero Lendix'tcux and his wife and sons, and how those Heroes were in turn transformed into mountains were as important to Antoine as the land itself. Life on the plateau was interwoven with the stories as closely as the berry-picking baskets fashioned by the women from plaited cedar roots. Antoine's duty was to pass on these stories to the following generations of Chilcotins. His grandfather's mythical stories were supplemented by the oral history his father told him of the Chilcotin Wars of 1864, and of how the whites said they were transforming the land, custom, and law for the benefit of the Chilcotins, but in the end introduced their form of justice, disease, and abuse of the land instead.

BORDY

It was July in the record-hot summer of 1937. The crowd at the Anahim Lake stampede grounds was betting that Dean Hanlon couldn't stay on Tornado, a black bronco that was red of eye and mean of spirit. Dean's son, Bordy, was minding the gate for his father, and in the stands whites and Natives from the full reach of the Plateau watched Dean adjust his stirrups, settle on the horse, and grip and re-grip his leathered right hand under the rope around the horse's withers. The bronco pawed and fidgeted in the chute, testing its muscle, anxious to buck the annoyance from its back.

In the ring, Antoine stood next to the fence, waiting for his boss to charge out of the chute. Stan Hewitt, in the stands near the chutes, sipped on a mickey of Walker's Special Old and thought that his client, who owned a good part of the Tatlayoko Valley, shouldn't be risking his neck riding broncos when there were pressing legal matters to deal with; matters that had brought Stan to the far corner of the Chilcotin from his law office in Williams Lake.

In this country where men were judged by how they handled horses or were handled by them, it meant something to wear the champion's silver buckle. Between father and son, who competed against each other in everything, it meant bragging rights for the next year. Now they were going at it like always.

Bordy laughed at his old man. "Careful, Dean! He has a double-kick that'll knock the breath out of your miserable hide."

A rodeo veteran, Dean spat chaw juice on the ground trampled by the bronco's hooves and snarled at Bordy. "This horse is going to win me the title. Just mind the gate and keep your trap shut!"

When Dean was ready, he signalled the timekeeper with his left hand. The bell rang. The gate swung open. Tornado sprang out of the chute. Dean's head was thrown back as he shouted to Bordy, "I'll beat you this time, you son of a bitch!"

Tornado crow-hopped across the ring, shaking the cowboy with each jackhammer jump. Dean dug his spurs into the horse's flanks and batted it on its head with his Stetson. Tornado's next move was the double-kick, but Dean came out on top. Again the bronco tried the double-kick, and again the veteran rider bested the animal. But Tornado was just warming up for his signature move, a fast clockwise spin that made even the judges feel dizzy, but still Dean Hanlon hung on. No rider had lasted this long on the bronco, and the crowd knew it. They shouted their encouragement; everyone except Bordy, who was cheering for the horse. If Dean could hang on until the bell,

Bordy would lose, and Bordy could tell by the set of Dean's jaw that no horse would unseat him today.

The mounted pickup man moved closer as the seconds wound down. When the bell sounded to end the ride, he moved in and wrapped his free arm around Dean's waist and hauled him off the horse. But Dean made no attempt to grab onto the pickup's saddle, as would be expected. Tornado had a few more kicks left, and as he bucked riderless, Dean's dead weight slipped from the pickup's grasp and slowly slid to the ground. Stan, who had had too many sips from his mickey, rose unsteadily from his seat. Bordy and Antoine ran into the ring and knelt beside Dean. They both heard Dean's last words to his only son—"Don't piss away the ranch"—as the judges' decision crackled over the loudspeaker:

"The winner and grand champion of the Bucking Bronco contest is Dean Hanlon!"

Antoine shook his head, unknotted the red bandana around his neck and placed it over Dean's face. Bordy looked up from his father and swore at the sun beating down on the arena. It was then that the crowd realized Dean was dead. It was shocked into silence by witnessing a man's death and at his son's apparent public grief. Stan saw it differently. He saw Bordy's expression not as grief, but as frustration that his father had beaten him for the last time with no chance of a rematch.

Stan wouldn't be talking about those legal matters to the owner of the Bar 5 Ranch after all: Dr. Hay pronounced Dean officially dead-on-arrival at the Williams Lake Hospital. The cause of death was a massive heart attack.

The funeral was held on the shores of Tatlayoko Lake. It was a sparse gathering, partly because Dean had bought out many of the neighbouring ranchers who couldn't survive the Depression and partly because of old grudges and range disputes. Besides Bordy and Stan, there was Dean's daughter, Clara, a few remaining ranching families who hoped that a miracle would happen before the bank foreclosed on their places, and a handful of ranch hands—both whites and Natives—including the Paul family, headed by Antoine. The only ranch worker who appeared sad about Dean's passing was Lady. The blue heeler cattle dog couldn't understand why Dean wasn't saddled up and punching cows; her barking could be heard from the locked barn.

Bordy was acting strangely. It occurred to Stan that Bordy had lost his sparring partner. He was subdued and had nothing to say about the loss of his father. When the procession walked up to the graveyard from the house, his limp from an old hip injury seemed more pronounced.

Even though the older Hanlon was a lapsed Catholic, Father Dumont—the Oblate missionary whose parish was the Chilcotin—read his last rites before he was buried in the family plot, which was circled by a white picket fence on a knoll overlooking the lake. Stan was called on to pay a tribute to Dean when the mourners gathered in the parlour of the ranch house for refreshments. He remembered not to drink anything before speaking, and kept his words short so he could get to his first drink of the day as soon as possible. He cleared his dry throat, grasped a glass of whisky in his right hand and began.

"Dean was a Chilcotin pioneer who had a stump ranch on the shores of this windy lake. He learned early on from his Indian neighbours"—and here Stan nodded to Antoine—"that this land gave a man nothing for free. He worked himself and his family hard to wrest a living from the dirt"—and here Stan turned to Bordy and Clara—"and with their help he built the Bar 5 to an eight hundred-head cattle operation. He was a good client and a man of his word. We will remember him with respect. Raise your glasses and drink a toast to his memory."

As the mourners raised their glasses, a half-dozen cars pulled into the ranch yard and people piled out, whooping it up and bringing their party into the house. They were Bordy's friends from Williams Lake, bolstered by strays they had picked up on the road. They were late for the funeral but in time for the free food and drink, and they partied all night.

Two days after the funeral, Bordy was in Stan's office. For the first time, Stan sized up the son as a man separate from his father. Here was the tree itself, he thought, and not the branch. He saw a swarthy, powerful, handsome man in his thirties. His curly black hair glowed with grease and he smelled of cheap aftershave. He was wearing a grey Western-styled suit and a matching grey Stetson, which drew attention to his luminous hazel eyes. Bordy had a reputation as a ladies' man, and Stan had heard the stories about husbands firing shotguns in the night at Bordy's retreating behind. There was never a dance in the Chilcotin that didn't feature his fun-loving smile. Bordy had worked on the ranch for his father since he was a child and knew how to raise cattle and ready them for market, but Dean had done all the business with the bankers, with the advice of Stan Hewitt.

In legal circles, Stan—when he was sober—was known as a careful man who could have had a brilliant career in Vancouver as a criminal lawyer, but for the double-martini lunches that sometimes affected his afternoon judgement. His firm had fired him and he had decided to take his talents to Williams Lake, where they would be better appreciated.

His wife had taken one look at her new surroundings and sued for divorce on the grounds of cruelty. Stan was now in his forties, and his continuing attempts to go dry often ended up with him in the drunk tank. Between bouts, however, he proved his early promise as a barrister and was eagerly sought after by clients throughout the interior plateau.

It appeared that Bordy had got over his grieving for his father—his only parent, since his Scottish mother Jean Somerville had died when he was in his teens. Many had asked why Bordy had put up with the older Hanlon, who was a tough, one-syllable rancher. Stan knew the real answer: it was lying on his desk, and here was Bordy, dressed up like a businessman to hear the news.

"Have a seat, Bordy." Stan motioned to the client's chair. "That was one hell of a way to go."

"He was a performer," Bordy said, pushing his Stetson to the back of his head and smiling.

"You're taking his death well."

Bordy tilted back in his chair. "I've got over it. The important thing now is that will lying on your desk. You know I worked like three ranch hands at the Bar 5 because I was promised the ranch."

"I figured that."

"So? What's the answer?"

Stan took his time opening the will, enjoying the impatient anticipation of the young rancher. Finally, he cleared his throat. "This will says—as clearly as I could draft it—that you inherit everything from the ploughshares to the two thousand deeded acres and miles of Crown Leased Land."

Bordy took off his hat and wiped the August sweat off his brow and face with a blue polka-dot handkerchief. "Damn, he kept his word."

"There is, however, one condition."

"What's that?"

"You must look after your sister Clara."

Bordy waved that aside and settled down. "What's the next step?"

"It'll take a month to probate the will. Your father had no money. All he had was the land in the Tatlayoko Valley."

"Land is all I need."

"There is something you don't know." Stan paused. "You recall that I came out to see Dean to speak to him about legal matters. The rodeo interfered with that. I was going to tell him that the bank has started foreclosure proceedings on his land."

"I'll sell some cows at the Williams Lake auction."

"The bank has put a lien on the cows."

"Dean was a good friend of Frank Walsh, the bank manager. I can buy some time," Bordy said confidently.

Stan shook his head. "Frank was fired last month for extending credit to Dean so he could buy up many of the smaller ranches in the valley that were being foreclosed on. The new manager has started the foreclosure action, and nothing but repayment of the mortgage in full will satisfy him."

Bordy jumped out of his chair and began to pace up and down. "That old bastard! He told me he had everything under control and that we would soon own the whole bloody valley. I should have paid more attention to the business. And why didn't you stop him from getting in too deep in the middle of a depression?"

"It would have been easier to stop a charging grizzly with a BB gun."

"He outrode me, and now he's left me with nothing after working me like a draft horse for the last twenty years."

He stopped pacing and pointed his finger at Stan. "You're my lawyer. Now, where the hell am I going to get enough money to pay off the bank when the whole country is broke?"

Stan thought a bit before answering. "Do you have any rich friends that you could partner up with?"

"The only friends I got are penniless girls who want to marry me for my money."

"What about relatives?"

"Yeah, I got my ma's cousins in Scotland, the Somervilles from around Lanark. They came out to visit us when Ma was alive."

"Give it some thought," Stan said as Bordy put his Stetson back on and left the office.

Stan held little hope that the party boy might salvage something from the tangled affairs of his father, but a week later Bordy dropped by to sign some papers and said, "I've given it some thought. I'm going to Scotland. The relatives are expecting me; I wired them and told them I'm looking for a wife. They are going to put me up and introduce me to the local girls. I'm leaving within the month. If I find what I'm looking for, there will be a few broken hearts in the Chilcotin. Oh, by the way: I'm changing the name of my ranch from 'Bar 5' to 'Empire.' Look after the paperwork, will you?"

BELLE

Stan was the first person Bordy saw on his return from Europe in February of 1938, a time when the world was about to erupt in war—a war that Bordy couldn't personally wage because of his hip injury. Fortunately, Bordy phoned from Vancouver to make an appointment, so Stan was relatively sober when Bordy came into his office with his bride, Isobel. Bordy called her Belle. Stan thought to himself that Belle wasn't a pretty woman. Her features were too strong for that, and her build was slight and wiry. Stan thought her expression seemed dour, and he hoped she had money. He did admire her soft, wavy, auburn hair, which she wore off her face. And then she smiled. It was a dazzling smile that wiped out the defects of her slightly freckled face and squared jaw. When she spoke in a lilting brogue he felt young again.

"Mr. Hewitt. Bordy has told me so much about you and

the good legal advice you've given him. My father gave me the money to pay off the mortgage on Empire Ranch, and against my wishes, insisted that I be made a co-owner. And Bordy—isn't he wonderful?—said that now that we are married, everything he has is mine."

All Stan could manage to say was, "Call me Stan. I hope you like our country."

She continued on as if she were an impressionable twenty-year-old, although Stan guessed her to be in her mid-thirties.

"I couldn't believe the Fraser Canyon. It made our Scottish glens seem so small. And the road twisted and turned so that if Bordy hadn't been driving I would have been in fear for my life. Last night we stayed at the 122 Mile House at Lac La Hache, where Molly and Gilbert Forbes treated us like family. Bordy tells me the hospitality and the scenery just get better when we get to the Chilcotin."

Bordy shook his head at her enthusiasm. "Now, darling! All I said was that the bench-lands along the Chilcotin River are made for grazing cattle and to me that's the best scenery around."

Belle left the two men to go shopping for Western gear at McKenzie's Store. After she had gone, Stan asked, "How did you meet such a charming woman?"

"At a dance, where I showed off my talent dancing Scottish reels. It's like square dancing without a caller. I even sang in a good baritone and held my liquor. I could tell she was impressed. When I invited her out, I told her all about Canada and the Chilcotin. Believe it or not, I was homesick. I told her that the Chilcotin is not just a place; it's a state of mind, where everything appears to move in slow motion until nature surprises you, and then only the quick survive. Energy is not generated from greed or machines, but from a delicate balance of survival in paradise."

Stan was surprised by Bordy's romantic description of his home. Of course, he thought, what Bordy had told Belle to win her over had no doubt been an act of necessity born of desperation. Perhaps a life charming women and competing with his father hadn't been wasted.

"Her fortune comes from her father's bottling business in Paisley. She's been married before: to a pilot in the RAF. He died, and she was just getting over his loss when we met. I proposed after a month of courtship and she accepted.

"She plays the piano and is a graduate of the London Conservatory of Music. She was a local prodigy—played for the King of England at Holyrood Palace in Edinburgh."

"Will she have much time for that on the ranch?" Stan asked, somewhat sarcastically.

"I promised she would. I even promised to have her Bechstein grand piano shipped to the ranch."

It was Belle's father who had set the terms of her dowry. Stan received the money and his instructions by wire. Mr. Stevenson insisted that Belle, his only child, own the ranch jointly with Bordy. Mr. Stevenson, Stan thought, was a canny man.

NOAH

Stan was invited to the homecoming. He followed Bordy's Buick in his old Ford on the four-hour journey to the ranch over rough roads. As the two cars approached the ranch house, Bordy and Stan honked their car horns. The plumes of Chilcotin dust were like clouds of white confetti. Clara came onto the porch. She removed her apron and called the hired hands out from the barn.

Father Dumont was standing by the Paul family's cabin, set well back from the ranch house. Maria Paul was holding two babies, one in each arm. Standing beside her were her husband, Alec Paul, and his father, Antoine. The priest held out his arms to Maria to accept one of the babies she was holding. She hesitated and looked at Antoine as if to say, "Shall I give this baby to the father?" Antoine nodded, and she allowed the father to take him. Clasping the remaining baby in her arms, she turned away.

Father Dumont proceeded to the porch with the baby just as the newlyweds pulled up to the front door.

Bordy was a non-practising Catholic, but Belle was a practising one. Bordy had told her there was a church in Redstone, an easy drive from the ranch. He had pointed it out to her on the way.

Clara was excited to see another woman on the ranch and rushed over to embrace Belle.

"It's wonderful to meet you too," Belle replied warmly. "I've heard many good things about you from Bordy."

The cowhands each formally greeted her, then Father Dumont stepped forward. "Welcome home, Bordy. I am anxious to meet your bride." Still holding the baby, he took Belle's hand. "Glad to meet you, Belle."

She smiled and said, "I look forward to seeing more of you, Father, but who is this adorable baby?"

"This is Mary's child."

"Well, Mary's child," she said, touching the baby's cheek, "I would like to see more of you too." The baby beamed at her.

At dinner that night, Belle turned to the priest. "Will you tell me about Mary's child?"

"Mary was a young girl from the people of the near mountains west of Tatlayoko. The Chilcotins call them Stonys. She died in childbirth. The father is unknown, and since Mary's mother couldn't look after the child, she came to Antoine to ask what to do. Antoine came to me to find a good home for him."

Belle looked at Bordy with tears in her eyes, and Stan could see the tenderness of this remarkable woman reaching out for the helpless baby.

"He is such a beautiful boy. Surely, Bordy, we can care for this child."

Stan could see that Bordy wanted to say "No." Instead he said, "I don't know, dear. We don't know about his health," as if he were considering a calf at auction. "For all we know, he could . . ."

Father Dumont interrupted. "Dr. Hay examined him and pronounced him a robust, healthy baby. Maria, the wife of one of your ranch hands, is wet-nursing him now. And his spiritual health is excellent. I baptized him myself yesterday."

In the silence that followed the priest's words, Bordy—who sat at the head of the table—mentally went over his narrowing options. The homecoming had gone so well. The pleasure of getting back to his ranch, the relief of paying off the bank, and the desire not to disappoint his bride were beginning to wear down his self-interest and his natural caution against complicating his domestic life.

"Very well," he finally said. "Let's give the little fellow a good start in life. At least we can care for him. What's his name, Father?"

"He was baptized Noah."

When Father Dumont took Noah from the wet nurse and brought him to the dining room, the child began to cry. When Belle took him and put him on her shoulder and patted him on his back, he stopped crying. Then he burped, drooled onto the back of Belle's dress—and grinned. Belle laughed, and Stan Hewitt—stiff lawyer with a drinking problem—felt there was hope for the Hanlons.

Antoine's daughter-in-law, Maria, cried when the priest came to say that the Hanlons would care for Noah. Alec, her husband, calmed her.

"We have our son Peter, and Noah will be close by. We will make other babies."

Antoine was pleased to hear that they were trying. They

would continue to try, but their daughter Justine would not be born for three more years.

*****

In the following years, Stan was a constant at the ranch, making himself as agreeable as it is possible for a divorced, alcoholic lawyer to be. What attracted him was Belle Hanlon. Her ready wit and talent enchanted him. He saw that she was becoming a doting mother to Noah, and as the next few years passed with no hope of having her own children, her attachment to Noah strengthened. Belle had been barren throughout her first marriage, and she and Bordy were concerned because she hadn't become pregnant since their marriage. She convinced Bordy that they should adopt Noah. She was determined to raise him with books like the children's classics Winnie the Pooh, Alice in Wonderland, and Wind in the Willows.

Noah played with Peter, who was the same age and the only other boy on the ranch, but Belle encouraged him to consider himself as white and therefore different. The white boys—the Johnstons at Tatla Lake and the Keiths near Eagle Lake—were regular visitors at the ranch, but it was Noah and Peter who shared secrets. They didn't consider Justine, Peter's little sister, a proper playmate until she was six and could stand up for herself.

Time was not a precious commodity among the Natives on the plateau. They moved with the seasons, not by seconds, minutes, or hours, which for a child growing up in the country was fine. But time meant something to a large ranch like Empire, connected as it was to the cattle markets of the world. This wasn't brought home to Noah immediately. He learned that lesson one day when he was six.

Stan was at the ranch for the weekend to fish and listen to Belle play her Bechstein. He was having dinner in the new ranch house, with company including the local MLA and Father Dumont, when Noah arrived late to the table in tears. He had been riding bareback with Peter on an old Clydesdale plough horse, Dobbin. He was supposed to be home for supper at five-thirty. It was six when he said goodbye to Peter at the Pauls' cabin. Antoine saw his grandson jump off the horse from his doorway and said nothing. Peter was never scolded for misdemeanours. Noah was full of fun from the ride as he came into the barn. He began rubbing down the horse like he'd been taught. He was standing on a stool, his little arms scrubbing down Dobbin, when his father came into the stall.

"Noah, you know your mother is worried about you. What time were you supposed to be in the house?"

"Five-thirty, Papa."

"Well, it's quarter after six. Where were you?"

"I was riding Dobbin with Peter and I forgot. I'm sorry."

"That's not good enough, son. Finish what you are doing and then come see me in the den."

Noah was puzzled, but he did what his father told him. He finished brushing down the horse and went to find his father. "It was wrong of you to disobey your mother. Next time you will remember to obey her. It is important to be punctual."

"What does punctual mean, Papa?"

"It means to be on time," Bordy said, and went to the desk where he kept his important documents, where Noah was never allowed. He grasped a piece of leather from an old harness and said, "Hold out your hand."

"Why, Papa?"

"Because you disobeyed your mother by being late."

"I won't do it again."

"I know you won't, son, and this will help you remember."

Bordy brought the strap down hard on Noah's little hand. The boy cried but stayed there in shock.

"Now the other hand."

Noah hesitantly held out his other trembling hand and received another blow. And then there were real tears.

"I don't want to have to do this again, so remember to be on time. Now go to the dinner table."

Life wasn't all heartache and tension for Noah. He had Belle to comfort him and show him another side of life from strengthening himself for the tests ahead.

That night when Belle read to Noah, he asked her, "Why is Papa so mean when there is no hurt in Alice in Wonderland?"

"Alice isn't in the real word, dear. But I will speak to your father about his striking you."

The next night she read to him from Grimm's Fairy Tales and Noah got to know more about the other side of the world, both the imaginary and the real. When she read Hansel and Gretel, Noah's eyes went wide with terror and he asked, "Mother, you know that woman who travels around by herself and doesn't have a home?"

"You mean Ta Chi, dear?"

"Yes. Is she a witch?

"No, dear, witches are evil. Ta Chi is a nomad. She prefers to live on the land by herself. That's not evil."

Noah was not so sure. Whenever he saw Ta Chi—and that was two or three times a year when he was out by himself—she would suddenly appear on a rise or at a corner on the path. She would just stand there watching him without saying a word. He wondered why she wandered about the Chilcotin by herself, and the thought occurred to him that maybe she had lost something.

Noah did not go to school that fall. Belle taught him at home through the provincial government correspondence courses. He spent the next six years excelling at his lessons and therefore pleasing his mother. He tried to understand his father, who was always on the move and talking about cows, grass and water, and when he wasn't cursing the hired hands he was talking about expanding the ranch.

Most days Noah spent time in the saddle, out riding with his father. He was expected to do his part on the ranch, along with his closest friend, Peter. Noah's chores started with bringing the haying crews fresh water and food, and if he was late his father called him out and punished him in front of the men. When he was given responsibility for the livestock, they came first, and no excuse was tolerated. A cow went missing in midwinter the year Noah was eleven. He was sent to find it and was told not to come back unless he did. Bordy, whose whole thought was on the ranch, was treating his son as he had been treated by Dean. In doing so, he was passing on to Noah how to raise a child who would hate his father and use that hate to beat the world.

The markets after the war were good for cattle, and Bordy wasn't satisfied with his eight hundred head. Some Americans had bought a couple of ranches by Big Bar and named their ranch the "Gang Ranch." It was reputed to be the biggest ranch in North America. They boasted three thousand head of cattle. The only way Bordy could get more was to work harder.

Belle kept the books and signed the cheques and kept track of their money. She supported the expansion up to a point. With it came a new ranch house, which she designed and furnished, but the cost of the continuous expansion was wearing her down. Underlying this struggle was Bordy's wandering eye. The tension between husband

and wife was building. Belle warned him many times that she would not accept his being unfaithful, and every time he promised it wouldn't happen again.

In July when Noah was twelve, they went to the Anahim Lake stampede to watch Bordy bronco-riding. Bordy was showing off, got thrown, and when he lost he came up to Belle—who was with Noah—and said, "Let's get the hell out of here."

"But Noah is competing in the roping contest."

"Have it your own way, then. I'll take the car and you can come later with the truck and horse trailer."

He didn't wait for a reply, but heard her say as he walked away, "We probably won't be back till tomorrow. Noah may win and be in the finals, and it will be too late to start home tonight."

Noah did win the trophy, and wanted to get back that night to show Bordy. They arrived after midnight, put the horses in the barn and walked to the house.

Noah said to his mother, "I'm going right up and telling Pa."

Together they went upstairs to the master bedroom. Belle opened the door. Noah rushed in and said, "Guess what, Pa?"

Bordy didn't guess. Instead he shouted, "What the hell!" and sat upright in bed with his arm around a naked strawberry-blonde.

Belle said in a chilled voice, "Sorry to interrupt. Come along, Noah! Your father is busy," and slammed the door on the bedmates.

Clara arrived from Vancouver on a visit the next morning. When Belle told her what had happened, Clara shrugged. "I have no influence over Bordy. The reason I left the ranch and the Chilcotin was to get as far away from him as I could. All I care is that he sends me an allowance every month."

The Hanlons didn't share the same bedroom again.

The final dispute, which broke the cycle of a driven man and a stubborn woman, was over Noah's education. He was twelve and had finished his elementary schooling at the ranch. To proceed further, his parents would have to send him to boarding school in Williams Lake, which to Belle was out of the question. Noah overheard them talking in the great hall one night.

"To be properly educated, Noah will have to go to a private school in Victoria," Belle stated flatly.

Bordy disagreed. "I went to school in Williams Lake and suffered no ill effects."

Belle, her voice rising replied, "Noah deserves a better chance."

"We can't afford it."

"You paid two thousand dollars for a prizewinning Black Angus bull from England last year. If we can afford that, we can afford to send him to a good school."

"Don't bring Sir Lancelot into this. He'll pay his way. Why teach Noah all that extra stuff, when all he'll do is raise cattle like me?"

"There's more to life than raising cattle."

"Not in the Chilcotin there isn't."

"Don't you see that when you were courting me, when you said that the Chilcotin was a wonder of the world, I believed you. Then I saw it, and saw that you hadn't deceived me. Now you spend your waking hours trying to figure out how much money you can make out of it. Then you said you loved me, and now you have deceived me. You don't love me; you only love the latest floozy that you've bedded. I'm taking Noah to Victoria and will provide a home for him there. We'll be back for Christmas, Easter and summer vacation."

Later in the summer, Bordy was in town for a Thursday

cattle auction and dropped by Stan's office. He told Stan that Belle was leaving with Noah. Stan could tell that Bordy was resigned to the move because he immediately began talking about the rise in the price of yearlings and his decision to hold back this year's calf crop to sell them as yearlings next year. Of course Noah would be back out on the range with him in the summer, learning everything Bordy had learned from Dean's beating it into him.

"What about Belle?" Stan asked.

"I'm not so sure she's coming back. All I know is that we've agreed that I will run the ranch and pay her a large monthly allowance."

The news of Belle's leaving affected Stan. He looked forward to regular visits at Empire Ranch, where he could talk to Belle and listen to her play Brahms in the evening, and fish during the day. It was a wonderful distraction for him, whose closest friend until he had met Belle was a whisky bottle. He invited himself to Tatlayoko that weekend to say goodbye.

They were in the great hall, which Belle had had designed to suit her Bechstein. The hall had a two-storeyed ceiling with a balcony on three sides which was over sixty feet long. The acoustics were marvellous, and after listening to her play Chopin that evening, Stan said, "You know if you go, you will be giving up your dream home and your piano."

"Noah comes first," she replied. "And, besides, I will still play the piano, and to a larger audience than just you.

"I can't believe Bordy is letting you go."

"Bordy is quite happy with the arrangement."

"I'm not. I am very unhappy."

"Then you will have to visit me in Victoria."

"But Noah can attend boarding school in Victoria while you stay here in the Chilcotin."

"It is not your place to question my actions," she said, showing him a different side of herself. "In fact, I resent your interference and will not tolerate it. I've thought of you as a good friend, and I hope, if you value our friendship, you will keep your thoughts about my marriage and Noah to yourself."

With that, she got up from the piano and left the large room, leaving him with plenty of time to reflect on how badly he had handled the situation. He was used to the hard-hitting debates of the courtroom and not delicate discussions about friendship and marriage. He remained where he sat, quietly drinking until the early hours of the morning. The goodbye had been a disaster. He had been critical when he should have been bracing, and negative when he should have been supportive, encouraging Belle to return with Noah on the holidays.

In the morning he woke up with a hangover, which he treated by slowly drinking some beer. He had planned to do some fishing on the lake, but Bordy suggested he delay until he was in better shape. He shrugged off the suggestion and was on the dock readying the rowboat when Noah showed up.

"Pa wants me to go with you."

"You tell your pa that I've been fishing for forty years and I don't need a twelve-year-old kid to help me."

Noah didn't move, but when Stan lurched into the middle rowing seat, almost capsizing the boat, he climbed into the stern. Stan made no further protests. He rowed out towards the middle of the lake, which was sandwiched between mountains and stretched miles to the south.

"Since you're here," he told the boy, "you might as well row. I'll fish."

They changed places, with Noah keeping the boat from

tipping by shifting his weight. Stan settled at the back, opened a bottle of beer and took a long swallow.

"I thought you said you were going to fish," said Noah.

"I'm trying to decide where the fish are."

"I know where the fish are. They are deep, and at this time of day near the cliffs over there." Noah pointed to an outcrop on the west shore.

"All right then. Row me over!"

A bottle of beer later, Noah signalled that Stan should set some line.

"You're not going to tell me what lure to use?"

Noah didn't understand sarcasm and said, "I would use some weight, a flasher, and fish eggs. There are some big char down there."

"I'm fishing for trout, so I think I'll cast for them."

"The wind is coming up a little. Maybe you shouldn't stand."

This was an invitation for Stan to rise to his feet with the fishing rod in his hand. He made a casting motion by drawing his right arm back and flinging it forward. In his drunken state, he lost his balance. Had he followed the rod into the water he might have cleared the gunnels, but he tried to check himself and got his feet entangled in his fishing gear. The boat capsized, spilling Noah and he into the glacial waters of Tatlayoko Lake.

They were a hundred feet from shore. Stan had no life jacket and couldn't swim; Noah had no life jacket, but could. Stan sputtered to the surface, flailing at the water. The wooden clinker-built was upside down and ten feet away from them, and the wind was gently moving it farther away. Noah was nearer the boat. Seeing it was their only chance, he swam to it and pushed it slowly closer to Stan, who was yelling and sputtering. He was beside Stan when the lawyer came up again. Noah made a last effort and shoved the boat towards him.

"Grab on!" he shouted.

Stan had sobered up enough from the shock of the water to make a lunge at the boat and get his fingers on the keel. They were still a hundred feet from shore and the wind was pushing them parallel to the shoreline. They would have to reach shore before the cold sapped their strength. Stan started to function. He moved hand over hand to the stern, where he was able to grasp an iron mounting for an outboard. Using this to hold onto, he began kicking the boat towards the shoreline, while Noah, exhausted from his effort, could only hang on to the upturned boat and be carried to the shore.

It took them ten minutes to reach a small pebble beach, where they collapsed and felt the sun slowly warm them to life. They didn't speak for the longest time.

It was Stan who spoke first. "Thank you, son. You saved my life. I'll never forget it."

"Pa would've been mad if I'd come back without you."

When they got back to the ranch, soaked through and having paddled the rowboat with pieces of driftwood, Stan told everyone how the boy had saved his life.

Bordy said, "It's only what I would expect of Noah," while Belle said, "You're a brave boy and I am proud of you."

Then she turned on Stan. "You selfish old drunk. How could you put my son's life at risk?"

Stan wished that he had drowned; it would have been a better fate than hearing Belle attack him. What Belle said was true. Her words gutted him. The one person he most admired—and if he told the truth, even loved—had found him out. When he left the ranch in his Ford an hour later, he made a vow to stop drinking that—with a few notable exceptions—proved more successful than his attempts at the Twelve Steps of AA.

VICTORIA

In Victoria, Belle's first priority was to arrange for Noah's education. She and Noah moved into a large house in the Uplands. Her next-door neighbour, Adele Buscombe, asked her to a welcome dinner. She met Adele's husband and another neighbour, Major Jack Parmenter. She was immediately attracted to him because he reminded her of her first husband, who had been a pilot in Royal Air Force. They were paired together at the dinner table.

"My son Noah will be entering grade seven and I am looking for a good private school. Would you happen to know of one?" she asked the major.

"Yes, my military friends say that All Saints is an excellent school for boys. It takes boarders and day students. I'd like to meet your son. Perhaps you could come over for tea tomorrow? I live next door to you."

They had tea the next day, and Noah fidgeted while they

explored each other's lives.

When the major had come to Victoria in his mid-fifties, she heard, his plan had been to invest in a small company, enjoy the society of the provincial capital, and perhaps find a compatible woman with whom he could hunt and fish. He had bought a house on the waterfront in Uplands—an upscale subdivision—and was getting acclimatized to a more leisurely pace when the house next door was purchased by Isobel Hanlon from the Chilcotin, a place he knew of as a remote, desolate part of the interior of the province, good for hunting mountain goats.

When his neighbours on the other side, Charles and Adele Buscombe—who were Victoria natives and owned the Cowichan Electric Company, which Charles managed—had invited him for dinner to meet Belle Hanlon, he had had no idea that she might be the compatible woman. The major had done all the necessary useful things to establish himself in Victoria. He had joined the Union Club, made contact with Royal Roads Military Academy, become friends with the commanding officer at HMCS Esquimalt, and made an effort to get to know the members of the provincial cabinet. But he had not settled on a business in which to invest his sizable fortune. Over tea, it hadn't take Belle long to get to know the major's interests.

Over the next few months, after Noah was settled at All Saints, Belle spent a lot of time with the major, who wooed her and won her heart with his little attentions—the kinds of attentions that Bordy had used to pay her before he put his cows before their marriage. One night over dinner at the Union Club, the major took Belle's hand and said, "My dear, I have never met a woman as vivacious and attractive as you. I would like you to be my fiancée."

The major's formal proposal was not unexpected. Belle

replied: "You know I am Catholic and I won't divorce Bordy. But I do like you, Jack, and could even learn to love you. Let's just say that you are my intended."

After that, Belle began to take a greater interest in the major's affairs. The Buscombes' business, she decided, was the ideal business in which to invest not only the major's money, but hers as well. Her father had recently died and left his estate to her.

Cowichan Electric was a privately held company. The Buscombes would have to agree to sell a part of it to their neighbours, and they were not yet aware of a reason to sell. That reason was conceived by Belle and carried out with the help of the major.

Charles Buscombe, a good administrator, was a shy man who built model trains in his spare time. The company was experiencing some political pressures which he was not capable of handling, and he had no interest in expanding the company. He needed someone to negotiate with the government, which was thinking of consolidating electric power in the province. He was also having to deal with a takeover offer from Nanaimo Electric.

The major had made political contacts since moving to Victoria and had experience dealing with a large bureaucracy: the army. By Christmas, Belle had convinced Adele Buscombe that Cowichan Electric should hire the major to help Charles steer it through the next few years. Adele, who controlled the company, talked to Charles. Within a short time, Major Jack Parmenter became the General Manager and President of Cowichan Electric, whose new majority shareholders were himself, Adele, and Belle, who was a silent partner. Knowing the provincial government's desire to consolidate the electric companies on the Island, he made a reverse takeover offer to Nanaimo Electric. With political pressure and the infusion of capital from him and Belle, the offer was approved. Two years later, with the government's blessing, they bought Campbell River Electric and the amalgamated company, renamed "Vancouver Island Power Company," became the biggest supplier of electrical power to mid and upper Vancouver Island and its growing population. Charles Buscombe retired to his real passion in life: keeping his model trains running on time.

In the Chilcotin over the next few years, Bordy came into town from time to time and would drop by Stan's office for legal advice or to talk about the continuing growth of the ranch. Bordy had it in his mind to make Empire the Chilcotin's largest ranch, one to rival the Gang Ranch and even the Douglas Lake Ranch in the Nicola Valley. This meant buying land on the Chilcotin River where the best hayfields were located.

Belle didn't object to this plan as long as Bordy kept up his payments to her. Although she left the running of the ranch to him, she had to sign the papers, and Stan used this excuse to travel to Victoria to see her. For her part, she was happy to see him as long as he arrived sober and offered no advice on how she should live her life.

MAJOR

At eleven o'clock one morning a few years after the boating incident, Stan arrived at Belle's house in the Uplands, an imposing white structure on the waterfront. Belle explained its size to Stan the first time she opened the carved oak door to him. "My father died and left me his fortune. Since I need a house for Noah and I like entertaining, this suits my needs."

"I am sorry to hear of your father's death. My correspondence with him when you were first married showed how concerned he was for your welfare in your adopted country."

"Thank you, Stan. I was at his bedside when he died, and with a host of his friends saw him piped to his grave."

Stan looked around the anteroom and asked, "Where's the piano?"

She led him into the front room, where the Bechstein

looked quite small in a room with floor-to-ceiling windows overlooking the Strait of Georgia. They conducted their business in the den before moving to the dining room, where the housekeeper, Alice, had prepared lunch. There were three places set. Stan asked, "Are you expecting Noah?"

"I am expecting Major Parmenter, who is my next door neighbour and a friend of mine. I hope you don't mind?"

"Not at all."

"Noah is boarding at All Saints, a boys' private school. He comes home on the weekends."

"How's he doing in school?"

"You remember that he used to draw quite good pictures of horses? Well, he's sixteen now and seems to have a talent for drawing wildlife, particularly birds. I am encouraging him. Last summer I took him to Europe for a month to see the art galleries."

The two friends were interrupted by the doorbell, which the housekeeper answered. Major Jack Parmenter was introduced and then went straight up to Belle, kissed her on the cheek, and apologized for being late. He was about Stan's age and a bustling, active man, very fit, with a ruddy complexion and a salt-and-pepper moustache.

"Sorry I'm late. We are in the middle of rate hearings, and the chairman wanted us to sit into the lunch hour."

"Jack is the CEO and majority owner of the Vancouver Island Power Company," Belle explained, "and the company is in the midst of a takeover of Nanaimo Power, so these are busy times for my neighbour."

But she couldn't explain the distinct odour of gin that issued from the major. The major didn't bother hiding it with mouthwash, for he was fondly remembering his gin at the club just an hour ago while he tried to be pleasant to the lawyer. It had been the major's first gin and tonic of the year. Jepson, the bartender, had taken a bottle of Beefeaters from his personal oak locker and placed it on a silver tray. From the cooler behind the bar he had taken a small bottle of Schweppes, and with a flick of the opener cupped in his right hand, uncapped it and placed it next to the gin. He had filled an ice bucket and sliced a lime into quarters, adding these ingredients to the tray. Picking up the silver tray, he had approached the major's corner table. The major had taken a keen interest in the preparation of his drink and had continued to observe the performance, making sure no detail was missed. Jepson had held the tray in the meaty part of his left hand and with his right removed the contents, arranging them on the table.

The major had appreciated Jepson's professionalism, for he was a professional himself and a stickler for detail; a military engineer who had fought in every theatre of war from Africa's desert sands to Italy, the beaches of Normandy to India, Burma to the Mau Mau in Kenya. When there was a pause in the wars, he had returned to Victoria. An observant military man would know from his bearing that the major had served in the Royal Engineers rather than the Royal Canadian Engineers, and that he had seen action in India, as his cheeks were red from countless gins consumed during the hot season. It was also evident that he had seen active duty, for at any sudden noise he would start as if a bomb had exploded. He continued to look at life as if he were on a war footing. Jepson, using the ice tongs, had dropped two ice cubes into the crystal, making a 'pinging' sound and misting the inside of the glass. He had splashed some gin over the cubes and they had made a satisfying crackle. Then he had added the tonic to within a half-inch of the top.

While Jepson had poured his drink, the major had recalled the gin and tonic served to him by the Maharaja of Jodhpur following a tiger hunt on the Prince's private reserve. Major Parmenter had just saved the Maharaja's life by shooting a tiger in mid leap, and the Prince was grateful. He had showed his gratitude by personally serving him a gin and tonic at the palace that evening. This was a memory the major would carry with him for life, as he would the gift of precious stones, which he had used to further his prospects in Victoria.

Jepson had finished his work by impaling a quarter of lime on the edge of the crystal glass. He had straightened and brought the empty silver tray up to his chest as a shield, saying deferentially, "Is everything to your liking, major?"

The major had raised an eyebrow, taken the lime from the edge of the glass, and squeezed it into his drink. He had raised the glass slowly to his lips and sipped. "Splendid, Jepson—the Maharaja couldn't have done it better. Now I must drink up and meet a boring lawyer for lunch."

Stan had wanted to spend more time with Belle and perhaps get her to play the piano, but he ended up trying to be nice to a man who was obviously her lover. Was Belle using him as a pawn? Had she invited the major so that he could meet him and convey his impression back to Bordy? Of course he had no intention of doing that, but if he had it wouldn't have been favourable.

Over lunch, the major talked about his North African campaign under Field Marshal Montgomery. Listening to the soldier getting worked up over his war years made Stan feel even more uneasy about the man who had captured Belle's affections. He thought ruefully that he could have been in the major's shoes had he wooed Belle, for Belle and he had so much more in common. He had to be content with being allowed back into her circle.

After lunch, the major left for his hearing and Stan found himself alone with Belle in the foyer. "It's been wonderful to see you again and to find you so happy," he said. "I would like to have heard you play."

"I would love to, Stan, but I'm expecting my bridge group any minute. I promise to play for you next time you are in town."

Stan took her hand and said, "Goodbye."

The major returned to his office in the city, a large corner office decorated with his war mementos. He was approached almost immediately by Ian Richards, one of his engineers. He had a high regard for Richards, who spoke and acted like a servant rather than a professional man in the presence of his chief.

"I need your advice, Major."

"Always happy to give it."

"Our electrical consumption projections for the Island for the next ten years show that we'll have to find and develop a new source of hydro power within the next five years if we expect to meet the demand. As you know, we've been considering a number of dam sites on the Island, and I have the report here. Once you've had a chance to review it, would you advise me on a course of action?"

Richards knew his boss and how to stroke his ego. He knew that the major had already made up his mind where to put the dam if one was needed, and Richards had shaded his report in that direction.

"Thank you, Richards. I'll read it and get back to you." The major took the report, but Richards remained standing before him. "Is there anything else?"

"I would like to get your advice on a personal matter involving my son, Ralph."

The major smiled. He enjoyed influencing the lives of young men. His advice was inevitably the same: enlist in the armed forces, because it was what he had done and it had served him well. "Of course, Richards," the major said.

It turned out that Ralph Richards was enrolled at Oak Bay High School. Ian Richards could not call his son a student, for that would imply that he studied. He lived in the shadow of his older sister Emily, an overachiever. Ralph and his friends played in a band, which was an excuse to drink and party. He could have continued this idyllic life through to graduation had he not crashed the family car while driving home from a gig. He had been arrested and charged with driving while drunk.

Ian and his wife had decided that the solution was to send him to a private school to straighten him out. Ian knew nothing of private schools, having been raised on a farm in Saskatchewan, although he had managed to squeeze through university on an ROTC program as a navy officer. He had met his wife, Enid, at university. They were surprised when—as Ian put it—their two children "came on board"; surprised when their daughter turned out so well; and terrified when Ralph—who had seemed to be so sensible and caused no trouble, keeping below their radar—suddenly became a criminal.

Of course, Ian didn't reveal the background when he spoke to the major. He only said, "My wife, Enid, and I have decided that our son needs the discipline of a private school. Perhaps you could suggest one?"

"I suppose he is too young to join the army," the major mused in a half-whisper, then out loud he said, "I have a few ideas and connections, but before I recommend anything, bring him around to my house tomorrow so I can size him up."

Father and son showed up at the major's house that Saturday. Ralph was a slouching teenager, self-conscious, wearing the baggy draped slacks fashionable in the early fifties, and not knowing what to do with his hands. He shoved them both into his pockets, but then had to drag one out to shake the major's hand.

The major grabbed onto it in a vise grip and wouldn't let go. "So you're the boy who wants to piss his life away?"

"No, I don't."

"Drinking and driving. What were you thinking? Your father has asked me to help. I know something about educating young men for war."

"We're not in a war," Ralph said, looking confused.

"Sir!" the major shouted in his face.

"Sir!" Ralph barked back.

"That's what you think, sonny. We've already had two world wars this century; the last one ended just eight years ago. Do you have a brain in your head?" The major answered his own question: "I think you do."

Ralph had never been spoken to in this way. Discipline at home meant being sent to his room downstairs, locking the door, and crawling out through the window to go meet his friends.

"I'll tell you what. I'll get you into a school that will change your life. You've heard of All Saints?" The major spoke while he crossed to an elaborate gun case. He pulled out a gold-inlaid, French, double-barrelled shotgun and put it in Ralph's hands. "See how light this is? I use it for skeet shooting. Come outside a minute."

He went to his desk and took out a handful of shells and some clay pigeons. Together they went to the terrace, where the major spotted Noah in Belle's yard next door and ordered him over.

"Come here, Noah, I want you to meet someone."

Noah reluctantly complied and was introduced to Ian and his son. The major said, "Ralph here wants to go to All Saints, and I'd like you to keep an eye on him."

Ralph spoke up. "I didn't say I wanted to go to All Saints."

"You're going to All Saints," his father hissed.

The two boys cautiously looked at each other. The major gave another order: "Ian, throw this clay pigeon out towards the sea."

The pigeon had hardly left Ian's hand when the major had put the gun to his shoulder, sighted the skeet, and fired, all in one motion. The pigeon burst into pieces. He handed the gun to Ralph.

"Now you try it."

Ralph eagerly took the gun. He wasn't able to hit the five pigeons that the major threw out for him, but the major praised his effort and said he saw some natural talent. He then handed the gun to Noah and said, "Now you try."

Noah missed in his five attempts. The major scoffed, but Ralph looked at Noah with real interest, because it looked to him like Noah had missed deliberately.

Back in the house the major said to Ralph, "There's more to guns than shooting them." He handed the boy a cleaning kit. "Clean the gun and put it back in the gun case."

When Ralph was placing the gun back in the cabinet, he noticed that all but one of the guns in the case were engraved and gold-inlaid. He took particular notice of the orphan plain gun because it seemed out of place and somewhat down-at-heel, which was much the same way Ralph was feeling these days. There were three notches on the worn stock of the gun.

"Isn't the major something else?" Ian asked his son on the way home.

"Yeah." Ralph nodded. "He's a crazy old bastard, that's what he is."

But the major had done one thing for Ralph: he had gotten him riled up. Ralph's anger got him through the years he attended All Saints. That and his friendship with Noah Hanlon were enough to see him through to graduation.

Noah was different from the other guys. By all rights, Ralph thought he should have given him a hard time by breaking Ralph into the school traditions. Instead, Noah sort of looked out for him. Ralph was a bit of a runt, which the rugby coach thought was just the right build for a scrum half. During the practices and games in early autumn, he was every player's punching bag. The only reason he survived was that Noah—who played wing, and ran so fast no one could touch him—was always there to pull Ralph out of the pile and tell him that he had made a hell of a play.

Soon the other boys started rallying around him, and resented it when the opposing teams roughed him up. Their team spirit was so strong that in the last season of Noah's graduating year, All Saints won the McKechnie Cup—a first for the school. The other teams called them the "All Whites" because of their white uniforms and the colour of their skin. Noah was the exception, and it galled them to see him run past, through and over their best players for a try. In the beginning they called him "the Indian," but by the time Noah graduated from All Saints he had taught them to call him "the Chilcotin."

That summer, as in other years, Noah spent most of his time at Empire Ranch. Ralph noticed that when Noah left for the ranch in July he was full of the Chilcotin, but when he returned at the end of August he was quiet and reserved, lean and hard, and talked very little of his time with his father and the ranch. Ralph asked him about it.

"Bordy is working out his demons," Noah said. "He doesn't just pick on me. He's that way with everything and everybody."

"Why do you go back?"

"I wish I knew. I'm like a moth to a flame. I can't keep away from the Chilcotin."

That fall, Noah entered the Fine Arts Program at Vic College. He had decided to major in painting and was over at Ralph's one day with his portfolio when Emily arrived home from her university in Vancouver. Ralph introduced them. She was amused. Ralph had told her about this fantastic rugby-player friend of his at All Saints.

Usually, she wasn't interested in any of Ralph's friends. As a scientist, she classified Ralph in the genus reptilian. She had had no interest in sweaty athletes . . . until she met Noah. He was six feet tall, dark, soft-spoken and an artist—all qualities she did not usually associate with Ralph's friends. Noah showed her his portfolio, and she was impressed. A few days later he phoned her up and asked her on a date, and out of curiosity she accepted. He took her to dinner and brought her home to meet his mother.

Belle was used to meeting Noah's dates, pretty girls with "little going on upstairs." She could not say that about Emily, who was in her second year at UBC majoring in ornithology. This discipline required that she study dead birds neatly filed in drawers. Noah's interest was to draw and paint living birds, not to kill and stuff dead ones; but love had nothing to do with birds, and for the next year they dated.

On Stan's visits to the ranch before Belle moved to Victoria he used to entertain the family and their dinner guests with stories about his court cases. He continued this tradition in Victoria to amuse Belle and Noah. On one occasion he went to the capital on an appeal and was invited for dinner. The major was there, as well as friends of Noah's—Ralph Richards and his sister Emily, whom Stan surmised was Noah's girlfriend. The major was full of his recent takeover of Campbell River Power. Stan sat between Noah and Emily and heard her say to Noah, "I like your new portrait of your mother, but I think you should have dressed your mother in chartreuse. It would have highlighted her colouring more."

"I prefer her in black. She looks more imperial," he replied, and turned to Stan. "What brings you down to Victoria?"

"I appeared before the Court of Appeal today in a civil case involving parents who sued their ten-year-old daughter, represented by a public trustee. They are a family from Alexis Creek who had bought an Irish Sweep-stakes ticket with their meagre earnings, and thinking it would be lucky for the whole family of seven, they placed the ticket in their youngest daughter's name. To their joy, they found that they had won a hundred thousand dollars. That the cheque was made out to their minor daughter was a mere formality, they had thought. But they hadn't counted on the law, which the public trustee interpreted as saying that it was the child's money, not the family's money. The father had recently been laid off and they desperately needed it. And although it was her money, she wouldn't be able to claim it until she legally became an adult at age twenty-one. In the interim it could only be spent on her necessities and education, but not on her family, who were living in poverty. The trial judge, Mr. Justice Deacon, agreed with the public trustee. He disregarded the intention of the parents and found that the ticket was a gift. The Court of Appeal gave their decision from the bench, accepting my argument that the intention was that the money be for the whole family, and divided the winnings into seven equal parts." He finished his story with a flourish. Had he been drinking, he would have quaffed a glass of wine with one swallow but instead ended by saying, "A truly biblical decision."

The dinner table guests with the exception of the major applauded him.

After dinner the men went for a smoke in the den. Noah and Ralph were ordered to join them, so they ended up with front-row seats to the men's talk. Stan took his filtered cigarettes from his vest pocket, extracted a cigarette, and fitted it into his cigarette holder. The major watched this show with some alarm and spoke gruffly while gesturing at Stan: "I find that holder quite affected. You should have a man's smoke."

Stan good-naturedly replied, "Oh, and what is a man's smoke?"

"A cigar, of course, hand-rolled in Cuba on the thighs of a nubile Cuban woman."

He offered Stan a cigar. Stan declined, thinking to himself that Belle's men were a vulgar lot.

The major took offence at Stan's turning down the cigar. "Not good enough for a back-country lawyer?" He carried on, obviously determined to insult the lawyer. "Perhaps it's not biblical enough."

Stan ignored the major's jibe and changed the subject. "How are you finding the change from fighting wars to running a power company?"

"There is no difference. I run the company as I ran my division. I set my priorities and objectives and achieve them. I let nothing stand in my way. As you can see, I have been successful," he said with a smug smile.

“So far,” Stan replied in an offhand way designed to get the response he wanted.

“Why don’t you blow that smoke out your ass?”

“Why don’t you read Cervantes?”

“What? What the hell are you talking about?”

“Cervantes—who was a writer, by the way—had a hero named Don Quixote, a mad knight who fantasized about jousts and ladies. Yet throughout his adventures, Don Quixote mainly harmed himself.” And with the major looking angry and belligerent, Stan stood up and left the room.

Noah smiled; he knew that the men had been sparring over his mother.

*****

The major was running out of options for a site for his hydroelectric project. The company was relying heavily on costly diesels to produce electricity, and political wrangling was holding up the sites on-Island.

He was explaining this to Belle one night when she said, “When Bordy and I were first married, he took me on horseback into the mountains west of the ranch. I remember following the Homathko River before it joins Mosley Creek. We climbed far above the rapids, dismounted, and clambered to the edge of a gorge that was hundreds of feet deep to the waters of the Homathko. I believe it is called Waddington Canyon. Bordy and I made our way down to the river and he showed me some iron pegs sunk into the walls of solid rock, which Bordy said were put there to suspend a road through the canyon. The road was intended as a route to the gold fields in the Cariboo. It would be an ideal place for a dam. Too bad it’s not on the Island.”

"I'm desperate for a cheap source of power. I'll look into this, but we have to keep quiet about it until we get approval for a water licence, otherwise some interest group will oppose it and the cabinet will get cold feet."

In late 1957 on a return to Williams Lake from a trip to Victoria, Stan received a call from Bordy on the radiophone. He demanded that Stan come out to the ranch. "We'll be branding tomorrow, and there's a dance in the evening. You can stay overnight."

Stan had not been to Empire since Belle had left and was surprised that Bordy was asking him now. Since the radiophone was broadcast and anyone in the Chilcotin could overhear the conversation, it must be urgent legal business.

The next day, Stan drove Highway 20 to the turnoff to Tatlayoko Lake. Thirty years ago when Stan had come to this country, Dean Hanlon had been struggling to live on forty cows and a quarter-section of land. Now, most of the twenty miles from Eagle Lake to Tatlayoko was Empire Ranch. But at what cost to Bordy and Belle and Noah?

The home fields were full of cows closely followed by their bawling calves, which were about to have the ER brand seared on their right flanks. Cowhands were riding in and out of the herd, lassoing the calves and dragging them to the fires and the red glow of the irons. The young male calves, soon to be steers, suffered the further indignity of having their testicles removed. Stan had attended these branding parties in the past and had always felt uneasy about celebrating the necessary ritual.

Mingling in the herd and watching from the fence railings was a good cross-section of the Chilcotin's peoples, white and Native, all rejoicing in Bordy's plenty. He was everywhere: giving orders, talking up the hands, showing off to the onlookers. The Pauls, with the exception of Peter, were there too. Alec was now lead hand, and his daughter, Justine—who was a fine horsewoman—took part in the physical work with much grace. Noah, too, was taking his part with Bordy riding herd on him.

Stan joined the rail-sitters next to Antoine. Where Stan buried himself in the law, giving him a more cynical approach to life, Antoine, the deyen, was connected to his surroundings; natural and unnatural. He was uneducated in that he couldn't read or write, but he was a person whose opinion Stan valued.

After acknowledging Stan's presence, Antoine turned his gaze back to Bordy, who was mounted on a palomino stud and was every bit the general in command of this branding. He had come a long way since his father died in the ring at the Anahim Lake stampede twenty years ago, and Stan could see a lot of Dean in him. The calf that Noah had lassoed slipped from the noose and went bawling back to its mother. Bordy yelled at Noah, "Don't you know enough to cinch up on that lasso?" Then Bordy lassoed the same calf himself and yelled, "That's how you do it."

Antoine leaned over to Stan. "Bordy is boiling water. He always scalds, never soothes."

The two men kept their eyes on Noah to see how he was taking his father's insult. Justine rode up to Noah and spoke to him. He appeared calmed by her words.

After branding that day, Noah met up with Justine in the barn. Since she had spoken to him in the corral and calmed him down he couldn't stop thinking about her. She had always been Peter's little sister and almost a sister to him. Now with Peter gone to Vancouver, he saw her for who she was: a spirited, independent Chilcotin woman who seemed to care a lot about him. He was rubbing down his horse in the next stall to Justine's and said, "Thanks for cooling me off over that roping miss today."

"Your dad can be a shit at times."

Noah laughed. "At times?"

They finished with the horses, walked to the front of the barn and sat on a hay bale. Noah asked, "Have you heard from Peter?"

"He sometimes phones Mum and Dad for money."

"I feel guilty in a way, because if I had stayed in the Chilcotin, he might not have been tempted to leave."

"No, don't blame yourself," she said, laying a hand on his arm. "Antoine says that Peter may come to his senses. He's planning on going to Vancouver to see if Peter will come back."

Noah took both of her hands in his. "This must be very hard on you."

Her heart stopped beating for a moment, and tears were in her eyes.

"Yes, I miss him."

He had never spoken to her like that before, nor held her hands so tenderly. She knew that Noah had a girlfriend in Victoria and she had been resigned to being just good friends with him, but when he reached out to her she was overcome. She flung herself at Noah and they fell off the hay bale in each other's arms.

There was a barbeque and a dance in the great hall that evening. Noah danced every dance with Justine. It was obvious even to Stan that they were a couple. Bordy was the life of the party. Towards midnight he approached Noah and Justine between dances when everyone was taking a breather from a strenuous square dance.

"Noah, I see you need more practice with the rope," he said, looking at Justine and winking.

She squeezed Noah's hand, and Noah said, "I'm doing just fine, Bordy."

"Well, it's time for you to go to bed now. We'll be up at dawn to finish the job."

"No, Justine and I are just getting started, but you have a good night's sleep."

Bordy scowled and walked away. A half-hour later, with the band taking a break, they were dancing a slow dance to Louis Armstrong's recording of Blueberry Hill. Bordy came up to them on the floor, having had a bit more to drink, and said, "I think I will dance with Justine now."

"No, thank you, Mr. Hanlon. I promised all my dances to Noah."

It was after this rebuff that Bordy motioned Stan into his den. Bordy went to the bar for a single-malt scotch whisky, not his first of the evening.

"Will you have a whisky?" he asked Stan.

"Don't think I will."

"That's not like you, Stan."

"I swore off it a while ago."

"Well, that's probably a good thing. You'll need all your wits to help me."

"What's the problem?"

"I've got news from our local MLA that the provincial cabinet has been secretly petitioned to give a water licence to the Vancouver Island Power Company for the purpose of damming the Homathko River at Waddington Canyon. If that dam is built, this valley will be flooded and you and I will be sitting under ten feet of water."

"Easy now. That's a long way off, and we have time to divert those plans. You do know of course that Belle is on very friendly terms with Major Jack Parmenter, the majority owner of the power company."

"I know that," Bordy spat out. "I can see her devious hand behind all this. I want you to use every legal trick you can to stop this invasion of my land."

"Well, they haven't made the decision yet. I'll start working on it."

Stan used the age-old lawyer's strategy of threat and delay to interfere with the government's plans. He wrote the premier and threatened legal action if a water licence was granted. He knew that it would take months for the attorney general to provide the cabinet with an opinion on whether its decision could be upheld in the courts.

Throughout the balance of 1957 there was silence from Victoria on the rumoured plan. Bordy was continually angry at the thought of the dam, and Stan believed that this was the main cause of Bordy's stroke that Christmas. Feng, Empire's cook, found Bordy in bed when he didn't come down for breakfast. Alec Paul drove him into the hospital, where Dr. Hay kept him for a week. The right side of his body was paralyzed, but he was mentally alert. The doctor warned him that if he continued to run the ranch in his condition he would certainly have a relapse. With proper exercise and a good diet he would see some improvement in the next year.

Noah came to Williams Lake to see his father. Belle wanted to come, but Bordy refused to see her so she remained in Victoria.

Bordy greeted Noah from his hospital bed. "I'm not dead yet."

Noah had never seen Bordy so vulnerable. He had learned to fear his father's rages. To see him lying there weak and with his face twisted on the right side made him sympathize with Bordy for the first time since he'd first ridden on his father's pommel as a child. Stan, who was hovering in the back of the hospital room, heard Noah mumble with some warmth in his voice, "You sure don't look well."

"I can't ride a horse now. How can I run a ranch without a horse?"

Stan, in the background, murmured, "My kingdom for a horse," then spoke out: "You'll have to find a good manager."

Bordy nodded and looked at Noah with apparent feeling. "The only person I would trust is Noah. What do you say, son? Will you to take over the managing of Empire until I get back in the saddle?"

"That would break up my year at college, but I'll think about it if you really need me."

"Start thinking!"

On his return to Victoria, Noah told his mother that Bordy had asked him to manage the ranch while he recovered.

"What did you say?" she asked.

"I said I would think about it."

She responded passionately. "He doesn't need you to manage the ranch. He wants to make life miserable for you and to humiliate me. You're an artist, not a cowboy."

"You should see him; he's paralyzed on one side and can't ride a horse."

"Can he talk?"

"Yes."

"Then he'll make your life a living hell!"

The major's response was more tactful: "I know you are a good artist. I've seen your work. I don't know about your ranching skills. Don't you and Bordy fight all the time?"

"That's his way of teaching me."

"If you want to be taught how to run a business—which I recommend, because you can't make a living as an artist—then I'll hire you to work at the company."

"Thanks a lot," Noah said sullenly. "That would kill any creative energy I have."

"And being a rancher won't?"

"No. I'm part of the Chilcotin. I'm going back to help Bordy, but it's the Chilcotin I'm committed to, and it's the Chilcotin that will give me the inspiration I need to improve my painting."

"Do you expect me to be waiting for your return?" Emily asked him when he told her of his plans.

"No, I meant to tell you that I am seeing someone else."

"Oh, I see! Your agreeing to manage the ranch is just an excuse to be closer to this someone else."

Belle's final words to Noah were even harsher. "Don't bother coming back to this house until you've rid yourself of the notion that you're a cowboy."

THANKSGIVING

Noah agreed to manage the ranch for a year. The first months of his stewardship—with Bordy confined to his room—were relatively peaceful. He found time to do some winter sketches and to visit Justine, who was a student at the Indian residential school St. Joseph's Mission about twelve miles southeast of Williams Lake. This idyllic lull ended with the start of the calving season.

The calving yard held fifteen hundred cows. The first calves came in March, and the season stretched into April. Noah slept in the barn to be close to the herd to assist those cows having birthing problems. After spring breakup the hay fields were harrowed and fertilized, and then the water systems had to be repaired. The busy summer months were full of riding the range, irrigating, and haying. He had no personal life, no time for Justine or his painting, and each day as Bordy's health improved Noah felt the sting of Bordy's verbal lashes.

When Bordy was up to it, they ate their big meal at lunch in the huge dining room that could seat twenty-four people. This civilized practice stopped in mid-June, when Bordy showed up drunk and his first words to Noah, who was spooning his soup, were, "I was at the Eagle Lake hay fields. You aren't getting enough water on them. I may be an invalid but there's nothing wrong with my eyes."

Noah, who had been up since four that morning, spoke right up. "Those fields have plenty of water. You're the one who needs more water and less whisky."

"Listen to me, boy. If you spent more time looking after the ranch and less time making eyes at that Paul girl you wouldn't be losing my money."

"If you don't like the way I'm running the ranch, then fire me."

But it wasn't Bordy's plan to fire Noah; he wanted to push Noah until he quit. Noah wasn't about to quit. He was going to finish the year and hand the ranch back to his father in better shape than he had received it.

The ranch crews hayed through the hot spells and in September hauled the hay to the winter fields and got ready for the annual roundup. Bordy made a practice of riding around in a buggy cursing at the hay crews and countermanding Noah's orders. He told everyone who would listen that his adopted son was ruining him and running the ranch into the ground.

A month earlier Noah wouldn't have spoken to his father that way. He would have been more respectful despite the abuse, but for the first time in his life he had experienced the loss of a close friend, and thoughts of his own mortality gave him a sense of purpose and fight. He had just buried—with Bordy's permission—his childhood friend,

Peter, in the Hanlon graveyard.

Since Noah had taken over the management of the ranch he found that he missed Peter's company. He had worked side-by-side with him and they had considered themselves brothers. When Noah left for Victoria, Peter had felt abandoned, especially when he had to attend St. Joseph's Mission School and was away from his family. Peter looked forward to Noah's coming back to the ranch in the summers when they would resume their friendship. But each year it got harder for Peter to accept his role. He drifted away from the ranch, dropped out of school and hung out and drank with other young men his age in Williams Lake. It wasn't long before the attractions of the big city lured him to Vancouver, and there, aside from a few phone calls asking for money, his parents lost track of him.

Then, in May, they received a phone call from the Vancouver police to tell them that Peter had died of alcohol poisoning. They made the painful journey by pickup to the city with a pine box to bring Peter back and bury him in the Chilcotin. Noah and Justine consoled each other over the loss of their friend and brother.

*****

Stan had not been invited to the ranch since Bordy's stroke. He had heard that Noah was working hard and that Bordy was making Noah's job more difficult. The word was that if he were feeling better he would have fired him by now. Stan knew Bordy well enough to know that Bordy was getting some enjoyment out of tormenting his adopted son. The question was whether Noah would be able to bear up under the pressure or if Bordy would break him like a wild mustang. Stan was planning on going out to the ranch after his annual Thanksgiving fishing trip at Puntzi Lake to see firsthand what was going on. He had heard nothing from the premier's office on the Waddington dam licence and was beginning to think the cabinet had other ideas for hydroelectric power.

The cattle drive was in the week before Thanksgiving. The crews drove the cattle to the home ranch from the ranges. Empire now ran over three thousand head. It took foreman Alec Paul, three cowhands, Justine, and Noah the better part of the week to round them up off the Potato Mountain, Chilko River, and Eagle Lake open ranges. Near the end of the roundup Bordy came in the buggy with Feng to one of the camps. He was drunk. He ordered Feng to drive the buggy right up to Noah and said, "You're nothing but a mother's boy. You're no help to me out here. You're fucking harassing those steers."

Noah replied in a matter-of-fact way, refusing to argue with his father: "That bunch of steers ran up the draw, and we're bringing them back to the main herd."

In Bordy's drunken state, any reasonable talk angered him more, so he said, "You goddamn breed. You've forgotten all I taught you."

He stepped off the buggy and fell on his face.

"Bordy, you're drunk," Noah said, and turned to Feng. "Take him back home. He could get injured out here."

The group of wranglers rode off, leaving Feng to deal with a humiliated Bordy, who cursed his cook, his crew and Noah all the way home.

In Victoria, Belle found that the major was becoming unmanageable. The delay in the cabinet's decision to grant his company the water licence was making him irritable, and he kept muttering to himself whenever the topic came up that Field Marshal Montgomery would have dealt with the roadblock directly. Of course the "roadblock" was Bordy Hanlon and his lawyer, Stan Hewitt.

Before Thanksgiving he dropped by Belle's house. He had already been to the club and was red in the face and excitable. She was at the piano practising for her recital that evening where she was performing Beethoven's Appassionato Sonata and Chopin's Ballade #1 in G Minor. She didn't look up when he entered, which irritated the major. He poured himself a drink, walked up to her and interrupted her playing.

He spoke loudly as if giving a command: "I won't stand for any more delay in getting approval from the government for my dam. Stan Hewitt, that tiresome lawyer who dotes on you, has threatened a lawsuit and injunction against the survey and is in a conflict of interest."

"Stan doesn't know I have an interest in Vancouver Island Power."

"You're a half-owner in the ranch. I want you to take action to force a sale. My lawyer tells me it can be done in a few months. Besides, Bordy is an invalid and not fit to run a large ranch."

"I can't talk about it now. Can't you see I'm getting ready for my recital?"

"This is important. The company needs the power. Bordy is causing a delay. You have to make a choice, Belle: either Bordy or me. If I don't get this water licence, then you and I are through. Give the word and I will have my lawyer start legal proceedings."

Belle threw up her hands. "I will take care of it in my own way. Now leave me be while I compose myself for the recital."

Mollified, the major had the last word: "See that you do."

*****

On Thanksgiving Sunday the ranch was quiet after lunch. All the able-bodied hands were in the hills for the last push into the home valley. The old cows knew the way and walked placidly to their winter quarters. By dinner, three thousand head of the finest Black Angus and Hereford cattle outside of Great Britain would converge on the home fields surrounding the main house. Antoine rested in his lean-to, which was attached to his son Alec Paul's cabin near the barn and set well back from the main house. It was a cool, still autumn day with a hint of snow in the sharp air. Age had not affected Antoine's hearing or his imagination, and he was alert for the sound of the lead cows, which would soon be followed by the thunder of thousands of hoofs descending on his valley.

He thought about Peter's death and wondered, as he did every day, what he could have done to prevent it. The boy who had once been the pride of the Paul family and their hope for passing on the Chilcotin's knowledge of customs and cures had died of alcohol poisoning. The chirping sparrows, making a fuss over seeds outside Antoine's window, comforted him. He took his mind off Peter and considered again the notion that Noah just might substitute for Peter as deyen.

The sparrows took flight. Antoine heard only his rasping breath, like the slow dip of a paddle across a still lake, and then a yell from his eight-year-old grandson Ben came from inside the cabin.

"Don't hurt her!"

Ben's yell brought the old man to his feet too quickly. Dizzy, he steadied himself, then looked out the cobwebbed window to see his granddaughter Justine, her blouse torn, run out of the cabin followed by Bordy. Justine ran for the barn while Bordy limped towards the ranch house. Gaining his balance, Antoine made his way to the door and pushed it open. He saw Ben, carrying his father's hunting rifle, go into the shed in the back and return empty-handed.

"I heard you yell, Ben. What happened?" Antoine asked.

"Nothing," replied Ben.

Then Maria's voice came from inside. "Go back to sleep, Antoine."

Antoine sat on the porch. Something had happened. Why was Maria telling him to go back to sleep? Did she think he was too old to protect his family? His breath came in little gasps and his chest tightened. He stayed on the porch for a while listening to the snowfall till his heart settled. Then he rose to his feet.

STAN

At five o'clock on the Tuesday morning after Thanksgiving, Stan Hewitt's long grizzled face stared back at him from a cracked mirror hanging above the kitchen sink. He never bothered to shave on the weekends spent at Puntzi Lake camp. He passed a hand over his three-day stubble, lathered, and with an ivory-handled straight razor scraped the whiskers from his lean, weathered cheeks, chin, and stringy neck. He rinsed in cold bracing water, and paused a moment to look at the effect. He was pleased with himself, not out of vanity but from amazement that after the life he'd led, he could still shave without serious injury to himself. He may not have to shave much longer. His smoker's cough had developed into a small throat tumour and Dr. Hay, who had arranged to treat him with radiation, had also given him some advice: "Stan, tidy up your affairs, stop working, and go fishing."

A line from the Rubaiyat of Omar Khayyam came to mind: "Eat, drink and be merry, for tomorrow we die." He was well-prepared for death, having spent a lifetime doing just what the prophet had suggested. He ignored his doctor's advice as he had ignored his priest Father Patrick's advice to prepare his soul for the afterlife. What kept him at his desk reading law and taking on cases was the conceit that a major case—perhaps it would be his next client—would benefit from his experience. He would be able to use his lifetime of knowledge at the bar and his full warehouse of wisdom to obtain for a client one last acquittal from a jury. Then he would put his affairs in order.

Mist was rising from the warm lake into the frosty air, and Stan should have been getting his gear ready for a day of fishing. Instead he was shaving to go into town to see Noah Hanlon, who was being held at the Williams Lake jail on the charge of murder. It was a three-hour drive over rough roads from Puntzi Lake to Williams Lake. He wanted to be at the jail when it opened at 9:00 AM.

The jail was in the basement of the Williams Lake Courthouse, the scene of many of his legal battles. Richard Snellgrove, the sheriff's deputy, met him at the desk. Richard's main qualification for the job of deputy sheriff was that he was Sheriff Gideon Snellgrove's nephew. He also weighed three hundred pounds, stood six-and-a-half feet tall and could intimidate most people by standing and staring down at them with his pig's eyes. Stan usually had a lot of tolerance for people, especially the misfits, for they formed the basis of his clientele. He took pride in finding some human warmth even in the worst offender.

Snellgrove was the exception. Stan enjoyed reading Charles Dickens. He thought of Richard Snellgrove as a Bill Sykes type of bully, who became Uriah Heep and snivelled when he didn't get his way.

Stan had told Sheriff Gideon Snellgrove a few years ago that his nephew was trouble. In particular he had roughed up a few of Stan's Native clients who were prisoners in his charge. Stan had advised Gideon to fire Richard, but his good advice was not acted on and got back to Richard. His natural mean streak was now directed towards Stan.

"What are you doing up this early, old man?" Richard asked.

"I'm here to see Noah."

"You mean that murdering breed that shot his father?"

"We'll see about that."

"Oh, we'll see all right. He must be desperate to think of hiring you."

"Just bring Noah to the interview room and then leave us be."

"Hey, Noah! Your lawyer the town drunk is here," Richard shouted on his way to the cells.

Stan moved into a room behind the desk. The deputy opened the door from the cells and shoved Noah into a chair. Stan looked across the table at Noah, whom he hadn't seen since Noah had taken over the managing of Empire Ranch.

He appeared physically strong. His face was leaner, emphasizing his high cheekbones, and his green eyes burned. He had lost his city softness. Living with Bordy could do that to a person. Stan shook Noah's hand. It was hard and calloused, but his grip was surprisingly gentle and he looked closely at Stan, keeping his eyes on the older man. In Stan's experience, his Native clients didn't look him in the eye much when they spoke or were spoken to. In their culture it wasn't polite.

Stan came to the point. "You all right?"

"Yes. Mother's been here a few times. It was good to see

her again . . . but not this way."

"The RCMP told me you've been charged with the murder of your father and that you asked to see me."

Noah listened to the older man's deep resonant voice, which had the timbre of a bass fiddle. He recalled Stan at the ranch and in Victoria, telling stories about his law cases that made him laugh and wonder how people could get themselves into such impossible situations. Now he knew.

"I need a lawyer. Is this the kind of case you do?"

"Yes, it is."

"Then I'd like you to represent me. My mother has agreed to pay for a lawyer. She suggested another lawyer from Victoria, but I prefer you."

Stan put his notepad on the desk and took out his pen.

"Tell me what happened."

"There isn't much to tell. We'd been rounding up our cattle for the last week. Last Saturday, Bordy came out to the range. He'd been drinking and we argued. He was mad. He went back to the ranch. The next day was the final day of the roundup. I met Justine in the barn at dusk. She had been crying. She told me that Bordy had sexually assaulted her in the kitchen of her parents' cabin. She was afraid of him. I told her to go back to her cabin, that I would speak to Bordy. I found him in the great hall in front of a blazing fire. I entered through the French doors. They were open, which was strange as the wind off the lake was near freezing and it was snowing. He was drinking. I told him that he was never to lay a hand on Justine. He challenged me, said that I had my eye on her myself."

Stan asked, "Is that true?"

"Yes, we're in love."

Stan nodded.

"Then Bordy laughed. 'That doesn't make her yours,' he

said. I told him to leave her alone, and he said I couldn't stop him. If he wanted Justine, he would have her. He taunted me. I came closer to him, and he said, 'Sure, beat up on a crippled man,' and flew into a rage. He said, 'You're just like your mother.'

"Then he picked up his rifle, which was stashed beside him like he was expecting trouble. I ran towards him as he was raising it and grabbed it. We wrestled."

Noah paused for a moment, and Stan said, "I know this is hard for you, but it's best I hear it now while it's fresh in your memory."

Noah continued. "I wrestled it away from him, and while the gun was in my hands it discharged. The shock of the sound startled him, so he loosened his grip. I threw the gun on the floor, turned and walked the length of the room towards the open doors facing the lake without looking back." Noah paused for a second to collect himself. "When I got near the open doors I heard a high-pitched, animal-like scream. Then the sound of a gunshot and the whistling sound of a bullet from the lawn. I looked out and saw a person in the dusk and snowflakes."

"Do you know who it was?"

Noah hesitated, then said, "No."

"What did you do next?"

"I looked back into the room, and there was Bordy lying on the floor, bleeding from a gunshot wound to his chest. I tried to stop the bleeding but he was already dead. I picked up his gun and ran from the room, right into two cowhands who'd come from the barn when they heard the shot. I had the gun in my hand. I was gone for a good long while, trying to track down the killer, when the RCMP found me and took me into custody."

"Did you give them a statement?"

"Yes."

"Did you tell them what you told me?"

"I left out the part where Justine told me she was assaulted. I don't want to get her involved in this. I just told them that Bordy and I had a quarrel about the cattle drive."

"Do you remember anything else?"

"I seem to remember a plane taking off from the lake. It wasn't loud. I was too distracted to think about it till now."

"Do you think that's important?"

"It's not unusual for floatplanes to land on the lake to deliver hunting and fishing parties."

The two men were silent for a moment.

"Do you think you can prove my innocence?" Noah asked. "I couldn't bear to have my mother think that I could do such a thing."

"We don't have to prove your innocence. The Crown has to prove your guilt beyond a reasonable doubt. They only have a circumstantial case."

"What does that mean?"

"It means that the Crown must prove to the jury that it was you who aimed the gun at Bordy with the intent to kill him and that it was you who squeezed the trigger firing the bullet that killed him. If the Crown had a credible eyewitness who saw this happen, that would be a strong case against you and could well be proof beyond a reasonable doubt."

"The only eyewitness I'm aware of is the person who shot Bordy."

"Then the Crown has to rely on circumstantial evidence such as witnesses hearing shots, seeing you with a gun in your hand, and Bordy lying dead on the floor. In your case there are other explanations for what the witnesses saw and the jury must take those other explanations into consideration, and that may lead them to a reasonable doubt about your guilt. The judge will instruct them that they then must acquit."

Noah nodded. He seemed to understand and take comfort from it.

Stan looked down at his notes and said, "One more thing. Can you describe the gun?"

"It was Bordy's Winchester automatic .30-30 hunting rifle. He kept it in a cabinet in the great hall."

It was now 1:00 PM and Stan had not eaten since 5:30 in the morning. At the Flying U Café, he had his usual fried-egg sandwich and coffee. Fran Harrop cooked him breakfast on weekdays, and he liked to use her as a sounding board for some of his cases. She had been around awhile and knew what was on the minds and tongues of the locals. While she was flipping his egg he asked, "Fran? You hear about Bordy Hanlon being shot and killed at Empire Ranch?"

"Yeah, that's no surprise. Half the Chilcotin had a grudge against him. "

"You know the police have charged Noah with murder?"

"Yup! Now I find that hard to believe. He's a nice Indian boy. I've served him since he was kid, and he was always polite."

Stan liked that answer. The jury would be made up of people like Fran, and her feelings about the case and Noah were probably the feelings of the town.

His next stop was the prosecutor's office. Acton Bates saw him from the open door of his office and told the receptionist to show him in. He had already heard that Stan had been retained.

"This case is a slam dunk, Stan. The crime lab technician phoned and said Noah's fingerprints are all over the gun, and ballistics tests show that a shell casing was ejected from the gun. And Noah has admitted to being in the room at the time of the shooting."

Stan shook his head. "You sure that's the gun that killed Bordy?"

Bates didn't respond and Stan continued. "You're going to have to find a lot more evidence than that to convict my client. In the meantime, I want all the witness statements and a summary of all your evidence as soon as you have it. I particularly want to take a look at that rifle when it gets back from ballistics, and I want a preliminary hearing and trial before Christmas."

"There are other cases on the docket."

"None as important as this one. I'm going to bring on an application for bail on Thursday."

Bates had expected Stan to apply for bail, which would usually be granted to a resident in good standing in the area. But this was the crime of the century on the plateau. Nothing like it had gripped the public's attention since the Chilcotin wars in the last century. Bordy Hanlon's adopted son, a Chilcotin Native, had been charged with murder. The press from Vancouver and Victoria were all over the story. The deputy attorney general in Victoria had been on the phone earlier that day to determine if the homicide arose from a family affair or from racial tension.

"You don't want the press to start speculating about this Chilcotin affair and the reasons for the murder," he'd said. "That could only cause unrest in the whole Chilcotin. It's too unsettling to have an unknown killer or killers roaming around loose on the plateau."

"We've got the right man," Bates had assured him, and now here was Stan Hewitt talking about bail.

"I've got instructions to oppose your bail application."

Stan had expected that response. "We'll see," he said.

Belle was staying at the Williams Lake Hotel. Stan phoned

her from the lobby and asked if he could come up to her room. He hadn't seen her for over a year and was wondering how she was bearing up under the strain of her son being charged with the murder of her estranged husband. It was late in the afternoon. He was tired, his head throbbed and he was due for his first radiation treatment later that week in Vancouver. But when she opened the door and he had a look at her, he forgot his troubles. When she began to cry, he put his arm around her.

She said while sobbing on his shoulder, "I got a call from the police on the night of the killing saying he was a suspect and could be charged with murder. I took the next plane to Williams Lake and rushed to the jail."

"Don't you worry. I will do everything in my power to clear his name."

He sat down on a chair. She sat on the bed opposite him.

"I told Noah not to take on the job of ranch manager. I told him if he did I wouldn't speak to him until he came to his senses. What more could I do to stop him? But I didn't think it would come to this."

"When you saw him in jail, did he tell you what happened?" Stan had to ask this question because anything Noah told his mother was not privileged and he didn't want to be sideswiped at the trial.

"No. All he said is that he didn't shoot Bordy. And I believe him."

"So do I. And it's my job to convince a jury of that. Did the major come with you?"

"No."

"In that case, and since you'll be here at least for the bail application, would you like to have dinner tomorrow night? I'll have to call you as a character witness for Noah. We could talk about your evidence."

"Yes. I would like that, Stan."

The day after Stan Hewitt's visit Noah had another visitor. She approached Deputy Snellgrove, who was lounging behind his desk reading a copy of Field & Stream magazine. He knew she was there but made no movement or response. She waited, knowing that he would expect her to be submissive in front of a white man with authority. Finally he looked up from his magazine and into the face of a young Native girl. Her hair was pulled back tightly from her forehead and braided at the back. She had a small oval face with large brown eyes which were alert and inquisitive, and although she was shy and didn't look directly at strangers, she spoke in a quiet, determined voice, carried herself well and walked gracefully.

"Who are you and what do you want?"

"Justine Paul. I'm here to visit Noah Hanlon. I am a friend of his."

"You know why he's here? He's charged with murdering his father. That's a hanging offence."

"Yes, I know," she said. "May I see him?"

"Why?"

She had phoned the sheriff's office before visiting the jail and had been told by the sheriff himself that she could see Noah, but she didn't want to say that to the deputy. To go over Snellgrove's head would make him her enemy, and she wanted to see Noah for as long as he was in jail. She didn't answer.

Snellgrove grinned. "Maybe he doesn't want to see you."

Justine felt like she was dealing with a child caged in a three-hundred-pound adult body. "Would you ask him? Please?"

The deputy believed that he had the best of her. She knew who was boss.

"All right, you can have five minutes with him, but I am keeping my eye on you."

He let her into a room divided by wire mesh and left the door open. Noah was sitting on a chair on the other side, and when she entered he got up and put his hands on the mesh. She did the same.

"God, I'm glad to see you," he said.

"I've been so worried."

They moved closer so that their lips were brushing the wire mesh that separated them.

"Hey, you two—back off!" Snellgrove shouted from the doorway. "I don't want you passing anything between you, even germs."

He whispered, "Justine, you know I wouldn't kill Bordy, don't you? All I did was warn him off you."

She nodded. "I knew it must have been an accident."

"It was no accident," Noah said, shaking his head. "He was shot by someone who was outside the room on the lawn."

"Time's up!"

"Will you come back?" Noah asked Justine.

"It will take more than him to stop me," Justine answered.

Within a week of his imprisonment and after the bail hearing had failed, Noah asked Justine to bring pencils, pastels, and paper to his cell. For the first time in months he had time for sketching. The portfolio of his drawings became his diary. His book filled with sketches of birds, animals and people. He drew Stan as a blue heron—thin and erect—in his black court robes, watching the little fish glide by. He drew Justine as a fawn. He showed the drawing to her, and she was flattered and asked to keep it. He didn't show his tormentor Snellgrove the drawing he had made of him: only a wolverine could convey Snellgrove. Justine shuddered when she saw it, for the fanged snarl and sinister cringing leer turned her cold.

Justine had grown to hate Richard Snellgrove. She visited Noah whenever she could get away from her studies at the residential school run by the Oblates and the Sisters of the Child Jesus. She was in her last year of high school and was granted some freedom by Mother Superior, who had great plans for Justine. Snellgrove, on the other hand, took every opportunity to insult Justine as a Native and as a woman. She didn't complain to Noah about the treatment she received because she knew that he was treated much worse. Although Snellgrove did not abuse Noah physically because he knew he would have Stan Hewitt on his case, he called Noah every dirty, racist name he could think of: breed, Siwash, and motherfucker. He wasn't inventive, but the repetition wore on the Native.

Noah's preliminary hearing began in December. The witnesses Acton Bates had were the ranch hands and Feng, who all said they had seen Noah outside the great hall, rifle in hand, within minutes of the shooting. They said that father and son often quarrelled and had done so at one of the camps a few days before the shooting. Then there was the fingerprint expert identifying Noah's prints on the gun, a .30-30 Winchester belonging to Bordy, and the forensic expert recreating the scene and the position of the victims and the assailant when the gun was fired. The report from the expert on gunpowder residue showed that Noah had fired a gun recently.

The Crown's case was not strong, however. A lead slug was found in the fireplace after the fire had burned out, but could not be identified as being shot from the Winchester either through the calibre or striations because the fire had reduced it to a formless lump. A casing was found in the room. It matched the gun's firing pin, but the exact position of the shooter wasn't known. But Noah had had the gun in his hands when the ranch hands had arrived on the scene. The ranch hands had heard only one shot and there was only one casing in the room and a piece of lead in the fireplace. Bordy was found lying on the floor with his head towards the fireplace.

With that information, the experts concluded that the assailant was standing inside the room, near the double glass doors, and that Bordy had been exactly fifteen feet in front of the fireplace, where the outline of his body was now chalked on the floor. The bullet was fired from near the glass doors and struck Bordy in the chest and then exited Bordy's back, struck the stone fireplace, fell into the fire and melted.

Stan cross-examined the witnesses to understand the Crown's case and to determine if there were any inconsistencies or flaws in their evidence he could exploit at trial. He wanted to make sure that there wouldn't be any surprises at trial and made only a perfunctory argument that the magistrate throw out the charges.

In his summation at the preliminary hearing, Bates said, "Your worship, I won't repeat the evidence you have just heard except to say that all the forensic evidence and the witnesses' evidence points to Noah Hanlon as the person who fired the gun that killed his father, and that he should be remanded to stand trial for murder."

The magistrate agreed.

"The accused, Noah Hanlon, will be remanded to stand trial without bail to the next assize in February."

Although Stan had told Noah that the magistrate would find that there was a prima facie case against him, Noah had hoped that Stan would be wrong and that he would be freed. He felt the disappointment. It didn't help that on the way back to the cells, Snellgrove took the opportunity to say, "I told you, you should get a different lawyer. You're going down."

Stan met up with Bates in the lawyers' robing room.

"If your client tells me the full story now and pleads guilty to manslaughter," Bates said, "then perhaps we can discuss sentence."

"That's not possible," Stan said.

Bates proceeded with the major charge. Stan was left relying on Noah to tell his story in a credible manner so that a jury, properly charged, would acquit. One afternoon before Christmas, Noah was surprised when Snellgrove's holiday replacement jangled his jail keys in front of Noah's cell and told him that he had a male visitor; as he put it, "A pint-sized boy with a bad attitude."

Noah walked into the interview room to be greeted by Ralph Richards.

"Ralph, it's good to see you."

"I'm sorry I didn't come sooner. I brought you some cookies my mum made, and Emily sends her best."

They spent the rest of the time talking about Victoria and the friends Noah had left behind but not heard from. Ralph came back to visit the next day and Noah told him, "My spirits rose yesterday to think that you cared enough to travel to Williams Lake to see me. Justine visits me, but she's at the mission school and can only come once a week. It's too bad you can't meet her." Noah told Ralph about the case and about his lawyer, whom Ralph knew.

As he was leaving, Ralph said, "I can't attend your trial, but I will be praying for your acquittal."

Justine visited Noah over Christmas, and the sheriff on duty gave them the privacy of the interview room where they could be together without bars or wire. Justine gave

Noah a few presents: some pastels, more drawing paper, and a painting of the Cariboo by Sonia Cornwall, a local artist.

He looked at it with a critical eye and explained it to Justine. "There's freshness in this painting. She has a strong sense of the understanding of life with space and movement. I'm working on a distinctive style of my own which will show the Chilcotin the way Mrs. Cornwall has found a style for the Cariboo. But here's me talking to you about painting nature's beauty when I'm looking at the real thing. I have a present for you," he added, handing her the complete works of Percy Bysshe Shelley.

"Mother brought it for me because he above all the Romantics best suits my mind and speaks my love for you."

Justine threw her arms around Noah. "Thank you, thank you," she said, and the book dropped to the floor as they embraced.

When they separated, Noah picked the book off the floor and opened it to a well-thumbed page. "Shelley died before he finished his best and last poem, "The Triumph of Life," but I've finished it for you."

"Read it to me."

"Shelley writes:

'Then what is life?' I said . . . the cripple cast
His eye upon the car which now had rolled
Onward as if that look must be the last. And answered,
'Happy those for whom the fold
Of . . .'

"Shelly didn't finish the stanza," Noah said, "but I did:

. . . And answered,
'Happy those for whom the fold
Of love hath embraced in the dew-filled dawn;
Life is a love story that is eternally told,
The curve of Justine's breast beautifully drawn.'"

Justine murmured, "I live to embrace you in the dew-filled dawn," and taking Noah's hand, placed it on her breast.

"Hey! It's awful quiet in there," the sheriff called out.

"Noah is explaining a painting to me," Justine called back.

They pulled apart and Noah, still holding her hands, said, "I have something important to tell you. You mustn't tell anyone unless I'm dead. You're the only one I can trust. I've been thinking about what happened when Bordy was shot. I told the police and Mr. Hewitt that I saw someone on the lawn after the shot was fired. The police don't believe that there was anyone. Mr. Hewitt believes me, and he's putting that forward as my defence. That night, I couldn't give anyone a description, and at the time I didn't have any idea who it was. All these months, I've been trying to connect what I heard and saw to the shadowy figure on the lawn. I think I know who it was."

"Who?"

Noah hesitated. He had second thoughts about telling Justine. "If I told you, your life would be in danger."

"You must tell Mr. Hewitt."

"I can't trust anyone but you and him."

JUSTICE

There were no Natives—Chilcotin, Shuswap, or Carrier—in the jury pool when the trial began before Judge Deacon that February. The lawyers had to pick a jury from the thirty-four white people sitting at the back of the courtroom, most of whom were from Williams Lake. It was more convenient for the sheriff to serve them with a jury notice and much more convenient for townspeople to attend in the middle of winter than those citizens living over a hundred miles away. The roads were icy and blizzards frequent and the sheriff would have had to put them up in a local hotel at the Crown's expense. Neither the distance nor the weather prevented a crowd of about fifty Natives from filling the balance of the courtroom and flowing out into the corridor.

Noah, in handcuffs, entered under the guard of Richard Snellgrove, who made a show of removing Noah's cuffs in front of the jury pool and the Natives. Justine was sitting in the courtroom beside her grandfather, old Antoine, and her father, Alec Paul. She waved to Noah when he turned. It appeared to Noah that the only whites in the courtroom were the jury pool and his mother. He had hoped that some of his friends from Victoria would be there and was disappointed when he didn't see any familiar white faces.

Stan Hewitt knew most of the potential jurors: a bank teller, a shoe salesman, an accountant, loggers, and housewives. Williams Lake was a law-abiding town, and sometimes when it was thought that the police weren't applying the law, its citizens took the law into their own hands. Guns were not the way they usually settled disputes unless there was too much liquor involved. He sized up this group of prospective jurors sitting quietly, waiting to know if they would be picked. He had had great success with Williams Lake juries. They understood the meaning of reasonable doubt. They also understood fairness, the struggle people had to survive on the plateau, their willingness to defend what little they had—including their pride—and their natural distrust of strangers.

Stan recalled that he had defended a few of the local boys last summer for assault causing bodily harm in front of a Williams Lake jury. That evening when he saw Noah in jail, he told him about the trial to raise his spirits.

"A motorcycle gang from the coast had rolled into a 150 Mile bar looking for refreshment after a long dusty ride. Full of high spirits, the gang thought they would show the locals a thing or two about big-city etiquette. To the guttural sounds of their engines they swept into the hotel parking lot whooping and hollering. Each of them had his girl sitting pillion except their leader. He was this big six-foot-two guy dressed in black leather, a metal skullcap, and a red ponytail and who had an empty saddle behind him that he figured needed filling.

"Entering the bar, he spotted a girl at a table and introduced himself by pulling out his dick and slapping it on the table. 'Hey there, pussy! I bet you've never seen anything this size in these parts!'

"His whole gang burst out laughing at exactly the same time as her cowboy friend launched himself at the biker's throat and his 'pussy' kicked him in the groin. The fight was on. The cowboys who grew up throwing steers and riding fence lines in minus forty degrees cleaned up on the east-end boys. A Williams Lake jury just like ours acquitted them of assault causing bodily harm and the courtroom broke into cheers."

Stan didn't tell Noah that his case was different. Guns hadn't been involved, nor father-and-son quarrels, nor death. Stan could not play the stranger card, nor could he emphasize Bordy's reputation as a hard-driving sonuvabitch. That would only serve to reduce the charge from murder to manslaughter. He had to rely on the jury to believe that his client was innocent, that he and Bordy had indeed quarrelled but that Noah had been leaving the room when a shot from a third person outside the room killed Bordy. The big question was, who would the jury believe was responsible for his death: Bordy's adopted son, or half the Chilcotin? You couldn't be indifferent to Bordy. People either hated or loved him, and there were very few who loved him.

Before the jury was selected, Stan made a motion to the court in the absence of the jury pool.

"My Lord, I have seen the jury pool, which is composed of thirty-four persons, all of whom are white and who reside in and about Williams Lake. There is not one Native among the prospective jurors, yet as you see there are at least fifty Natives seated in this courtroom. This pool is not representative of the Chilcotin territory where this offence was alleged to have taken place."

Judge Deacon turned to the prosecutor. "What have you to say to that, Mr. Bates?"

"The sheriff picks the jury pool at random, My Lord. This is a large jurisdiction."

The judge turned to Stan. "Your client is the son of a white couple. Why is it that you require Indians on the jury, Mr. Hewitt?"

Stan, who found the high falsetto and the precise manner of the judge irritating, didn't know that he was colour blind.

"My client was adopted, My Lord. As you can see, he is a Chilcotin by birth. Most of the gallery who are present today live on the Chilcotin plateau, and by their presence show that they have a great interest in this case."

"Very well, Mr. Hewitt. Mr. Bates, I'm inclined to have the sheriff increase the jury pool by adding a few Indians. I can see by the gallery that this would not be difficult. I will stand this case down for an hour. Mr. Sheriff, will you make those arrangements?"

His first victory in the trial proved useless to Stan's defence. Three Natives were added to the pool. Stan used his challenges on the white jury selections in the hopes of getting at least one Native onto the jury. When Joe Willieboy's name was pulled from the box of names by the sheriff and read to the court, he stepped forward and walked to the bar. Stan said, "Agreeable, My Lord."

Bates immediately said, "Challenge, My Lord."

Willieboy was told to return to his seat. Stan had used all his challenges. The twelve seats in the jury box quickly filled with an all-white, ten-man, two-woman jury.

Stan was not discouraged. Noah, a young man with no

stain on his life, would take the stand and explain what had happened. His mother would verify his gentle nature and good character. Even a white jury would be moved.

One of the shields a defence lawyer had in a tough case was sympathy, even if the judge told the jury to erase it from their minds. Because the case involved family and guns, this jury might be unduly influenced. If Stan had had his pick of judges he would not have chosen Judge Deacon, but this was all hypothetical. His mind was fixed on acquittal.

Acton Bates opened the case for the Crown on the afternoon of the first day by telling the jury, "The Crown will prove beyond a reasonable doubt that the accused, Noah Hanlon, murdered his adoptive father Bordy Hanlon on that fateful Thanksgiving Sunday at their ranch house in the Chilcotin. The evidence will show that there was a quarrel between the accused and the deceased on the range a few days earlier. According to two ranch hands, the accused went to the ranch house at about 6:00 PM. Shortly after, they heard a shot and ran to the house from the stable area about three hundred yards away. It took them a few minutes to get to the house. On entry through the door into the great hall they saw the accused with a gun in his hand. They went into the room and saw the deceased lying on the floor with a wound to his chest.

"We will be presenting forensic evidence that will show that the accused's fingerprints were on the gun that fired the fatal shot, that he had powder residue on his hands, and we will show through reconstructions how the one shot would have been fired by the accused while he was standing in the room by the double doors. The Crown will be asking you to find the accused guilty of second-degree murder or a lesser charge of manslaughter."

Over the following days, the jury heard the evidence of

the two ranch hands and the cook. Cobby Evans, one of the ranch hands, was a big man with drooping white moustache yellowed with cigarette smoke. His rounded shoulders and muscular arms, linked by his clasped hands, framed his belly when he sat down in the witness box facing the jury. He had a meandering mind and the judge had to keep him on track.

"Tell the jury what you heard and saw when Bordy Hanlon arrived on the range."

"Me and Charley Hopkins—he's called Hoppy on the ranch on account of his being twitchy—he's a nervous type is Hoppy. I remember just last year . . ."

"Please, Mr. Evans, what were you and Mr. Hopkins doing on the range?"

"I was just getting to that. We were rounding up cattle at Choelquoit Lake when the Old Man came up in a buggy and chewed us out for harassing his steers."

"Who do you mean by Old Man?"

"Well, I thought everybody knew that. Isn't that what this trial is all about: the death of Bordy?"

"Carry on, witness."

"We never argued with Bordy. He was apt to fire you on the spot. As we were jawing, up rides Junior—that's what I call Noah—and the old man turns on him and says, 'You better go back to your mother in Victoria because you're no damn help to me.' He used stronger language than that, but I'd better not say it in front of the ladies. And Junior says, 'Those steers got away from us. We'll walk them in from here.'"

"What was Mr. Hanlon's reaction to that?"

"This reasonable talk really got to Bordy. He just got madder. 'I'm taking over my operation,' he says, and he swore some more, referring to Junior as a 'goddamn breed."

"Go on!"

"Then up rides Alec Paul, the lead hand. The Old Man says to him, 'You're taking orders from me now,' and he gets out of the buggy and falls on his face. Junior says to him, 'Bordy, you're drunk.' Then he turns to the cook, Feng, who is driving the buggy and says, 'Take him back to the ranch house before he has another stroke!' and we all ride off 'cause the cattle are starting to wander."

"Did Noah say anything else before you rode off?"

Evans sat sphinx-like without moving a muscle and then spoke slowly through his moustache. "Yeah. As the buggy moved off, he said, 'Better watch out, Bordy! You could get yourself killed out here.'"

Bates then turned to the night of Bordy's death. He asked Evans, "Where were you when you heard the shot?"

"Near the barn, about three hundred yards from the back of the house. I can tell you I was winded when we got to the house. If a horse can't carry me over any distance, I'm in trouble."

He started to expand on horse-riding versus walking when the judge interjected, "Try to keep your answers to the point, witness."

"All right, Judge. We was just coming up to those fancy glass doors at the front of the house when Junior runs out of the big room with a rifle in his hand and heads for the lake like he was pursued by a pack of dogs."

In cross-examination, Stan—in his conversational style—got Evans to say that Noah was at the ranch to help his father. That he was a mild-mannered person who got along well with Alec Paul, and was not as close to the ranch hands but treated them a lot better than Bordy did. When Stan asked if there were any other people in the area the day Noah and Bordy had words, Evans thought a bit and said, “No one except maybe Ta Chi, whose camp was a hundred yards away. She was probably catching suckers in the creek.”

On hearing Ta Chi’s name, the Natives whispered to each other, so that there was an audible sound in the courtroom like wind rustling aspen leaves.

“Who’s Ta Chi?”

“She’s a crazy Native woman who is part of the landscape. She shows up at the darnedest times.”

“Could she hear anything?”

“I dunno, I didn’t see her. I just know she was camped there.”

“Now turning to the day of the shooting. You say you were at the barn and heard one shot?”

“Yeah.”

“Did you hear any other sound coming from the direction of the house before that?”

“No.”

“I take it there was a lot of noise around the barn with cattle milling about?”

“Yeah.”

“Then you could have missed the noise of a muffled shot?”

“I coulda.”

“Thank you, witness.”

Hoppy took the stand next. He was the opposite of the large and garrulous Dale. He was short and wiry and couldn’t sit still in the witness box. Bates found it hard to get words out of him, and whole sentences seemed impossible.

“You were on the range rounding up cattle when Bordy rode out in the buggy?”

“Yeah.”

“Did you overhear any conversation between Bordy and Noah?”

"Yeah."

"Tell the court what you heard."

Normally, Hoppy put his hat on with his boots in the morning and only took it off in his bunk at night. In the courtroom, he had to give his evidence hatless, and this confused him. He moved his right hand to his head as if to lift his Stetson and scratched his head with the other hand before setting the imaginary hat back on his head.

Finally he mumbled, "They had words."

"What were the words?"

He repeated the hat-and-scratch manoeuvre. "I guess they wasn't happy."

"What weren't they happy about?"

He was about to go for his imaginary hat again when Judge Deacon, at the point of exasperation, said, "Mr. Hopkins, is it possible for you to answer a question without scratching your head?"

Hoppy was startled by the judge's voice. He hadn't expected him to say anything, so he stared at the judge. His left hand came up to remove his hat and the right smoothed his hair.

The judge answered his own question. "I guess not. Carry on, Mr. Bates."

The court reporter read out the question to Hoppy, whose face was furrowed in concentration.

He finally answered, "I guess they were unhappy about t'other."

Bates gave up at this point and Stan began his cross-examination.

"Mr. Hopkins, I guess most people in the Chilcotin were unhappy with Bordy Hanlon?"

Hoppy smiled at this simple question, which didn't require any hard thinking or head-scratching, and said, "Yeah."

"Did you notice Ta Chi's camp nearby?"

"Sure did.

"What did that mean to you?"

"Trouble."

"Why is that?"

"Cause it explained a whole lot."

"What, for example?"

"Cattle spooking the way they did."

"What did she have to do with that?'

"Bad things sometime happen when she's around."

Stan had found a rich vein of defence evidence in Hopkins. He could see the jury taking notice.

"Now you were at the barn when you heard a gun go off?"

"Yeah."

"It was quite loud?"

"Yeah."

Hoppy was starting to enjoy his role now. His shirt with its mother-of-pearl snap-on buttons wasn't as tight around his throat.

"Why did you run?"

"You don't hear gunshots from the direction of the big house every day."

After the court adjourned that day, Bates took Stan aside in the lawyer's changing room. "I'm going to call Justine Paul to the stand tomorrow morning."

"Why would you put her through the ordeal of testifying against Noah? Besides, what can she say that hasn't already been said?"

"Getting at the truth is always a painful experience," Bates intoned.

"Well, what about Miss Ta Chi? She isn't on your list of witnesses. Did you interview her? We believe she may have seen or heard something that may help the defence."

"This is the first I heard that she was in the area. If you can find her, you call her."

Stan spoke with Noah that evening in the jail. "The Crown will be calling Justine as its last witness."

"Why would she give evidence against me?"

"Justine has no choice in the matter. She's been subpoenaed so she must give evidence."

"What will she say?"

"According to her statement and what she told me, she will say that she heard only one gunshot from the house and that she is your girlfriend."

"But what if he asks Justine about Bordy assaulting her?"

"They know nothing about that. Besides, Mr. Bates may be bluffing just to unsettle you."

"Well, he's succeeded."

But Noah quieted down after Stan's explanation, so Stan raised his next concern. "You and I have gone over your evidence many times over the last few months preparing for trial. I will be calling you to the stand tomorrow."

"I'll have to sleep on that."

This was the first time Noah had indicated he wasn't fully committed to telling his story to the jury, and Stan tried not to let his anxiety show in his voice. "Noah, our defence is based on you taking the stand."

When Stan left the cell he felt that Noah understood and would probably accept his advice.

Justine visited Noah in the jail after dinner that night. She was agitated, and as soon as she sat down opposite him and the guard left them alone she said, "Mr. Bates wants to put me on the stand tomorrow, but I'm going to tell him I'm not saying a word."

"Stan says you don't have a choice, Justine, but I do. Stan wants to put me on the stand, and I intend to refuse."

"Why? It's your chance to tell the jury what happened."

"I've got to find out who killed Bordy." He leaned forward and quietly asked, "Will you help me escape from the white man's justice?"

"How?"

"I have a plan."

*****

At ten the next morning, after the judge had settled on the bench and the jury—anxious to hear the next act of the drama—were seated, the prosecutor rose and said, "That's the Crown's case, My Lord."

Stan smiled to himself. He turned to look at Noah, who appeared relieved that his lover would not be put through this ordeal. Stan had thought that Bates was bluffing. Bates probably suspected that Justine knew more than she let on, but Justine wouldn't tell him about Bordy's attack and to call Justine without that evidence would only strengthen Noah's case, as Stan would have a right to cross-examine on all Noah's good qualities.

Judge Deacon pursed his lips and looked at the ceiling. He had not been sleeping well. This little town hadn't much to offer for lodging and nothing in the way of decent food unless one enjoyed egg foo yung. He thought he saw a bird looking down at him from on high. He dismissed it; after all, this was his courtroom. The trial was not moving at the pace he would have expected in the city, where the younger lawyers kept things lively and were at each other's throats. Here in the interior it seemed that they were much too friendly. Hewitt had been around forever, although there was no sign of his usual drinking. The judge brought his eyes down from the ceiling and looked at the jury.

"Yes, members of the jury. As I told you at the beginning of this trial, the Crown rests its case, and we are now in the capable hands of Mr. Hewitt, who will present the case for the defence."

Stan was wary of judges who paid him compliments—there was usually a stinger at the end—but he rose, and using his rich baritone addressed the jury.

"The defence expects to call three witnesses to show that the Crown's theory that Noah Hanlon shot his adoptive father Bordy is wrong. The Crown's web of circumstantial evidence is weak and cannot hold up under scrutiny. What happened at the ranch house was a tragic accident that occurred between father and son. The defence will show that Noah had spoken to his father in the great hall and that they had indeed quarrelled. His father produced a gun and Noah disarmed him. During the tussle, the gun discharged in the air and the bullet was not found because it exited the room through the open doors. As Noah left the room through those same doors, his father was still alive. As he cleared the doors there was a shot from the lawn, and that was the shot that killed Bordy Hanlon. Noah picked up his father's gun and gave chase to the murderer. That was when the ranch hands arrived."

Stan was about to call his first witness when two birds perched high on a window-ledge in the courtroom began twittering. The judge hadn't been imagining things. The birds had flown into the courtroom through a broken window thirty feet above the bench in that high-ceilinged room built forty years ago to convey the majesty of the law. They were the sort of sparrows that winter on the plateau and were using the courtroom as a roost. The Natives in the gallery smiled and nudged each other; they looked upon the birds' appearance as a good omen. Judge Deacon took this avian intrusion personally as an affront to the dignity of his court. He interrupted Stan before he could call his first witness and spoke to the RCMP officer in red serge sitting in the courtroom.

"Officer, do my eyes and ears deceive me, or are there birds in the courtroom?"

"There are birds in the air, My Lord. Sparrows, I believe."

The lightness of the officer's response angered the judge and provoked a testy reply: "I don't need to know the species. I just want them removed immediately. I shall adjourn court for five minutes and I expect them to be gone by then. Do I make myself clear?"

"Yes, My Lord."

Everyone left the courtroom except the RCMP constable and Snellgrove. There was a flurry of activity inside. The minutes ticked away. The birds refused to be captured. The judge's five-minute deadline went past. Stan, who was in the corridor talking to Antoine, was startled by a shotgun blast from inside the courtroom. The doors opened to the whiff of gunpowder and the sight of Snellgrove running out the back of the courtroom with the shotgun.

The constable was on his knees scraping up the shattered remains of the dead birds. This wanton execution changed the mood of the Natives and shocked Noah, who came up from his cell below the prisoners' box to see the officer cleaning up the carnage. Judge Deacon and the jury returned. The judge glanced at a ceiling peppered with birdshot, flecks of blood, and feathers and said, "Mr. Hewitt? I believe you were about to call your first witness."

"I call Belle Hanlon to the stand."

Belle entered the courtroom. Stan thought Belle looked magnificent. From the small black hat atop her long auburn hair to her simple black dress and patent-leather high heels, she gave the impression of a person completely in control of herself despite the situation. Stan knew that she would not have worn the hat in Victoria, but this was Williams Lake, and she knew that the impression she had to give the jury was that she was just one of them. Noah turned in the prisoners' box and watched his mother enter the courtroom. As she passed him, he was overcome by the fragrant scent of white heather perfume. She hadn't worn that perfume in years. It had been part of his childhood, his protection when he was too young to protect himself. Then he remembered the last time he had smelled that scent: in the great hall on the night of the shooting. Could Belle have been there? Suddenly he felt lightheaded. If she had been there, why hadn't she told him? When the blood rushed back to his brain, he reasoned that his mother would now tell the truth on the stand and he would be a free man.

He looked at the notepad that Stan had given him to write down anything he thought might be useful during the trial. He had drawn the judge as a hawk, a large bird of prey perched on the bench, and the jury as shrikes, smaller birds of prey waiting on a wire for their turn at the chickadee: himself. As Belle was being sworn in by the court clerk, Noah made a rough sketch of her while she intoned that she would tell the whole truth and nothing but the truth . . . " . . . so help me God."

The sketch was of a raven with one raised eye crouched on a field of snow.

The jurors, the spectators in the gallery, the courthouse staff, everyone except Judge Deacon knew that there were two ranches in the Chilcotin that ranked among the biggest cattle operations in North America: Gang Ranch and Empire Ranch. The Gang was owned by two Americans who didn't come up to Canada that often; Empire had been owned by Bordy Hanlon. But no one knew what Stan Hewitt knew—that the person who had saved the ranch and financed its expansion over the years was Bordy's wife, Isobel Hanlon.

Stan started his direct examination. "Madam, are you Noah Hanlon's mother?"

"Yes, I am."

"Noah was adopted by you and Bordy when he was less than a month old?"

"Yes. On the day that I arrived at the ranch as a bride from Scotland, Father Dumont presented us with a perfect child. His mother had died in childbirth and his father wasn't known. We cared for him, and after a few years with us I insisted that we adopt him."

"And you raised him as if he was your own. You schooled him as if he was your own, did you not?"

"I taught him through correspondence school until he was twelve. Then we decided that the best thing for him was to attend a private school in Victoria, so I moved down with him to give him a home. Bordy stayed with the ranch he loved and Noah came back in the summers to help with the haying and all that."

"You left your husband?"

"No. It wasn't like that. In Victoria, I developed a career on the coast as a pianist, so I couldn't get back to the Chilcotin as often as I would have liked."

"What sort of relationship did Bordy have with Noah?"

"Bordy was a hard-driving man. I think that in the Chilcotin, in order to survive you've got to be a bit hard-driving, and Bordy did more than survive. He thrived. He demanded a lot from everybody and especially Noah, but

Noah loved Bordy and would do anything for him."

"When Bordy suffered his stroke a year ago last December, what did Noah do?"

"Noah was in his second year of fine arts at Victoria College. He's an artist. A gifted painter. But his father needed him, so he gave up his studies and went back to Empire to run the ranch."

"Is Noah a violent person?"

"Noah is as close to me as a natural-born son. He doesn't believe in violence towards any living thing. His friend Peter used to chase grasshoppers and put them in a jar. Noah, who was six, let them go because he felt the jar was like a prison. He is very sensitive and prefers to draw birds rather than shoot them." As she said this, she looked up at the blood-stained ceiling and then at Judge Deacon. The Natives in the gallery nodded at Belle's reference to the dead sparrows and Stan, sensing that the jury had got his point, turned to Bates and said, "Your witness."

Bates did not waste time on pleasantries. "You and your husband had not lived together for nine years?"

"That's true, but we were still friends."

"You haven't seen your husband for years? Not even when he had his stroke?"

"I would have seen him, but I was in Europe. I sent him my good wishes for a speedy recovery. It was sad to know that this robust man was reduced to walking with a cane. He couldn't get on a horse, and he had lived his life on a horse."

"Do you know what happened in the ranch house when Bordy was killed?"

She looked at the jury and almost pleaded with them, saying, "No! All I know is that my son didn't kill him."

"How would you know that your son didn't kill your

husband? You weren't there!"

"I know my son, and he is not a murderer."

Noah watched his mother give her evidence in the self-assured manner reserved for people with money and standing in the community. Why hadn't she told the jury that she was there at the ranch the day of the shooting? Was he mistaken? Or was she lying to protect someone? Perhaps Stan Hewitt was in on it. Noah had to find the answer.

As Belle left the witness stand, Judge Deacon thought to himself that she was a fine-looking woman. But he could tell that the jury was not as impressed with her as he was. He had hoped that this trial would go to the jury that day and that he would be able to catch the 6:00 PM plane to Vancouver; that was not to be.

"My Lord, I will want to discuss the case with my client and therefore I require an extra fifteen minutes at the break."

"Very well then, Mr. Hewitt. The court will reconvene at 3:30."

When Stan entered the holding cell, he thought Noah appeared calm, like he had come to terms with what he had to say in court. It was, after all, the truth. He was about to say, "Just tell your story as you have told it to me and nothing the prosecutor can say should shake you from it," when Noah said, "I've decided not to take the stand."

Stan had seen and heard too much in his over thirty years of practice to be surprised by any twist or turn on the road to a verdict. He remained seated, lit a cigarette, and took a drag.

"Can you tell me why?"

"I could. But I won't. My reasons are personal."

"Look, if you are trying to protect somebody, tell me and it won't go any further. You can trust me. I am here to advise you and I have to know your reasons to be able to advise you. You don't have to accept my advice, but at least you should hear it and consider it."

"I have considered everything. I've had four months to consider everything. I know what I have to do and that's to remain silent. It's for the best; not just for me, but for everyone."

"Noah, I believe you are innocent. But if you don't give the jury an explanation of what happened, there is a good chance they will convict you at least of manslaughter, and you could go to jail for ten years."

Noah looked down at Stan with a tight-lipped smile.

Stan tried another way to shake Noah from his decision not to take the stand.

"You know, son, I took this case because I thought you wanted me to represent you. I also had my own personal reasons. I'm repaying the debt I owe you from when you saved my life the day the boat turned over at Tatlayoko Lake. I figure that by taking on your defence the fates have given me chance to repay you, and now I feel that I am letting you down."

"That's not the way I see it. When you came into my cell that first day I was surprised and pleased that someone was there to help me through my ordeal. If it wasn't for Justine and you I would have given up a long time ago."

The young man had to ask his lawyer a question and he didn't want it to sound like an accusation. "Mother looked strained when she gave her evidence. Is she all right? Is there anything troubling her?"

Stan was surprised. He hadn't been thinking about Belle. "As far as I know."

"Where did she say she was at the time of the shooting?"

"She told me she was in Victoria. Why do you ask?"

"I can't think of the great hall without her and the Bechstein."

"I know what you mean." Stan stood up. "I tell you what I'm going to do. I am going to adjourn the trial over the weekend. That will give you more time to think over your decision."

When a client made a fundamental decision against his advice—like Noah had just done—Stan usually took the precaution of drafting a note to that effect and having the client sign it just to cover himself against accusations of professional negligence. In this case he wouldn't. If things went wrong, Noah could use that as grounds for appeal. But Stan was not ready to concede. He wanted to delay the trial over the weekend to allow Justine, the only other person in whom Noah had some trust, to talk to him and perhaps get him to change his mind. He would ask to speak to the judge in the absence of the jury.

Richard Snellgrove opened the cell door. "Break it up, you two—the judge is waiting."

Stan made his way to the courtroom. Snellgrove moved Noah in handcuffs from the interview room to the holding cell beneath the prisoners' box. He unlocked the door and entered. Noah followed and turned towards the door so that he was between it and the deputy with his hands near the lock. Snellgrove kicked the holding cell door shut. The clang of metal on metal masked whether the lesser telltale click of the spring lock had sounded, which would confirm that the door was locked. He shoved Noah in front of him and took his cuffs off at the foot of the stairs leading up to the prisoners' box.

With Noah in the prisoners' box and the judge on the bench, Stan rose to his feet.

"My Lord, during my cross-examination it came to my

attention that there is another witness the Crown did not reveal to the defence before the trial: a Miss Ta Chi, who may have some relevant testimony. I am seeking an adjournment until she is found and I can speak with her."

Bates jumped to his feet. "I wasn't aware of her presence before the trial, My Lord. I don't see how she could have overheard anything even if she was in her camp. It was over a hundred yards away, and the evidence about the quarrel does not appear to be in dispute."

Judge Deacon was annoyed and thought a lecture was in order. "Gentlemen, this is all very unsatisfactory. I had expected that a week would be enough to hear the evidence and that we would be addressing the jury on Monday. Now there is this surprise witness. I thought that was what preliminary hearings were all about, to sort out these witness problems well before trial. I suppose you should have a chance to speak to her if she can be found over the weekend. I expect, Mr. Hewitt, that you will continue the defence on Monday whether she is found or not."

The motion and the long recess had taken some time. It was five o'clock, an hour past the usual court rising time of four. The judge advised the jury that the trial would be adjourned for the weekend and told them that they were not to speak to anyone about the evidence or about the trial.

FLIGHT

The judge rose. The whole courtroom rose in deference to his authority. Noah turned to Justine, who was sitting behind him in the gallery separated by a glass partition; he looked at her and scratched his nose. No one else noticed. She immediately left the courtroom ahead of her father and Antoine, walked around to the back of the courthouse and waited.

The sun—which had barely made an impression on Williams Lake during the day—had set, leaving the town in the dark with only a few streetlights to guide the people leaving the courthouse. The Natives from the plateau left in a group, heading out to their pickup trucks to return to their reserves and ranches. Once home, they would tell their families what had happened and everyone would come to his or her own conclusions about Noah's guilt or innocence.

Richard Snellgrove escorted Noah from the courtroom

without putting on the handcuffs. It was Friday night, and he was in a hurry to have his usual after-work drink at the Legion. They went down the stairs in the prisoners' box to the holding cell directly below.

Stan watched them go.

"I'll see you tomorrow," he said to Noah.

In the holding cell Snellgrove paid little attention to his prisoner, who had been docile and appeared beaten down by the process and saddened by the slaughter of the birds in the courtroom. It was Snellgrove's job to move him from the holding cell to the jail in another part of the building along a corridor which ended in an exit door. Snellgrove, as he had done before, took out the handcuffs and ordered Noah to put his hands behind his back. Noah was between Snellgrove and the door to the corridor, which opened inward. He started to put his hands behind his back as Snellgrove was sorting out the cuffs. Snellgrove, with his head down, felt rather than saw Noah move and then the metal door hit him in the face as Noah flung it open and ran down the corridor towards the red exit sign. Snellgrove was stunned. He staggered out of the cage, pulling at the revolver on his hip. Noah hit the exit door as Snellgrove fired. The bullet struck the wall, and Noah was through the door to freedom.

Snellgrove ran to the exit door and saw Noah headed for the back of the building. He raised his gun just as Noah rounded the corner out of sight. Still in pursuit but losing ground, he reached the corner of the building and saw a retreating figure crossing the field that led to the city park north of the courthouse.

The sheriff, who had heard the shot from the jail, called the police. He followed his nephew outside and yelled at him, "The RCMP will respond with two cruisers to circle the park. Keep him in sight but don't shoot. I'll give you backup."

The sheriff watched the dark shadow disappearing into the woods heading north and was confident that Noah would be captured in the park, which was surrounded by roads. It would be just a matter of minutes before they would have him back in custody. Although his nephew was responsible for the escape, he knew he would have to bear the ultimate blame. Corporal Leblanc, who was in a patrol car on Highway 97 on the park's eastern boundary, saw a person run out of the park two hundred yards away to flag down a passing car. The corporal turned on his siren and flashing lights and the person retreated into the brush and back towards the park where the foot patrol was advancing. Squeezing in from the west was the other squad car, in contact by radio, cutting off escape from that direction. They had him trapped. They saw him—exhausted from running through the snow—fall to his knees, bend over and cover up his head.

Richard Snellgrove was the first there. He pounced on his fallen prey. "I got ya, you no-good breed. No Indian has ever got the best of me!"

His uncle, Sheriff Gideon Snellgrove—out of wind and panting hard—caught up to his nephew, who grasped the fugitive by the parka and yanked him to his feet with the intention of giving him a beating. Instead, he found himself staring into the face of Justine Paul.

*****

The Chilcotins, still socializing in the parking lot down the street, weren't aware of the escape. They were getting into their pickup trucks to start the long drive back to the plateau and their reserves of Anaham, Stone, and Toosey. Some would have to overnight at Riske Creek or Redstone. Some would return to the courthouse on Monday to show support for one of their own. Alec Paul could not return because the cows were starting to calve and he was needed at Empire Ranch. In each pickup, nine in all, there were three or four people crowded into the front bench seat, with the canvas-covered boxes full of groceries and supplies. The caravan headed out of Williams Lake past the rodeo grounds, across the flats, past the stock yards and sawmills with their beehive burners lighting up the night sky, and up the hill heading west towards the Fraser River. The pickups were old and tended to break down, so the drivers went slow and kept in sight of each other as they strung out along the road. Alice and Joe Willieboy were riding in the last truck in the caravan with Rose Cochin and her son George from Eagle Lake squeezed in between them. They all knew Noah. George and Joe had worked at Empire when the big ranch needed extra help during haying. "Too bad that judge killed those sparrows, eh?" Alice said to Rose.

"Pretty bad spirit, I think," Rose said back.

"That defence lawyer Hewitt not very good. Pretty old, eh? He should put Noah on the stand right away to tell his story. Bordy drank a lot, I think. Must have been trouble from the drinking. Can't see the reason why Noah would kill him on purpose."

"What about Belle, poor thing?" Alice asked. "Pretty hard on her, eh? Maybe we give her a hand."

They crossed Sheep Creek Bridge, the only bridge across the Fraser for seventy miles in either direction, and were heading up Sheep Creek Hill when Joe spoke up. "You girls put on any weight at the Lake?" Then, after shifting into low gear: "The old truck is having a hard time getting up these hills."

The caravan was the only traffic on the road. Joe could see the taillights of the other trucks climbing the hill a half-mile ahead of them, but in low gear it would take them a while to crawl up the five miles to the Chilcotin plateau, at which point it would be another half hour to Riske Creek, where the caravan would break up, some heading south towards the Gang Ranch, some stopping at Toosey, others—including Willieboy—heading further west to Alexis Creek where they would stop for the night.

A few miles from Riske Creek, Willieboy heard a police siren behind him and within five minutes a police car passed him moving at speed and kicking up clouds of snow. The squad car passed every truck in the caravan and pulled in front of the lead truck to stop the caravan. It would take Willieboy a few minutes to come up to the stopped vehicles. He was only going twenty miles an hour when his truck crossed a small bridge over a frozen creek fringed with willows and surrounded by snowfields. The truck swayed crossing the bridge and Willieboy looked into his rear view mirror to see if he had lost any cargo from the back under the tarp, but it was too dark to tell. He carried on, and Alice and Rose—who were still talking about Belle and her shock—didn't seem to notice anything. He pulled in behind Len Shand's truck, left the engine running, and walked up.

"What's up, Len?"

"The police are searching our trucks. Won't say why."

The two RCMP officers quickly moved down the line of trucks, shining their flashlights in the faces of the occupants and looking under the tarps and into boxes. After they had completed their search, the corporal in charge spoke to the gathering of men near the lead pickup.

"Noah Hanlon escaped from the courthouse just before you people left. Have any of you seen him?

No one in the caravan spoke up.

"If you have helped him in any way, you could be charged with giving aid to a fugitive, which is very serious. Speak up now and there won't be any trouble. Did any of you see Noah around the courthouse or on the road?"

Again, there was silence.

"If you see him, contact the RCMP. There'll be a reward if you do."

NOMAD'S LAND

On the day of the escape, a disinterested setting sun provided a high cloud-filtered light but no warmth to any living creature brave enough to be outside. Nothing moved on the bleak plateau during the day, for man and beasts were holed up in their lairs and shelters. As the sun slipped past the horizon, there appeared—as if it had emerged from the land itself—a lone figure casting a long shadow and leading a horse—*qiyus*—and cow—*sek'i*—along a streambed. The figure moved without effort through the snow. Fifty yards ahead around a bend in the willow-draped stream, a lop-eared, black-and-white dog barked. Ta Chi approached the bend, where a frame of bleached willow and poplar branches were lashed together under the lee of a sheltering bank. It was a familiar place to stretch a tattered canvas and spread blankets on the hard ground.

Covered in layers of clothing and capped by a blanket

shawl, Ta Chi built a fire the size of a handkerchief a step away from the opening of the shelter. She removed her shawl, revealing the strikingly delicate features of a Tsihlqot'in. Her white-flecked black shoulder-length hair was held off her face by a headband of tanned deer-hide. Her copper-coloured face was unlined except for crow's feet at the corners of her wide black eyes. Her features, from her broad forehead and high cheekbones to her slightly squared chin, were perfectly proportioned.

Ta Chi was completely focused on skinning the rabbit she had snared at her last resting place. She held a sharp paring knife in her quick fingers and removed the fur, exposing its lean carcass. Then she cut it into quarters, pierced them with willow sticks, and pushed them into the fire to roast.

She planned to camp in this spot a few days so that her qiyus and sek'i could eat borrowed hay from a nearby rancher's haystack. They were now browsing like moose on purple shoots of willow. A billycan of melting snow was suspended above the fire and a piece of tinfoil reflected the small heat towards the opening of her shelter.

Her wanderings over the land followed the routes her ancestors had taken in their search for food. They had wintered in pit houses then. Now most of her people were in frame houses in the six reserves throughout the plateau. All she had in the world was the Chilcotin. She had no house, no possessions except her own person and the clothes on her back and in her bags. Winter didn't interfere with her constant communication with the land. In a few days, if the weather allowed, she would follow the creek down to the Chilcotin River where her animals could scrape away the snow and feed on the wild hay of the river bottomland. It was better than moose-browse.

The rabbit was roasted. She ate it with her hands, gnawing meat from bone, squatted in front of her shelter, and washed her meal down with boiling tea. Finishing, she rose from her haunches and stretched her arms to the clouded moon. A coyote—her competitor for the small game—howled, and she spoke English and Tsihlqot'in to her animals.

"Eat willow shoots, qiyus; see how sek'i nibbles them. Tomorrow you eat hay from Rafferty's haystack. She won't miss it." Rafferty was a man, but Stonys like Ta Chi referred to males as "she" and females as "he."

Her camp was in a hollow out of sight from the vehicles travelling the road between Williams Lake and Anahim Lake. There was little traffic on the road. She could identify most of the vehicles by the sound they made as they passed. Johnny Setah's old Chevy clanked by sometime after sunset and woke her from a light sleep. Shortly after that she heard the rumble of a number of vehicles heading west from Williams Lake. The first vehicle was a pickup truck creaking under a heavy load. It sounded like Fred Quilt's. Then, a few minutes later, another pickup, and another. Farther east, a good mile away, where the road dipped onto the prairie, she heard the wail of a siren that became louder as the convoy of pickup trucks passed her hidden campsite. Before the last pickup passed her shelter, the police car caught up with the convoy, passing each vehicle, and continuing on to the lead vehicle and cutting in front of it to force it to stop.

The straggler, Willieboy, was well behind the others; he seemed to be having some engine trouble. As it came level with her camp where the bridge spanned the creek, she heard a thump that sounded like a deer carcass thrown onto the road followed by a muffled cry of pain, then a shuffling, dragging sound.

Later, the police car silently and slowly retraced its route, crossing the small bridge, heading back towards Williams Lake. The night returned to the creatures of the plateau both great and small.

Under the bridge, Noah—dressed in a jacket and tie for his trial—was wrapped in a blanket he had found in the truck. Tucked in his belt was the portfolio of drawings he had worked on in jail. After his charge through the open door of the courthouse, he had circled it and ducked under the canvas in the back of Willieboy's pickup. He was worried about Justine, who had decoyed Snellgrove to allow his escape. When he jumped from the truck he had landed heavily on his right leg, which he now believed was broken.

Even after the police had driven off, Noah remained huddled under the shelter of the bridge. He would have to take his chances on flagging down a car whose driver would help him and not turn him over to the authorities. The excitement of his escape and the stress of avoiding capture had left him exhausted. Despite the cold and the pain of his broken leg, he began questioning how he had arrived at this low point in his life. Half-awake, trying to be alert to any sounds on the road, he began to try to piece together why his adopted white world, having made him in their image, had turned against him.

He thought he heard an animal at one end of the bridge. He sat up and drew the blanket around himself, facing the sound. The moon was up and shining so that he could see the frozen creek and the overhanging branches beyond. There was nothing there. Another rustle caught his attention and he saw, silhouetted in the opening, a creature: human or animal, he couldn't tell.

"Who's there?" he whispered, taking a chance.

"You're in a lot of trouble."

"Who's there? I'm armed."

"Hell you are. You're hurt and weak. I guess if I left you'd die."

He didn't reply.

"Course she could go back to jail."

"How do you know I was in jail?"

"You're Noah, I know the voice. You jump from pickup while ago."

A coyote yelled at the night, and her dog yipped.

"Shut up." The dog cowered and lay down.

"You're Ta Chi," he said.

"Lucky I found you."

POSSE

Belle had left the courthouse that evening believing that Noah would take the stand when the court reconvened on Monday, and that after a short deliberation he would be acquitted. She ate dinner alone at her hotel, and when she got back to her room at eight there was a call waiting for her from Stan Hewitt.

When she called, he told her that Noah had escaped and that he was in grave danger if he didn't give himself up.

"Do you know where he is?" Stan asked.

She sat down on the bed. "No, no, I don't. This is terrible. He must tell the jury about what happened."

"Noah asked me today after you gave your evidence if you were all right. He was concerned about you. Then he asked me where you were the day of Bordy's murder, and I told him, as you had told me, that you were in Victoria. Am I right about that?"

Belle without a pause replied, "Yes. Of course."

She didn't pursue it or offer any fuller explanation and Stan left it at that. ". . . Stan, are you still there? What can I do, go on the radio and beg him to surrender?"

"I doubt he's listening to the radio. My concern, besides over him being shot by the police or by a trigger-happy vigilante, is that if he is captured alive he will refuse to take the stand."

"Why?"

"Because I think he believes that if he takes the stand, he would put someone else at risk of being charged with Bordy's murder."

"Who's that?"

"He didn't say, and even if I did know I couldn't tell you because of solicitor-client privilege. I'm going to ask for an adjournment. The best thing you can do is return to Victoria until he's found. I'll keep in touch with you."

"I want to go to the ranch for a few days. Noah may contact me there."

"If he does contact you, call me immediately."

*****

Early Saturday morning at the sheriff's office in Williams Lake, Luke Parsons—the regional supervising sheriff from Prince George—was summarizing the verbal report he had received from Sheriff Snellgrove and Deputy Sheriff Richard Snellgrove. The other man in the room was Staff Sergeant Boyd of the RCMP, the chief investigator in Noah's case. Parsons had left Prince George at five in the morning to make this seven o'clock appointment and was in bad humour.

"Deputy, let me get this straight: you were in charge

of the prisoner, who was on trial for murder and who had been denied bail because he was considered a danger to the community and a flight risk. The Crown had closed its case and the defence was in the middle of its case when the trial was adjourned for the weekend."

Deputy Sheriff Richard Snellgrove nodded and Parsons continued. "The prisoner was not handcuffed in the courtroom and you allowed him to leave the courtroom without handcuffs."

Snellgrove nodded again.

"Do you want to tell me why?"

"He was going into the locked holding cell."

Exasperated, Parsons said, "But the cell wasn't locked. The prisoner kicked the door open. How was that possible?"

"I shut the door before I brought the prisoner up to the courtroom after the adjournment. The door didn't lock because the prisoner had jammed a wad of paper in the lock."

"Do you have the paper?"

Richard dug into his pocket, pulled out a crumpled piece of paper and threw it on the desk. Parsons picked it up and carefully unfolded it. It was a torn piece of drawing paper with a pencil sketch of a wolverine that bore the unmistakable image of the man standing before him.

"For the last four days I moved the prisoner without shackles. The jail is in the same building as the courthouse and I didn't think they were necessary. I was going to put on the cuffs. I usually do, but that one time I didn't. If he hadn't jammed the lock it wouldn't have mattered." No one said anything, so Richard—being a talkative man and seeing his three seniors staring at him—continued. "That Indian never showed any sign of wanting to escape. He was dumb. I couldn't get a rise out of him. I figured I knew him."

His voice changed from assertive to whining. "Besides, the sheriff knew I didn't put shackles on Noah and he didn't say anything."

Sheriff Snellgrove turned his back on his nephew.

Parsons continued his recap. "The prisoner ran down the corridor towards the exit and instead of following him in hot pursuit you wasted time going for your gun. Thank God you didn't shoot him, but the delay allowed him to get away."

"I followed him. It was pitch black but I swear it was him running like a scared rabbit up the hill to the park. I figured we had him cornered. And we did corner him."

"Trouble was, it wasn't a he, but a she. Where is Justine now?"

Sergeant Boyd replied, "She's in jail. I'll have her brought in."

Justine was escorted into the room by an RCMP constable. She hadn't slept, but it didn't show. Her dark eyes burned. She looked defiantly at her jailers. She knew her rights.

"Justine, I am Sergeant Boyd, the officer in charge of the RCMP investigation. Tell me why you were at the back of the courthouse when the prisoner escaped and why you ran from the police."

"I was going back to my school dorms. I was late because the trial didn't end till five, so I was running. Suddenly I saw men chasing me; I ran harder and tried to flag a car. I heard sirens. The police chased me and threw me in jail. But I haven't done anything wrong. Can I leave now?"

Richard Snellgrove, who had receded into the background, hated her because he knew she'd been the decoy for Noah's escape. He thought to himself that life would not go well for Justine if he were to lose his job over the escape.

It was against the sergeant's better judgement, but he let Justine go. He knew that she would probably try to help the prisoner, but that was all right. She could lead them directly to Noah.

"She's not telling us the whole truth," Snellgrove said after she'd gone.

Sergeant Boyd now took over the questioning from Parsons. He looked disdainfully at Snellgrove. "Oh, and what's that?"

"I don't know, but she helped him escape."

"I thought he escaped from your custody. If she helped him it had to be on the spur of the moment, unless she knew you were not going to secure the prisoner. Now let's get back to Noah Hanlon. He's out on the Chilcotin plateau and it was ten degrees below zero last night. We have limited resources for a manhunt. In the next hour, I'll instruct my search team to drive every road in the area, plastering the country with posters offering a large reward. We'll question every person who was in that caravan last night. I believe that they transported him back to the Chilcotin and that he got off before the roadblock. We didn't have dogs last night, and that was an oversight. Today we'll get them to sniff each truck, and then we'll search along the road and the sides to see if there has been any sign of him. A big reward and a thorough search should be enough to flush out our man."

What he had said to the sheriff about Justine being an innocent hare to the sheriff's hound masked his real assessment of her. He would keep a close watch on Justine, for she was much too clever to not be involved.

The meeting broke up and the sergeant left the room. Luke Parsons asked the sheriff and Richard to stay behind. "Richard, I've looked at your personnel file and it doesn't give me any confidence in you. You have a series of complaints from lawyers about your conduct towards prisoners.

And with your background, I can't overlook this serious breach of regulations which has led to a prisoner's escape. You leave me no alternative but to fire you. Gather your things and leave."

"Old Hewitt has been on my case. Don't forget he's the town drunk."

"Not anymore."

Richard turned to his uncle. "You can't let him do this, Uncle. Don't I get a second chance?"

Gideon Snellgrove said nothing. The door slammed shut and Parsons turned to him. "You've given good service over the years, Gideon, but you slipped up badly by hiring your nephew and not disciplining him in the past. I urge you to consider early retirement."

That evening ex-Deputy Sheriff Richard Snellgrove told his friends at the Legion—where he was respected on account of his size, strength and sheriff's badge—that he had been fired, making himself look like the one wronged.

"I showed the breed some leniency," he said. "Then he took advantage of me, and with the help of his girlfriend, escaped. I could've shot him but I showed a little mercy. I'm forming a posse to find him. Who's joining me?"

A number of his unemployed friends agreed to join his posse. Richard bought a round for the house and raised his glass shouting, "Here's to the Snellgrove posse! Here's to the reward! Here's to success!"

TA CHI

With the help of her dog, Ta Chi dragged Noah to her shelter. She put an extra stick on the fire and a pot of water full of shredded roots on to boil, and then rummaged in her bags for some clothing and dressed him to withstand the sub-zero temperatures. While she was dressing him, she noticed his right leg was swollen. She probed it and found it was a simple fracture of the small bone of the lower right leg, which she immobilized by making a splint from two sticks bound in place by spare rags. She packed it with snow to reduce the swelling. The pain from her poking and prodding made Noah sick and lightheaded. He cursed her. She ignored him and went about her treatment, then removed the pot from the fire, all the while talking to herself as if he wasn't there. "Here blankets and belts and a jacket. She need something. I had other sek'i, she take place now. Look at leg, there no bone showing. I fix. Now some roots to take away pain."

She removed the roots from the cooling water and made him drink the liquid. The roots had an effect.

It was light the next day when Noah woke with a start to see her on the other side of the fire looking at him. She gave him some tea and porridge and said, "We move now. First I go to road. Wipe away marks."

She meant the marks that he had made dragging himself off the road and over the windrow left by the snowploughs. She knew the police would return with dogs, and those were the signs they would be looking for. When she returned, she doused the fire by stomping on it and burying it in snow. She fashioned a travois out of two long poles lashed onto her horse. While she pushed, he pulled himself on to it. She covered him with bags and blankets so that it would look like he was part of her baggage.

They moved south away from the road on an old trail. Her intention was to get off the exposed prairie and go down into the Chilcotin River valley, which had many draws and hideaways. She knew of an abandoned cabin on the other side of the river where he could stay for a while.

Noah had no choice. He felt like her papoose in a cocoon strapped onto the travois, moving away from any connection with people and onto the land. If she left him now, he knew he would die. . . .

The court reconvened at Williams Lake on Monday morning. Belle was there. Bates advised Judge Deacon, for the record, that the accused had escaped custody. Stan requested an adjournment until his client was found. He also reminded the judge of the missing witness. "My Lord, Mr. Bates tells me that the RCMP have not been able to locate Miss Ta Chi. Until she is found and I have had an opportunity to speak to her, my client would not have a fair trial."

Judge Deacon did not call on the prosecutor to respond. "Mr. Hewitt, your client has shown by his conduct that he holds this court in contempt. I am issuing a bench warrant for his arrest. If he has not been captured and returned into custody by next Monday, the trial will resume without him. As for Miss Ta Chi, the police will continue to look for her, but if she cannot be found in the next week the trial will proceed. I cannot keep the jury waiting any longer. I trust that your retainer allows you to continue to represent him in any event."

"Yes, My Lord."

"Very well. Sheriff, call the jury in and I shall advise them of the adjournment."

Stan spoke to Belle in the courtroom after the judge and jury had filed out. "There is no need for you to stay here. The judge has said the trial will be adjourned for a week, but it would be highly unprecedented if the trial proceeds without the accused. Go back to Victoria and wait till you hear from me."

Belle followed Stan's advice. Stan spent the next few days in bed trying to recover from the fatigue caused by his cancer treatment. On the off-chance that the judge would force him to proceed with the trial in the absence of the accused, he turned to revising his closing argument to take into account that without Noah there would be no explanation of what had happened at the ranch house last Thanksgiving. He reflected on the evidence from this new perspective, and woke up on the weekend before court was to resume with an inspiration. On reviewing the transcript of the trial evidence from the cook, he discovered that his evidence at trial differed from both his written statement to the police and the one he gave at the preliminary hearing. In both those cases, Feng had said that he was in the kitchen cooking Thanksgiving dinner for the whole crew when he heard "a bang." He had run into the great hall and seen Bordy lying dead on the floor in a pool of blood.

Stan read aloud from the transcript of his cross-examination at the hearing:

SH: "How many bangs did you hear?"

W: "Just bang(s)."

SH: "Did you hear more than one bang?"

W: "I don't know, can't remember."

At the trial, Stan had heard the cook refer only to the singular bang, and in the cook's statement to the police he had referred to the singular. But the court reporter in transcribing his shorthand notes thought Feng might have said bangs—plural.

Stan subpoenaed the cook to appear on Monday morning. He also had an investigator conduct an experiment in which a similar rifle was fired in the great hall and outside the room while a person was in the vicinity of the barn, with the doors to the hall both open and closed. For both shots from inside the room, the person could not hear the rifle discharge. But the rifle shot was clearly heard when the shot was fired from outside the room.

*****

Noah and Ta Chi moved at a slow pace. Noah had a fever for the first few days and the animals were hungry. He was in constant pain.

The main threat of detection was from the air and Ta Chi was alert to that, making sure that there was always some cover near the trail where they could hide. She didn't speak much to Noah except to give him orders. When she spoke to herself, it was in the third person. They camped on the north bank of the Chilcotin River at noon to wait till dark to make the exposed crossing of the high, timbered bridge at Farwell Canyon. With no moon, conditions were perfect for a crossing.

She waited until midnight, then strapped Noah onto the travois and covered him up again. With the dog keeping the cow in line, they started across. They were at the mid-point when a sweep of headlights made an arc on the snow banks: a northbound vehicle was snaking down the canyon and slowly advancing on them. There was nowhere to hide. Before the headlights caught them she turned the horse around so it would appear that they were heading in the opposite direction.

The headlights of Alex Auld's pickup lit up the procession, which looked to him like a travelling manger. As he drew closer, he and his very pregnant wife, Darcy, recognized Ta Chi.

"Hey there, Ta Chi!" Alex said, drawing up beside her and rolling down his window. "Whatcha doing out on a night like this?"

She didn't reply.

He looked at her horse and cow. "Stock looks pretty lean."

"Um. Ta Chi look for hay."

"Well, I'm heading for Williams Lake. Darcy here has got pains. I think the baby's coming. I'll be back tomorrow and I'll haul some hay out to ya. Oh, and keep a sharp eye out for Noah Hanlon. The police are looking for him. Say he might be dangerous."

He rolled up the window and drove off.

This was Noah's first contact with anyone since Ta Chi had rescued him from under the bridge. It was good to hear another voice. He had felt like calling out to Alex, "Take me with you," for he knew that nothing would be the same after he crossed the Farwell Canyon bridge. Instead, he just watched the red taillights receding, imagined the warmth of the heated cab and wondered why he had made a run for it and why this simple woman was so determined to care for and hide him.

He couldn't forget that she had, after all, given him the promise of life. He could endure just a bit longer. The procession carried on to the south end of the bridge, left the road, found the trail, and climbed the bank two hundred yards before Ta Chi made camp.

In the morning there was no fire. Noah ate cold porridge and drank water, and decided he was improving because he was questioning the quality of his rations. Ta Chi was talking to herself and appeared agitated. He was concerned and trying to make out what she was saying when she stopped eating and looked at him and said, "Last night she come to bridge crossing the river as Noah. In middle of bridge, we meet woman in labour. We come to this side of bridge, she now *Wawant'x*."

He didn't know what to say. She was giving him a Native name. Was that her way of accepting him as a Chilcotin? She didn't wait for a response.

"I bring sek'i to the road. Leave with rancher. Get hay for qiyus. She can see the road from here."

He watched her lead the horse and cow back to the road and across the bridge and settle there as if her camp was on the other side. The.few vehicles that passed on the road stopped or slowed down and honked. She was a landmark in this country, a sentry. People were on the lookout for her and pointed her out when they saw her, which was usually from a distance. Often times it wouldn't be her but a gnarled stump or a black bear scurrying into the trees. Children were told that if they didn't behave Ta Chi would get them. Yet she harmed no one and asked nothing from the people, only from the land, which maintained her and her spirit.

Alex Auld came back from Williams Lake just before noon. Noah saw him stop, exchange words with Ta Chi, and carry on. Half an hour later he was back with some hay for the horse. He forked out the hay and backed his high-box pickup into a rise and loaded the cow and left. Ta Chi was packing the hay onto the travois when a car drove up to the bluff overlooking the bridge and stopped a good five hundred yards above her. The occupants would have a clear view of her and the bridge. She gave no indication that she was aware of being observed and carried on with the loading. When it was done, she started moving off the road, heading east towards the Fraser River at its junction with the Chilcotin. Noah knew then that she was aware she was being watched.

The car came down the hill very fast and intercepted her before she got far from the road. Two men got out, and even at a distance Noah could recognize Richard Snellgrove. They walked up to Ta Chi, who stood her ground. They yelled at her. Noah couldn't hear them shouting, but Snellgrove—who towered over the twig of a woman—waved his arms, and then pushed her down into the snow and waved at her some more while the other man held him back. Noah wanted to help her but couldn't move—shouldn't move, or he would cause further damage to his leg. He felt sick at not being able to protect her from Snellgrove. The two men returned to the car and went back in the direction of Williams Lake. Ta Chi raised herself from the snow, took the horse's halter rope and led it back across the bridge to Noah.

*****

The court reconvened on the following Monday. The police had not found Ta Chi. Snellgrove had located her, but he wasn't telling because he thought that Ta Chi would lead him to Noah and the reward.

With Noah still at large on Monday morning, Stan made another motion for an adjournment before Judge Deacon. Surely the court would not proceed without the accused—that is what Stan believed, and that is what he had told Belle. "My client would not have escaped if the sheriffs had been doing their jobs. The Crown is to blame for his escape and the trial should not proceed until my client is found."

"I've given your client a week to reconsider his ill-advised escape and turn himself in. Please proceed with your case, Mr. Hewitt."

Stan had no choice. After the jury filed in, he recalled Feng Chan to the stand.

"Mr. Chan do you remember your evidence about the bangs you heard from the kitchen on the day of Bordy Hanlon's death?"

"Yes, I remember."

"Your evidence was—and I am reading from the transcript, My Lord . . ." Stan then read to the point in the transcript where the witness said he couldn't remember how many bangs there were and continued. "Mr. Chan, can you describe where you were and what were you doing, and what you heard the day Bordy Hanlon was shot?

"In kitchen. Head in oven. See if roast cooked for Thanksgiving meal. Heard bang sound like something drop on floor."

Stan nodded and smiled at the witness, encouraging him.

"Later, did you hear another something being dropped on the floor?"

Bates, in a slow, deliberate manner, unwound himself from his chair and stood up.

"I object, My Lord. This witness has already testified that he heard only one bang. My friend is trying to confuse the jury as he has confused me."

Judge Deacon raised an eyebrow, inviting Stan to speak.

"My Lord, this witness's evidence is uncertain. If you read the transcript, you will see that the court reporter was not clear on the plural or the singular of the word bang." Stan then read to the point in the transcript where the witness said he couldn't remember how many bangs.

The judge shifted uneasily in his seat and took a moment before saying, with a touch of impatience, "Oh, very well, Mr. Hewitt. Ask your question!"

The jury was on the edge of their seats. They had rested from their labours for a week and now were plunged back into the murder case. Stan was determined to create as much confusion in the jury's mind as possible, as that was the best defence he had left.

Stan turned back to the cook. "Did you hear another something being dropped on the floor after the time you had your head in the oven?"

"Yes," Feng answered. "I peel potatoes. Not long after I hear another something being dropped on floor. Not as loud. Maybe dropped outside. And then I go see what's making bang, and find Mr. Bordy dead."

"Thank you. Those are my questions."

Bates slowly got to his feet. He looked at the jury. He looked at the judge and shrugged his shoulders. Finally he turned to the witness, who appeared to be cowering in the witness box.

"Mr. Chan, when you swore to tell the truth at this trial, did you understand what the truth is?"

"Yes. Tell what happened. Don't make up things."

"When you gave evidence last week you said you heard only one bang, didn't you?"

"Yes . . ." And before Bates could say "That's all, Mr. Chan," the witness continued ". . . but I heard two noises like something being dropped on floor."

"So you didn't hear any bangs. Is that what you are saying?"

"I don't know. I just tell the truth."

When Feng Chan left the stand, Stan shook his hand warmly and offered his heartfelt thanks for the confusion he had sown in the minds of the jury. Stan next called his expert to give evidence on the failure of a person by the barn to hear a gunshot from within the house with the doors open or closed, and their ability to hear a shot clearly from outside the house. This was all he could do, without his client to tell the story, to bring home to the jury that an indoor shot with the doors open or shut at the time of the shooting would not have been heard by the cowhands at the barn, but a shot from outside the house would have.

Acton had no questions, and Stan, with a heavy heart, said, "That is the case for the defence, My Lord."

In his summation, Stan made it clear to the jury that there was no direct evidence as to what had happened in the great hall of the ranch house. The Crown's case was that there were two people known to be in that room: Bordy and Noah. But the Crown had not accounted for the third person—the gunman—who had been outside the room on the lawn.

The glass doors on the front of the house facing the lawn and the lake were open, and the barn from where the ranch hands had heard a gunshot was three hundred yards from the back of the house, a solidly built log structure. The ranch hands could not have heard in the barn a rifle fired from within the house. Their testimony was that the gunshot was loud and sharp, and it brought them running. That meant the gun must have been fired from the outside of the house by a third person who had gotten clean away. Therefore the gun that had Noah's fingerprints on it was not the gun that killed Bordy. He then referred to the cook's evidence by saying, "Don't forget the evidence of Mr. Chan." Stan finished his address to the jury, his voice filled with passion: "There is a reasonable doubt, and as his Lordship will tell you, if you have a reasonable doubt it is your duty to acquit."

Acton Bates summed up the Crown's case in a more clinical, matter-of-fact way. He was a methodical man with a detached manner befitting a prosecutor, and when he spoke to the jury or judge during argument he closed his eyes from time to time giving the impression—whether it was true or not—that he was drawing on his vast inner resources and providing the jury with the benefit of his extensive legal learning. He assumed that the jury would not be impressed by the accused, Noah Hanlon, who had not bothered to stick around to tell his story and hear their verdict. His most telling argument was that even if the shot was fired from the outside of the house, Noah Hanlon was the person who fired it, not some mystery person.

Judge Deacon was also short and to the point. He outlined the law and summarized the facts. There was in evidence only one gun, one shell fired from that gun and one lead bullet. The accused's fingerprints were on the gun, the analyst had detected powder residue on his hands indicating that he had recently fired a gun, and finally, the ranch hands had seen him with the gun in his hands. Whether the rifle was fired from outside or inside the room was of little consequence, for it was open for them to decide that Noah Hanlon had fired the gun and the bullet which killed Bordy Hanlon. The motive was a quarrel between father and son, and as the Crown had argued, there was no evidence that Bordy Hanlon was killed in the heat of the moment.

Justine, who had received permission from the school to attend, sat through the evidence and argument, confident that the jury would acquit, for it was plain to her that whoever had shot Bordy must have been outside the great hall and that was not Noah, just the way Mr. Hewitt had explained.

The jury took the afternoon to come to a verdict. They entered the courtroom and the clerk asked them, "Have you reached a verdict?"

The foreman answered, "We have, My Lord."

"What is your verdict on the first charge of murder in the second degree of Bordy Hanlon?"

"We find the accused not guilty."

The gallery was all smiles. Noah was acquitted. But the clerk went on, "What is your verdict on the second charge of manslaughter?"

"We find the accused guilty as charged."

The Natives in the back of the court—the ones who had sat through the trial, who did not rely on newspaper accounts and wanted to see justice done with their own eyes and hear the evidence with their own ears—said in one voice, "No! No!" The judge called for order and their cries quieted. Judge Deacon thanked the jury.

The foreman of the jury turned to his fellow jurors in the box and they whispered to each other. Heads were nodded, and the foreman stood and spoke to the judge.

"We recommend mercy in the sentencing, My Lord. This was a horrible accident."

The judge thanked the jury again and they filed out, nodding to Stan, who was on his feet as soon as the door closed.

"My Lord, the jury's verdict is perverse. I move to set aside the guilty verdict and order a new trial. The foreman just called their verdict an 'accident,' which indicates that the jury didn't understand the essential elements the Crown must prove in order to convict on a charge of manslaughter."

Mr. Bates rose and said with his eyes closed, "When twelve men and women come to a difficult decision after due deliberation it is not for us to question their verdict. The evidence is there for them to accept or reject. As to the word 'accident,' that was just a layman's way of saying it was a tragedy."

Judge Deacon gave his ruling: "The Court of Appeal will have to consider your arguments, Mr. Hewitt. The verdict will stand. I sentence your client Noah Hanlon, in absentia, to ten years imprisonment for the manslaughter of Bordy Hanlon."

The jury's verdict left Stan drained. He had taken on Noah's defence thinking that he would get an acquittal. He was convinced that Noah was innocent of the crime and equally determined to have the decision reversed.

Dr. Hay's advice to tidy up his affairs would have to wait.

PART II

The intelligence that Mr. MacDougal conveys in regard to Alexandria is not very agreeable. The Indians in that quarter, having some serious misunderstandings a few years ago with the Chilcotins, the latter in revenge lately murdered three of the former when they were hunting in the vicinity of the Chilcotin River. This event I am afraid will be an obstacle to the establishment of a post on the Chilcotin River for the present.

William Connelly, The Hudson's Bay Journal, 1826

POWER

On the day of Noah's verdict and sentencing, the major got the good news he had been waiting for and was celebrating the cabinet's awarding of the Homathko River water licence to Vancouver Island Power at his club after work. Now he could dam up the river and flood Bordy's ranch. Jepson poured him the usual stiff gin, and as he turned to go the major said, "By the way, I am expecting a guest at seventeen hundred hours. Show him to my table and ask him what he wants to drink."

Ian Richards was late for his meeting. That morning, while Ian was trying to balance his family accounts at his work cubicle, the major had phoned and invited him for a drink at the club at 5:00. The balancing had been made more difficult by Ralph being enrolled at All Saints on the recommendation of the major. Although it wasn't featured in their brochure—which showed healthy boys studying hard and playing rugby—All Saints prided itself on straightening out problem rich boys through strict discipline. Major Jack Parmenter, having no children himself, had continued to take a keen interest in Ralph by questioning his father from time to time.

Ian proudly wore the civil engineers' iron ring on his little finger, but he had clung to his desk in Victoria throughout his career as firmly as would a shipwrecked sailor to a piece of flotsam, not willing to challenge himself by venturing into the field. He did take the trouble of chatting up the major whenever he dropped by his office. He kept reminding the major that the company should be making a decision for new sources of power on the Island, as the projected tourist boom would create a heavy demand over the next decade. On that same day, Ian's wife, Enid, had phoned him just before 5:00 to remind him of all the things he had to pick up on the way home from the office, and then went on about what her hairdresser had told her of an affair between two deputy ministers whom they vaguely knew. He couldn't get her off the phone. Finally he said, "Enid, Major Parmenter invited me to meet him at the Union Club and I'm late."

"Oh, that stupid old fool—let him wait."

"He does control the majority of stock in the company, and don't forget he got Ralph into All Saints."

"Yes, and the school fees are bankrupting us. Never mind, go have your drink with that madman."

Jepson ushered Ian into the club's lounge at ten minutes past five. Ian Richards was a man who had been waiting for greatness to be thrust upon him, but he would not be disappointed if he waited in vain. He polished his shoes, wore blue blazers, HMCS Esquimalt ties, and buttoned-down shirts, and bought his flannels at Straith's on Government

Street. He fit very nicely into a foursome at the Uplands Golf Course and tried not to embarrass Enid when they played bridge. He had caught the major's eye because he kept his hair short, had gone through college on the ROTC program, and was a good listener whenever the major told his war stories. The major was thinking that Richards was the man to head up his biggest campaign. That notion may have changed had the major been aware that Richards was late, which he failed to notice because of a diversion.

At five sharp Colonel McGowan—head of the Liquor Control Board—had entered the club and instead of walking directly to his table, which was at the other end of the lounge from the major's, took a circular route which brought him by the major's table, a change of routine so profound that the staff and a few of the members scattered about the lounge remarked on it later that evening. The colonel's recognition of Parmenter in such a public way could only mean that Parmenter had recently been favoured by the government, for the colonel's connections with the party in power kept him well-informed. They knew each other and would nod when their paths crossed. The major was on his second gin when the colonel walked up to him, paused and said, "I say, Major; I've received a shipment of one-hundred-percent-proof Jamaica rum. I thought you might like a few jars before the boys water it down."

"That's decent of you, Colonel. Yes, I would."

"I've just heard that your company has been granted a water licence on the Homathko River. Congratulations!"

"Thank you, Colonel. By the way, I believe you know the coastline at the northern end of the Island."

"Yes, I sailed up there a few summers ago."

"Tell me: Is Bute Inlet still navigable to the outfall of the Homathko River?"

"Yes! Yes, it is, but it's a long way to go for nothing. If you intend to boat there, the squalls off Mount Waddington can be dangerous."

The major bridled. "Danger, you say? Danger is landing with the Canadians at Dieppe in rough seas under German fire. A little wind from Mount Waddington is nothing."

After a few more broadsides the colonel moved off, just as Ian Richards entered the lounge. The major, stimulated by his encounter with the colonel, stood up to greet Richards, and said, "Richards, just the man I want to see. I am appointing you my field commander in our campaign to dam the waters of the Homathko River."

"And where is the Homathko River, sir?"

"That beautiful river, Richards, is in the Chilcotin, and you will find out where that is presently. First, let's have a drink."

*****

The circles of Victoria's society—social, business, and political—intersected at the Union Club. The deputies, who effectively ran the government, the bankers and businessmen who benefited from government contracts, the lawyers, the lawmakers, and the social hangers-on were all members, and there in the lounges and dining rooms of the venerable institution was where the members firmly believed that the decisions which shaped the province of British Columbia were made.

They deceived themselves. Persons who were by the rules of the club banned from membership—although they could be entertained as guests—made many of the real decisions. They were not Asians, nor Natives, nor Jews, all of whom were excluded: they were women. And four of the most influential women in Victoria were playing bridge at Belle Hanlon's on the day the major was told that the cabinet had approved his company's application for a water licence to survey and build a dam on the Homathko River at Waddington Canyon.

Belle's bridge partner was Adele Buscombe. Their opponents were Sybil Crosstairs, the wife of the Minister of Energy and Mines, and Samantha Eggers, the wife of the deputy minister of finance and senior deputy minister. Belle's north cards were fanned out in her left hand. She was looking at a weak hand with barely enough to open. She said, "One no trump," and then carried on to say, "I'm so pleased, Sybil, that Reggie obtained cabinet approval for the permit to survey the Homathko. It will make the major's day, don't you think, Adele?"

Adele laughed. "He's probably at the club right now planning his campaign." She went to the sideboard and picked up a dish. "Now, I want you all to try some anti-pasto I made fresh this morning." She went around the table offering it with crackers.

Samantha took a bite. "Mmm. Adele, this is delicious. You know it wasn't a sure thing that the licence would be granted. The cabinet was divided, and I doubt that it would have been granted if Bordy were still alive. He and his lawyer were putting up quite a fight."

Sybil had married an ambitious lawyer. She had decided early in their marriage that he should run for reeve of Oak Bay because she enjoyed entertaining. She found herself in Belle's inner circle at the bridge table because her political instincts were beyond any that Belle had previously encountered. Bordy had used his influence over the sitting member from the Cariboo Chilcotin, Eric Manson, to protect his ranch, and Belle had hosted a number of political picnics and dinners at the ranch house. Eric knew how to get elected and to keep his own seat in the backbenches of the government, but in Victoria Sybil had a better command of political power. As she explained to Belle, "I am a better organizer than most men. I understand how half the population thinks and I can manipulate the other half. My political philosophy is simple: the basic unit is the family. What's good for the family is good for Victoria and the province. Who runs the family? Women do."

She had made that speech to the Women's League on many occasions when she was president. Before she bid she said to Adele, "You must give me the recipe for this delicious antipasto." With six spades king-high in her hand, she bid two spades.

Adele, south with the AKQJ and two small hearts, knew that Belle would not cooperate with any six-level adventure and made the practical decision to bid slam on her own. "Six hearts."

The strong bid from Adele didn't startle Belle, who was familiar with Adele's take-charge attitude in life and bridge. Adele had been left with the Cowichan Electric Company by her father, and rather than sell the company she had married Charles Buscombe, a man whom she thought could run it while she retained control. When it became obvious that Charles had his limitations, she agreed to have the major take charge and had never regretted that decision.

Sybil led a spade, and the table was silent as Adele set about making her twelve tricks. After winning the spade lead with the ace, she drew trumps and had to decide how to develop the extra tricks she needed to make the contract. She found them in diamonds, giving Samantha her diamond jack and smugly ruffing the spade return, crossing to the table with the club ace and discarding her club losers on the six and three of diamonds. The table erupted in praise and congratulations.

"Oh, well done, Adele."

"I thought you would go down."

"I'm glad we didn't double."

With the tension of the hand over, Sybil turned to Belle. "What's happening with Noah's trial?"

"I don't know what to think or do anymore," Belle replied. "His lawyer, Stan Hewitt, says that the trial shouldn't proceed without him, and Stan is expecting another long adjournment, otherwise I would be in Williams Lake today. I'm convinced that he is innocent. I warned him not to give up his art to take over the ranch, but he insisted and now look what's happened."

She sighed, but wasn't allowed to dwell on her emotions long before Samantha asked, "Why do you think he is innocent? We all know that Bordy was an impossible man to live with."

Of the foursome who enjoyed sorting the cards and divining the future, Samantha was the quiet one and appeared out of place in the colourful group. She brought a rational mind to their avian flights. Last year, Adele had mentioned the problems of Vancouver Island Power, which—thanks to the major—had expanded too quickly for its electrical power base. She had told Samantha that he was looking for a source of hydro power in the Chilcotin. Samantha knew that before a water survey could be done, they would have to get approval for a water licence from the highest levels of government. It was she who had suggested to Sybil that it would advance Reggie's career to be seen to secure the power for Vancouver Island, his own political power base.

When Belle didn't answer her question at once, Samantha

continued, “You’ve told us that Noah hasn’t told anyone except his lawyer what happened at the shooting. Perhaps he escaped because what he has to say in court may affect too many people?”

Belle was shaken by this suggestion. “All I can say is that he is my son and that I know him to be innocent.”

It was just before five when the phone rang in her den. Belle excused herself. She picked up the receiver in the den and, anticipating the call, said, “Hello, Stan. Did you get the adjournment?”

“I have bad news. Noah has been convicted of manslaughter.”

Stan heard her sigh and catch her breath. She was always a composed woman, very bright and intense and not given to emotional outbursts. The pause on the line convinced Stan that she felt this verdict deeply.

“I’m devastated. It doesn’t make any sense.”

“I think there are grounds for appeal. I don’t believe he’s guilty. There was another person who shot Bordy.”

“Who?”

“We’ve been over this before, Belle. This is your family. Do you have any new ideas?”

“No, I have no idea. As you so well know, Bordy was not well-liked. But if you are successful in your appeal and Noah goes free, will it matter any more?”

“Well, yes. Yes, it will. The best I could do for Noah on appeal is to get a retrial. We don’t want to put Noah in jeopardy again. Besides, there is a killer out there on the plateau and the police should be looking for him or her. You are all in danger until this person is caught. Belle, you are paying my retainer. Noah can’t be found. Do I have your instructions to appeal his conviction and to find the answer to the question that you’ve asked: Who killed Bordy?”

"Yes, of course, Stan. Please proceed."

Belle hung up the phone and remained sitting at her desk in the dark, unable to move. Since Bordy's murder, she had been torn between her devotion to Noah and Jack Parmenter's obsession over building a dam on the Homathko River. Then, on the very same day she learned that the government's approval for the survey had been awarded, she had also learned that Noah was convicted of manslaughter. The news kept her sitting in the dark long after she'd hung up the receiver, even though her bridge partners were in the other room waiting for her to return and take command. Her conscience, guilt-ridden and over-exercised, could not come to terms with the two driving forces in her life. She made a decision: she would hide her grief, attend the major's celebrations over the awarding of the licence that evening, and speak to the major afterwards to get his advice on what she should do.

When she returned to the bridge table, her players said in unison, "What happened?"

"Noah has been convicted of manslaughter and sentenced to ten years." Then she straightened up and said, "Never mind! Noah will be found and his appeal will be successful."

Samantha asked, "How will this affect the dam on the Homathko?"

"The major will proceed, of course." In a fit of bravado Belle carried on: "And you are all invited to the ranch in July to play bridge. The ranch is at its best at that time of year."

The irony of Belle's invitation was not lost on Samantha: the ranch would be flooded in a few years and all that beauty would be submerged.

The major had invited a select number of influential people—politicians, bankers and would-be investors—to his house that evening for a barbeque dinner. On occasions such as these, when people of like mind who have backed a winner gather to confirm their good fortune, there seems to be no obstacle that cannot be overcome by planning, selecting the right people to execute the plan, and money of course. That had been the major's formula, along with Belle's silent financial backing. The taking over of Nanaimo Electric, whose owner had fought through the courts to prevent it, was followed by a harder fight, with allegations of corruption from the owners of Campbell River Electric. Then Bordy Hanlon had proved a problem, as Belle knew he would. Stan Hewitt's letter questioning the legality of the licence and threatening to take the government to court if a licence was granted had proved effective. The cabinet had delayed the announcement, which was vital to the power company's existence . . . but Bordy's opposition to the dam had died with him. Belle now was the sole owner of Empire Ranch.

On hearing about Noah's conviction, the major thought it a shame that everything had turned out so badly for the boy. He was a good lad and had attended All Saints, a good prep school, and that was in the major's estimation a wonderful preparation for life. Noah had even asked the major for his advice on whether to go back to the ranch after Bordy's stroke or to finish his schooling in fine arts. Of course the major hadn't seen any use in a fine arts education for a young man. At the same time, he hadn't encouraged him to go back to the ranch. He had suggested a third alternative: join Vancouver Island Power and work his way up to the top of the ladder.

Noah hadn't taken his advice, and the major hadn't held it against him. Yet the major couldn't help thinking that things would have turned out much better for Noah if he had. Noah had told the major at the time, "The Chilcotin is in my blood. I'm not keen on running Empire Ranch, but my father needs me. I would prefer to go back to the Chilcotin as a painter. Perhaps next time I will."

The major was also surprised that the jury had convicted Noah, for the boy knew very little about guns and had no interest in hunting. But that was all the thought he could spare for that unfortunate lad until he and Belle settled down to talk after the last guest had gone.

"Thank you, Belle. I know it took a lot out of you to be gracious when your family is in such turmoil."

She brushed aside his thank-you. Belle was a performer. What she needed was his advice. She had been tormented by guilt since last October. She had confessed her sin of omission to her confessor every week for months but had done nothing to rectify it except to say a few Hail Marys. The major was someone in the practical world she could lean on. She began by saying, "Jack, you must understand that I was just trying to help deal with Bordy as you had suggested I should do a few days before Thanksgiving on the night of my recital. That's why I decided to go to the Chilcotin that weekend to confront Bordy and to tell him that if he didn't stop his opposition to the licence, I would force a sale of the ranch, which I owned in joint tenancy with him."

The major became a little testy. "What possible connection could that have with your husband's murder?"

"I was at the ranch when Bordy was shot. I heard the gun go off as I was leaving the house after he threatened me with it. I ran to my car, which I had parked out of sight away from the house, and drove off. I didn't know that Bordy was dead until I called home that evening and my housekeeper, June, told me that Sergeant Boyd had called.

I called the sergeant from Lac La Hache and he told me that Bordy was dead. I left the impression with him that I was phoning from Victoria and I would arrange to get to Williams Lake the next day, which I did."

"Have you told anyone else you were at the ranch?"

"No. I told the police, Stan, and the prosecutor I was in Victoria. I swore under oath in court that I was in Victoria at the time. I thought that if it were known that I was at the house at the time of the murder, the chances of us obtaining the licence would have died because of my association with you. Stan believes that there was another person outside the great hall, but he doesn't know whom. I didn't see anyone. You are the only person who knows the full story. I lied because I believed that it didn't matter to Noah's case whether I was there or not. When I left the hall, Noah wasn't there, and the shot was fired about five minutes later when I reached my car hidden in the woods. I didn't lie to harm Noah but to protect the company and all that you have worked for."

She looked at the major, imploring him to help her resolve her conflict. He returned her look rather coolly and after a pause said, "Are you sure that there was no one else in or outside the house besides Noah who could have seen anything?"

"I was in a panic. I thought I was going to be shot. I didn't see or hear anyone else, although I had a strange feeling on the long drive back to Lac La Hache that there could have been someone there. I thought it was my guardian angel. I believe Stan thinks it was Ta Chi."

"Who is Ta Chi?"

"A Native woman who lives off the land and turns up when you least expect it. The Natives say she is the embodiment of the Chilcotin. I say she is a bit deranged."

The major had found his true mate in Belle. She was the equal of any man, a real partner in business and at home. He was pleased that she trusted him and sought his advice in the most difficult crisis of her life. He had forgotten that he had given her an ultimatum to remove Bordy's opposition to the dam. They were sitting on the sofa before a dampened fire. He shifted towards her and held her hand to reassure her that he would do anything to support her; that he would do anything to protect her.

It was midnight at the end of a busy, hectic day full of the excitement and anticipation of planning a campaign. The next two months held the promise of many more busy days as he readied the survey party for the Chilcotin. "You've been carrying this secret far too long. I'm glad you spoke to me. I'm sorry I was away fishing that long weekend. Perhaps if I had been in Victoria, you would have told me of your plans."

"I did mention I was going up to the Cariboo."

"You did? I had forgotten."

"What should I do, Jack? If I come forward at this late date, the press will play up the connection between me and you and the company, which may ruin our plans. Yet I can't let Noah's conviction stand, for a crime that he didn't commit."

The major was noted for making quick decisions, but now he hesitated. He was trying to control his emotions, for he knew that this day which brought such triumph could come to nothing if Belle's involvement, no matter how innocent, in Bordy's murder were made public. He spoke slowly and distinctly. "My dear, the first thing you must do is to fire Stan Hewitt. You will then hire the best criminal lawyer in Victoria, who will have the verdict set aside and who will successfully defend Noah at a new trial when he is found.

I suggest Jack Cuthbert. You will recall he defended me on the fraud charges related to the takeover of Campbell River Electric. Oh, you should also have Cuthbert act as the lawyer for the ranch. You live in Victoria and it's more convenient for you. As for Noah: he is a dreamer, but he showed a bit of pluck by escaping custody. It reminds me of my escape from the Nazis in the Italian campaign by swimming the river Arno. God, that water was cold."

He began to shiver and his eyes narrowed to pinpoints. He noticed that Belle was looking alarmed at his digression. He shook himself. "As for you, my dear," he said and squeezed her hand perhaps a little too hard, "there is no need for you to breathe a word about this to anybody. Do you think that Noah saw you at the ranch that day?"

"I don't know. When we met in the jailhouse, he didn't mention it. But he escaped before giving evidence. Why do you ask?"

"I suggest that we arrange to find Noah on our own, so that we can help him through this ordeal."

"What do you propose?"

"I'll ask Charlie Rainbow to track him down."

She felt better. Charlie had moved into the major's basement suite the year before and was now doing odd jobs for him. Private Charlie Rainbow, an Iroquois from Ontario, had been his batman during his campaigns. Charlie was very quiet and very helpful and Belle knew that there was nothing Charlie wouldn't do for the major. They went to bed on that settling note.

In Williams Lake, a hard-blowing, snow-packed west wind pushed Stan Hewitt down Third Street towards his office. He was thinking that it would be hell out there on the plateau for Noah if he had no shelter and was living rough.

In the Legion two nights previous while waiting for his wife's delivery, Alex Auld had told Snellgrove that he had seen Ta Chi at Farwell Canyon. Eager for the reward, Snellgrove had followed up on the tip and boasted in the Legion that he had found Ta Chi and convinced her to keep an eye out for Noah.

Stan had phoned Sergeant Boyd, told him what he had heard and warned him that he had better keep Snellgrove under control. Auld had said that Ta Chi was heading east towards the Fraser, but it was now March and Stan was told by the Chilcotin that she, like the deer and the caribou, would instinctively follow the migration route west towards the foothills and higher land as winter retreated. Stan wanted to speak to her. He believed she held the clues to the death of Bordy Hanlon. He arrived in his office stamping the snow off his feet as the phone rang in his office. It was Belle.

"I've slept on the bad news you gave me last night," she started. "You've done a wonderful job for Noah. He has such trust in you and so do I, but you have not been well and I think this is too strenuous for you."

"Nonsense, I rise to the challenge."

Belle changed her tactics. "I think the appeal and the retrial should be in the hands of a more experienced appeal lawyer. Do you know Jack Cuthbert?"

"Yes I do. He has a fair reputation."

"Well, he has agreed to take the appeal and the retrial. I will of course pay your fee up to date. There is no need for you to do any investigative work either. I want to thank you for being there in our darkest hour. I've also decided that Cuthbert should act as lawyer for the ranch since I'm in Victoria."

Stan mumbled something into the phone and hung up.

He knew perfectly well that Noah was his client and his mother's permission to act was not necessary, but he had wanted to keep her in the game. For the last four months, Noah's defence had consumed him. Now he was told that his services were no longer required. He had been fired in the past because he was drunk, but never because he was inexperienced. He desperately needed a drink. Instead he rang up an old fishing buddy of his, Tom Barton, at the 122 Mile House on Lac La Hache and invited himself down for some ice fishing on the lake, which was noted for its kokanee.

Tom had been following the trial in the local paper, the 100 Mile Free Press. That evening he and Tom's sister Dorothy questioned Stan about the verdict. They had been good friends of Belle's when she was living in the Chilcotin. Belle often stayed over at their place or at their sister Molly Forbes' next door when she and Bordy drove down to Vancouver. They were reminiscing about those days when Dorothy said, "You know, I saw Belle up here last fall. She stayed at Molly's place for a night or two. I don't remember when."

Stan held his breath. "Dorothy, would you mind giving Molly a call and asking if she remembers the date?"

Stan had his answer within minutes. She'd been here, and at Thanksgiving. Molly had remembered that Belle had gone to Quesnel and returned too late to eat pumpkin pie hot from the oven. Belle had lied to him. She had not been in Victoria when the shooting occurred. She'd been within a six-hour drive of the ranch.

Over the next few weeks Stan talked to Cuthbert and briefed him on the case and his thoughts about the appeal. He was very frank with him. "I won't be offended if you tell the Court of Appeal that I am a doddering, negligent old fool. It's the truth. Noah's conviction must be overturned, and I'm sure once Noah is found there will be sufficient evidence to acquit him; evidence that was not available at trial."

Cuthbert pounced immediately on this. "Can you tell me what it is? It will be helpful on the appeal."

Stan couldn't tell him because he didn't have it yet, and he was not prepared to voice his suspicions. He didn't tell Cuthbert that he was continuing to work the case to clear Noah's name. Noah had never dismissed him, therefore he was still Noah's lawyer. He would bide his time, wait till spring came to the Chilcotin, and then he would find Ta Chi.

JUSTINE

Ta Chi returned to the camp to find Noah on the ground in pain. She adjusted his splint and boiled him some root juice to sedate him. His pain could not stop their journey. They had to keep moving west away from Farwell Canyon, where she'd been sighted.

They headed upriver with the horse breaking trail. When they camped that night she explained in her halting English, "Those men don't hurt. They warn me watch out for Noah and if I don't tell 'em where she is then they hurt me. Noah is gone. Wawant'x lives."

It wasn't as cold that night. The small fire was between them and the stars were very close. "Next few weeks I show her how to snare rabbits so we eat, and trap beaver and martin so she can trade for food."

Noah asked her about the morning star in the southern sky, and she told him a story that old Antoine had told her.

Once, three young men who hunt with dogs live with old woman grandmother. When come in from hunt, young men give old woman a little caribou liver and other good bits. One day, after hunting all day they kill nothing and come home to old woman, take some rotten wood, give it her and say, "Here, grandmother, here is some caribou liver for you." Old woman is blind, take it and try to eat it and when he see trick very angry. So next day, when young men start out, old woman take bear's foot and heat it in fire and dance about camp and sing his song; in this way by his magic he stop young men from coming back, and turn them into stars. After this, young men live in sky; and one day, while hunting, they find tracks of great moose and follow them several days. As young men track moose, they look down and see earth, and eldest brother decide to try get back to earth. So she tell her brothers to cover with their blankets, and not to look. Then she start, but when only partway down, youngest brother look through hole in his blanket. So her brother can go no farther, and they live, all three, in sky ever since, and you can see to this day, as well as moose and dogs. Morning star is old woman with torch looking for young men, her grandsons.

Noah forgot his pain while she told her story. Listening to it under the stars and starting to think about where his next meal was coming from made him even more aware of his condition. "Thank you, Ta Chi. I'll remember that story when I see those stars." Then he asked, "Do you practise magic?"

She smiled and said, "Better rest up; we move soon."

"I was told by Belle that when Father Dumont brought

me to them he said that my birth mother was Mary and that she died at childbirth."

"Yeah."

"Was Mary my birth mother?"

"No."

"Do you know my birth mother?"

"Yeah. Your mother is Ta Chi."

Noah stared at the small placid figure in front of him who without emotion had just declared that she was his mother. He, who had endured four months of jail and over a week of being hunted like an animal, was overcome and couldn't stop the tears from welling in his eyes, spilling down his cheeks and freezing there. He had wanted to know something about his real mother ever since he fell in love with Justine. He couldn't speak. Ta Chi's attention was directed to the fire. Going back to the time he could first remember, she was always there in the landscape, just as the land was always on his mind and in his heart. He believed her. All he could think to do was to reach out and touch her on the hand and say, "Thank you." After some time he said in an offhand way, not wanting to disturb her but having to ask, "And who is my father?"

She looked away as if she hadn't heard the question. Then she said, "Chilcotin."

He accepted that and didn't press her further. From then on he knew he would be able to tolerate memories of Bordy because he knew that Bordy wasn't his real father.

They moved upriver along the Chilcotin Valley trail. Supplies were low and chances to trap rabbit and squirrel were few. After seven days of low rations, when hunger was turning into starvation, they were near a small lake feeding Big Creek when they heard a wolf pack in full chase under a waning moon. They listened for a half-hour to the din. Suddenly it stopped. Ta Chi interpreted the sounds: "Wolf flush deer from cover. Chase onto lake and bring down. In morning we follow the sound of raven. Find kill and take our share."

"The wolves won't like that."

"They eat good."

In the morning they followed the ravens to the wolf kill, just as she had said. It was a fine-looking stag which had wintered well. The wolf pack had chased the deer onto the lake, where it had lost its footing and slipped. After the pack had brought the stag down, they'd eaten their fill. A lone wolf now stood guard to keep the ravens away, who would have finished the deer and deprived the pack of a second meal.

Ta Chi moved out on the lake with the dog while Noah stayed behind with qiyus. He had trouble controlling the horse, which had gotten wind of the wolf. Getting close to the kill, Ta Chi raised her arms and shouted, firing her .22 rifle in the air. The lone wolf slunk off. Ta Chi hacked off a hindquarter of the not-quite-frozen meat that would feed them for a week. She tied the bloody meat to the horse, leaving the balance of the red carcass to the ravens and the wolves. While they walked through the pine forest, Ta Chi gathered what appeared to be pieces of bark from the branches of the trees lining the trail. Noah didn't understand the reason for this until they camped that night. She made a stew of the venison and placed the pieces of dried bark into the stew. They tasted like mushrooms. She explained, "In summer squirrels pick mushrooms on trail and carry to branches to dry. In winter squirrels and Ta Chi eat mushrooms."

By the end of March they had travelled as far as the Taseko Lake road, close to Hanceville on the other side of the river. Noah was starting to walk with the help of a staff. They were on the outskirts of the Stone Reserve, where Ta Chi's cousin lived. She waited until dark and then went to his house.

"I come to ask buy tea, sugar, oats. Pencils and paper."

He was puzzled. "Pencils and paper?"

"This letter for Justine Paul at the mission school; deliver to her, no one else."

She handed him a letter. He accepted these jobs without further question and agreed to look after her horse.

*****

At his office in Williams Lake, Sergeant Boyd met with the three constables who patrolled the Chilcotin. His first priority was the capture of Noah Hanlon. There had been a number of break-ins over the last month at Anahim Lake, Redstone and Hanceville: all of them were unsolved. The victims and the press were attributing them to Noah. The Williams Lake Tribune editorials were asking pointed questions about why there wasn't any trace of the fugitive or any leads. Justine was to take her Easter break the following week, and a special constable would be assigned to follow her. Boyd had some advice for his men.

"Richard Snellgrove wants the $25,000 reward that has been posted for Noah's capture. I expect he'll be out there and I don't want him interfering with our search. Keep an eye out for him and warn him off if necessary!"

*****

Although she knew it by heart, Justine read the letter for the tenth time, in her bed at St. Joseph's. She would burn the letter tomorrow, but she had to sleep with it tonight. The envelope was folded paper gummed together with pine sap. It was addressed to her at the mission school and given to her, without explanation, by a Chilcotin from the Stone Reserve.

The printing in pencil appeared to be the stick letters of a child. The brief message inside had the same printing:

> *Hope school goes fine,*
> *Pick you up at Anaham*
> *On Easter break.*
> *Love Mother.*

Justine's mother couldn't read or write, so she knew it was from Noah and that he was safe. She put the letter under her pillow and went to sleep. When she woke in the morning the letter was gone. She boarded the bus at Williams Lake and didn't notice the men who were following her. Dale Pope, the Native special constable, boarded the bus and sat a few seats behind her. Richard Snellgrove, in a car with two other men, watched from across the street. Pope was there on instructions from the sergeant to follow Justine in hopes she would lead them to Noah. Snellgrove was there because his informant at the school had stolen the letter and given it to him. Pope was aware of the other's interest in Justine.

The Anaham reserve was a cluster of houses strung out along the road to Anahim Lake on the north steppe of the Chilcotin River. The bus took two hours to make the trip from Williams Lake. Justine was impatient to get off and see her relatives. The bus driver knew her stop and pulled up. "I see you have a welcoming committee." Running down the muddy road came a swarm of young children, shouting and waving at Justine. She waved back. They formed a ring and jumped around her, their eyes open wide and each one demanding her attention.

"Justine, look at me! I have a tooth missing."

"Johnny Hance broke his arm when he was bucked off his horse."

"Are you going to ride in the stampede this year?"

"What did you learn at school?"

"Granny is not well."

She answered each question, squatting down and hugging the girls, and tousling the boys' hair.

"What about Granny?" she asked.

"She came here last night and took to bed. She wants to speak to you."

"All right. Johnny and Matthew, you can help me with the bags and then I'll give you all a treat."

The welcoming committee walked back up between the two ruts made by the Bennett wagon—a horse-drawn buckboard mounted on car tire wheels, adapted by the Chilcotins to navigate the mud during spring breakup and used year-round to haul hay and the family. A couple of their best Appaloosa horses were tethered in the field in front of the house. The children prattled and chatted. They told her all she needed to know of how things were on the reserve. Their treat was a bag of Werther's candies they were told to share amongst themselves.

On entering the one-room shack, Justine saw her cousin Del Lalulà and his wife, Cecilia, seated at the table. They nodded, without getting up, showing a reserve which was common amongst Natives. It was not taken as, nor meant to be, a slight; it was an acknowledgment of her presence in their house, a form of greeting, and with it she felt welcome. There was a wood fire burning in the cast-iron cook stove in the middle of the room. It was uncomfortably warm. A curtain of blankets partitioned off the corner of the room where the parents slept. In the other back corner was a pallet of straw, and on the pallet, watching her every move, was a small woman. The woman was like a caged sparrow, uncomfortable inside, waiting for Justine to release her.

She whispered, "Justine," and reached out and touched Justine on the arm with her sinewy fingers.

"Are you not well, Granny?"

"I don't like indoors. I bring news of Wawant'x. She's reborn. You will see her tonight."

"Who is Wawant'x, Granny?"

"She used to be called Noah."

Justine had not expected that Ta Chi would tell her where to find Noah. It was remarkable that Ta Chi, who refused to be housed and wandered the land alone, would lend herself to such a meeting.

"Granny, I will wait forever for the chance of seeing Noah again."

She placed her hand in Ta Chi's. Ta Chi was not her grandmother, but like many others, she called her that as a term of endearment. Some called her a witch.

Special Constable Pope got off the bus a few houses down from Justine's stop and walked to a hill at the back of the house where he had a good view of the shack. As dusk settled, he saw the Snellgrove posse leave their car and surround the shack. They waited for two hours. Pope watched them and waited. No one came or went from the house, and Snellgrove, who had no patience for the waiting game, finally motioned his two comrades forward. He and the second one burst in the front door while the third entered through the back.

Snellgrove's rush into the private home of Del Lalula was a gross trespass. The force of the entry startled Del and Cecilia and their children, but they had suffered abuse and disgrace before at the hands of the whites and sat still while Snellgrove cornered Ta Chi and Justine.

He was disappointed at not finding Noah there.

"All right, where is he?"

Neither woman spoke.

"I know that Noah is to meet Justine here."

Justine said, "Leave now or I will send someone to call the police."

He ignored her and spoke to Ta Chi, who was lying in the corner with her eyes shut as if asleep. "I told you to report Noah to me when you see him. I know you've seen him. Where is he? Things will go bad for you if you don't tell me."

He towered over her, and she would have seen him raise his fist if her eyes had been open. But Del Lalula saw. He stood up. A short man with bandy legs, his eyes were level with Snellgrove's chest, and he had to tilt back his head to speak to him.

"You're not welcome in our home or on our land. You threaten Ta Chi, you threaten our land and us. Get out!"

Snellgrove realized he might have gone too far. He snarled, "Noah is a fugitive and no one should help him." He motioned to his men. As they left, Ta Chi opened her eyes, and to her the men appeared as wolverines slinking away in the night.

Special Officer Pope came closer to the shack after he saw the posse make their move and heard the commotion inside. He retreated before the posse left. He figured Justine would leave soon and he would follow her. He failed to notice that he himself was being watched.

At midnight, Justine left the cabin and walked towards the woods in the back of the cabin. There was no moon, but Pope could just make her out as she approached his lookout. She would pass very close to where he was sitting, and he knew it would be easy for him as an experienced tracker to follow her and find out where Noah was holed up.

When she passed by, he followed behind. The trail was a rough one. He was clambering over and under deadfalls. Within two minutes of taking up her trail, he was crawling on his hands and knees in the snow under a fallen log. When he straightened up, he placed a foot on some loose brush lying on the snow and was jerked upwards by a rope tied to a young spruce. His ankle had been caught in a snare. It took him five minutes to cut himself down, and by then Justine had slipped away. It was a good half-hour before he got back to the road, found a phone, and called the Tatla Lake RCMP detachment to advise them that Noah was in the vicinity and to send a patrol and dogs.

An hour later, the dogs picked up Justine's scent, which they followed in a circle back to the road, where the trail was lost. It was clear that a passing vehicle had picked her up. It wasn't possible to determine in which direction they had gone. Pope reported back to Sergeant Boyd, who commented, "We can't prove that Noah was the person she intended to see, but it sure looks suspicious."

Del Lalula, the brave man who had stood up to Snellgrove, arranged to have his cousin pick him up and drive to Anahim Lake—another hundred miles west on the road, a journey back to the beginning of the Chilcotins' existence on the land. They met at a clearing a half-mile down the road from Lalula's cabin. Even though Snellgrove was parked out front of his cabin, Del and Ta Chi had no trouble leaving unnoticed. They arrived at the same time as Noah and Justine. This was the first time since Christmas that these two could touch, look, and speak to each other outside of jail. They had only a few minutes. Justine clung to him.

"I want to go with you and be with you. Nothing else matters."

"No. I can't place you in danger. I need to know that you are safe."

"But I love you. I want to be with you."

"Do as I say. I promise to meet you on Potato Mountain in June when you have finished school. We'll meet at that special place we knew as children, on the slopes of Potato Mountain overlooking Tatlayoko Lake."

As he steered her towards her father's waiting truck, he kissed her and said, "I wanted to spend time with you and let you know I am alive and in good health thanks to Ta Chi. Justine, you can trust her. She is my birth mother."

Noah put her inside the truck, and before he shut the door kissed her again on the lips and said, "I love you. Meet me in June."

She looked out the back window at him standing on the road in the moonlight, waving until they rounded a curve. Del had told his cousin that he was going to visit his mother at Anahim Lake and when his cousin stopped for Del a few minutes later he asked him, "Do you mind if two of my friends and their horse hitch a ride in your box?" If anybody had a vehicle in the Chilcotin, they doubled as free taxis for those who didn't.

He got into the cab and his friends, Noah and Ta Chi—with their bags and baggage—got into the box of the pickup with the horse.

His cousin asked after a while, "Who's your friends?"

"Oh, a couple of guys drinking at my house."

Ta Chi knew of an empty cabin on a bay of Charlotte Lake where Noah could hide till the end of May. They were dropped off at Towdyston and Ta Chi left Noah at the cabin, promising to return to guide him back to Tatlayoko Lake.

*****

Sergeant Boyd came knocking at Justine's parents' cabin door at Empire Ranch early the next morning. Her father let him in but stayed in the room while the sergeant interviewed her.

"I see you have made it home safely."

"Yes, I have."

"You were seen with Ta Chi yesterday at Anaham reserve."

"I was there, but I didn't see Ta Chi."

"Oh, then my informant must have been mistaken."

She didn't reply.

"Why did you stop off at Anaham?"

"I was able to get a ride from there to my home."

"Did you see Noah Hanlon at Anaham at all in the last few days?'

"No."

"I want to remind you again that if you are seeing Noah you must tell me. You know it's an offence to help a fugitive, and I don't want to see you spend time in jail."

"Thank you for telling me."

He turned to her father.

"Alec, if you love your daughter, keep her away from Noah."

Alec nodded, and Sergeant Boyd opened the cabin door

and left. He said to the constable who was driving the police cruiser, "We were close to getting him this time. He'll slip up soon."

*****

Settling into the cabin and free from detection for now, Noah was able to pause and consider, as an artist, his westward flight from Farwell Canyon to Charlotte Lake through the heart of the Chilcotin. He was thinking of the Chilcotin as a huge house with many rooms connected by long corridors—the rivers—and interlaced with secret passages—the trails. This reminded him of a bible passage drilled into him during his Catholic schooling: "In my father's house there are many mansions." He didn't know who his father was, whether he was still alive or whether his father would be proud of him. Although he was born and raised for twelve years in the Chilcotin, during that time he had been confined to one room—the area around Empire Ranch circumscribed by his adoptive mother and father's war. He had left there for the civilizing influences of Victoria for eight years, interrupted by his summer work and then as ranch manager, destined never to experience more until he was charged with and convicted of manslaughter. Now with the help of Ta Chi he was becoming familiar with the whole house and its inhabitants.

For over a month in the cabin, he was able to reflect on his experience and his art. In Victoria he had drawn and painted in the Audubon style. His paintings were anatomically correct but they lacked life. He had tried with some success to detail the birds' surroundings and make their natural settings vivid. He had also studied the Native West Coast art of a Victoria painter named Emily Carr and watched Mungo Martin, a Native carver from the coast, carving totem poles next to the legislative buildings, and was familiar with the art form of the ovoid and inverted U's. He was starting to experiment with more interpretive drawing of birds in larger landscapes combined with west-coast Indian motifs before he took a year off to be a rancher. In jail he had taken up his drawing again, and with the pencils, pastels and paper brought by Justine his portfolio of sketches and portraits had grown. He had escaped with what he had produced in jail and during his journeys with Ta Chi had added to it.

In the few hours each week that Justine visited him in jail, he had talked of Victoria and she had told him about her Chilcotin and her relatives. When she was asked where her home was, she wouldn't say "Tatlayoko Lake" or "Empire Ranch." She would say "Chilcotin," for that was her home—all of it. One day as Noah was sketching her she had said, "You should draw your home."

"What do you mean?"

"Well, the Chilcotin is your home."

"Yes, but I don't know it well enough to paint it."

"When you get out of here, I'll show it to you."

Now, after two months of wandering the rooms and corridors with Ta Chi, he had a better idea of what Justine had been talking about. With time to think, he began drawing and planning for a project about what she referred to as his home. When all his troubles ended he would paint this land. He had decided that he would never again ranch Empire.

SPRING

Spring came to the high Chilcotin three months later than to Victoria. First there was a tonic in the air, then the booming sound of cracking lake ice, a trickle of water in the rivulets, a flow in the streams, and a gushing torrent in the rivers.

The government didn't think it was necessary to consult the Chilcotins on the cabinet's decision to grant the water licence to Vancouver Island Power. Bordy had opposed the project to save Empire Ranch, not the Chilcotins' land and water. It was thought in Victoria that the Natives would not be directly concerned because their reserves were in the Chilcotin River watershed. The flooding of the Homathko watershed would affect only a few Chilcotins—the Stonys, including Ta Chi, who were still semi-nomadic. Empire Ranch and a few smaller ranches in the fertile Homathko River valley north of the ranch that Bordy had not succeeded in buying would be flooded. Empire Ranch would cease to exist, and so would the jobs of the lead hand Alec Paul and the Natives who were hired on hay crews and as cowhands.

The power company's intentions were not made known to the Chilcotins through more conventional forms of communication, but Antoine had his own way of divining the future of his land. With the coming of spring, Antoine went into the mountains to a cave that had been shown to him by his grandfather. This was where deyens for generations had sought visions. There, perched on a high cliff above the Homathko, with snows receding in the warmth of April, Mount Waddington looming to the west and Potato Mountain to the east, he fasted and waited for his vision, a foretelling of the year ahead for the land and the people.

The winter bird-sounds of the brash crow, the crackle of the raven, and the rasp of the jay were answered by the warble of the mating thrush, the distinctive sound of the killdeers and mergansers. The frozen river had broken and the deer and moose were moving from the lower valleys to the western mountains. The does were heavy with their unborn, some with the promise of twins. With winter's privation ending, Antoine was thankful to be alive, but he was concerned with what the spring awakening would bring. He drank only spruce tea and ate some dried salmon. His ancestors had starved at this time of year before the salmon runs. If one had food to share, now was the time to share it. That spirit of sharing had been forgotten a long time ago.

Antoine remembered the wound as if it were yesterday. His father, who had taken part in the Chilcotin War, told him that the ferryman on the Waddington survey had refused food to two starving Chilcotin hunters. In a rage they had shot him. The main hunting party was nearby and when they were told of the shooting, they had decided to form a war party to stop the incursions of the whites—*midagh*—into the Chilcotin. The war party had been led by *Klatsassin*, a war chief, who incited his band to follow him. They fell on the survey and road-building crew, killing all but three who escaped.

The mercenaries and settlers who had been sent there by the government in New Westminster—then the capital of British Columbia—in turn had hunted the Chilcotins. Klatsassin and his men could not be found on the vast plateau. On a promise of safety should they turn themselves in, the Chilcotins did so and instead of freedom found themselves put in chains, tried by Judge Begbie, and convicted. Six were hanged at Quesnel as common criminals: a tooth for a tooth, an eye for an eye, and a life for a life.

Antoine chanted the trials of his people since the coming of the midagh: the first sighting of Simon Fraser; the failed attempts of the Hudson's Bay Company to establish a fort in the heart of their lands; the distinction of being described in the Company's journals as "troublesome and disorderly;" the long association with the Oblate Missionaries, who persevered and finally converted many to their faith; the smallpox epidemics which wiped out over half the population; being assigned to reserves; watching children and grandchildren—including his grandson Peter—forced to go to residential school and then turn to alcohol, go to Vancouver, and be lost to the ghetto. Life had been hard for many of his people; there could be no letting down their guard for a promised heaven. This was his chant.

"What is Raven's message for the Chilcotin this year?" he asked. "Where is the next threat coming from?"

Raven answered by swooping low over the clearing by

the river. Another raven flew from its perch by the cave entrance and they joined—plummeting, swirling, and falling into the swift river in a feathered embrace. One managed to escape, shake its wings and fly off; the other was caught in an eddy and was swept away.

"It is the river," Antoine said aloud.

The threat was coming from the river that cut through the mountains. It was a natural weakness to be exploited; in Klatsassin's day for a road, now perhaps for a dam. It had caused the war years ago. What would happen now? His son Alec and other members of his tribe joined him that evening and he told them what Raven had told him.

Noah was away from the cabin for a few days climbing a nearby mountain to get a better view of the land, to sketch the landscape and to determine his escape routes should he have to leave in a hurry. Under the stars, watching them move across the heavens, he began tracing and naming them, not by the myths of the Greek gods but by the stories that Ta Chi had told him of the Chilcotin myths.

He had not seen anyone since being led to the cabin by Ta Chi, who had said she would return to guide him to Tatlayoko. He was coming down the lake by canoe and approaching the cabin when he saw smoke coming from the chimney. He paddled to shore, stashed the canoe and approached close to the cabin on foot. He would wait till whomever was inside came out. After an hour, the cabin door opened and a Native came outside for an armload of wood for the fire. He straightened up and looked out onto the lake. It was old Antoine.

Noah gave him a signal that he was there so that Antoine could tell him whether he was alone. He waved Noah in. Noah Hanlon, named Wawant'x by Ta Chi, sat with Antoine in the cabin. Wawant'x gave the old man a meal of roasted squirrel, rainbow trout and potato, which they ate in silence. After, Antoine lit his pipe and quietly smoked while nodding and smiling at Noah. Ta Chi said that Antoine, whom Noah had considered a babysitter for Peter and Justine when he was growing up on the ranch, was a deyen who was much respected by the Natives. He had seen Antoine at the trial but had not spoken to him and of course he remembered him from the times when Peter and he were companions at the ranch.

Antoine waved his pipe at the drawings tacked to the walls. "I see you draw."

"I have found time to draw."

"You have discovered our land?"

"Yes, from Ta Chi, my mother."

"Do want to learn more?"

"Yes, I have to know more to finish this painting."

"What do you want to know?"

"How the Chilcotins found this land, the stories that sustain them, and, I guess, most important to me: Who am I?"

"I answer last question first. You is Chilcotin, born of Ta Chi in mountains near lake like this. Your mother could not raise you. Leave you with me. I ask Father Dumont to find family to raise you. Maria, your wet nurse, would not let Father Dumont give you to anyone but the Hanlons, where she keep an eye on you."

"I know my mother is Ta Chi. Who is my father?"

"I can't tell that. Ta Chi will tell."

"Ta Chi's told me that my father was the Chilcotin. She wouldn't say more."

"If she don't say, I don't say. Now I tell you of our beginnings." He took some tobacco out of his pocket, stuffed it into the bowl of his pipe with his thumb and picked an ember from the fire to light it, drawing in the smoke and exhaling. Then he looked at Noah and said, "I tell you story of Lendix'tcux, the transformer. He readied the Chilcotin for our people. Since you returned to us, you hear it. It help you to know our land. I tell the story to Peter before he taken from us. It maybe help answer all your questions. Perhaps you use story in drawings."

"I think so."

"I will make start."

Long ago, before my time, before our people find Chilcotin, a chief's daughter had a lover. He visit her during night but not show himself. She discover identity of lover by marking his shoulder with white paint. He turn out to be a dog. The woman later give birth to three pups. Her father in anger desert her, take villagers with him, and leave the woman alone with pups and dog father, whose name is Lendix'tcux. The mother one day surprise dogs playing in house in human form, and she destroy dog blankets of three children and half the blanket of Lendix'tcux. Then children remain in human form, and father is half-dog, half-man.

Noah got up and put a log on the fire and asked, "Which half was man and which half dog?"

"Man is above waist."

Boys grow up and taught by mother to become skilful hunters and lay up great stores of meat. On return of villagers, all are happy. But Lendix'tcux and boys become restless and wish to travel to Chilcotin country. Their mother warn them, in the Chilcotin country animals kill people. But they start out anyway after receiving full instructions from their mother and come towards the Chilcotin country, where you sit now.

They come first to ford in the river guarded by great Moose. Moose swallow Lendix'tcux, who kill it by cutting his way out of Moose and roasting the heart and from the carcass they make all sorts of small animals. After many failures he succeed in making Frog from brain.

Next they come to Seagull. It was spearing salmon. Lendix'tcux turn himself into salmon and Seagull spear him, but Lendix'tcux cut off head of spear and swim away. He come to the Seagull's camp when Seagull is mourning loss of spear. His wife is weeping bitterly, because, being pregnant she must die. Because at that time in Chilcotin the only way to give birth to children was by a section of abdomen. Lendix'tcux give Seagull spear point in return for sweathouse and teach woman how to give birth to children with safety.

Noah marvelled at the medical knowledge as Antoine, engrossed in his story, continued.

Next he obtain Eagle feathers from nest and is carried up and back again by Eagles. He make them harmless to men. Lendix'tcux lost last part of his little finger in stone door of Marmot's house, now short of that part of finger. Next he obtain tobacco from tree. He has intercourse with a woman after breaking out teeth in her vagina with magic staff. Then he overcome Moose who kill men with dust raised by running race around mountain. Lendix'tcux pretend to be old and feeble dog. He tie arrow points in his hair, which fly out as he run and kill Moose. He bring to life again and make harmless to men.

He next come to Chilko Lake, where he is swallowed by Beaver. He is found by three boys after long time and is rescued. From Beaver flesh they make fishes. A messenger from mother overtake them, but messenger not speak. Finally, in anger Lendix'tcux kill him. He then try to catch Chipmunk, but fail, and Chipmunk has stripes on its back where his fingers scratch. Because he is a failure, Lendix'tcux and sons transform to stone.

To south of Potato Mountain and Nemiah Valley is Lendix'tcux with three sons watching over Chilcotin. The mountain we call Ts'yl-os.

Antoine's voice, which had filled the cabin, fell silent, and the two men watched the open fire of pine logs in the hearth and thought their own thoughts. Antoine remembered the effect of his story on Peter, his chosen one, as Peter listened to how the land and animals were transformed. He was thirteen at the time and Antoine had taken him to his cave on the Homathko to explain the mysteries and myths of their people. They had fasted and Peter was overcome with the ghosts of his ancestors.

Noah was also thinking of Peter and asked Antoine, "Would Peter have become a powerful deyen?"

Antoine response was quick: "Yes. His mind was open to the Chilcotin."

Noah, sensitive to the stories of the religion in which he was brought up and of the ancient gods that he had studied, was amazed by the taming of the land in such a fierce way. But he was more receptive to the message after surviving with Ta Chi for many months.

Noah again broke the silence, "I would like to ask where

you were when you first heard the story of how the animals were created."

"My grandfather told me, and I have been telling it around our campfires for many years."

"You know there is another story in the Bible about how the animals were saved."

"Yes, I know it. Father Dumont told it to me. But that story, it seem, does not fit our land or our people. You should know our story if you are going to paint our land."

The next morning, Antoine left the cabin after promising to meet Noah on Potato Mountain, from where he would show him Lendix'tcux and his three sons. Noah walked with him to the highway where he was going to hitch a ride. He said in parting, "I have been thinking about Lendix'tcux and how he was transformed into the mountain. My experience since my escape from jail seems to have been a transformation."

The old man smiled and nodded, "Midagh intends to dam the Homathko at Waddington Canyon."

"When?"

"I think they come soon."

"Does my mother know this?"

"The Raven, she know."

It was May. Noah was expecting Ta Chi. They would be leaving the cabin and returning to Tatlayoko Lake at Noah's wish. He had told her that was where he would find Bordy's killer. He was getting impatient. He wanted to see Justine. He wanted to confront Belle. He was cutting wood outside the cabin in the afternoon. It was quiet, and as he methodically split the silver birch for his fire, he thought about the mural and how Ta Chi would be part of it. Finishing the job, he set the axe aside and gathered an armful of dry birch, walked to the door, and pushed it open with his back. As he backed in a strong arm grabbed him from behind in a chokehold. He struggled, but his air was throttled. A voice said quietly, "Don't struggle or you will black out. I want to talk to you, but I have to tie you up or you will run away."

Noah knew any further struggle was futile, so he relaxed and let his attacker blindfold him, wind rope around his waist and pin his arms so he couldn't move. Noah caught his breath.

"You're after the reward. I'll pay you double if you let me go."

"Not the reward. I have instructions to speak to you and to bring you in if necessary."

"Who are you going to bring me to?"

"I can't say. It's near suppertime and I'm hungry. I'll get some food for both of us."

The stranger heated up some beans and toasted bannock on the fire, which they both ate with tea without speaking. He looked at Noah, sizing him up, and said, "How did you survive in the wilderness for so long?

"This is my land."

"It's not important. What I want to know is who you saw on the lawn the night of Bordy Hanlon's shooting."

"No one."

"You told the police that you saw someone."

"I lied."

The stranger slapped Noah across the face with his open hand. "I don't believe you."

Noah wasn't expecting the blow and shook his head to clear the stars. "What do you care about who it was I did or didn't see?"

"Maybe someone wants vengeance."

"Bordy didn't have too many friends. Who would want

to avenge his death? Maybe it was me that killed Bordy."

"We've just met. Already I know you couldn't have done it."

"I can't tell you any more. You're going to have to take me to your people."

"We'll wait till morning; then you and I will go to Nimpo Lake resort and go for a plane ride."

Noah didn't sleep well. His captor had taken the precaution of tying his feet together. He was more professional than Snellgrove. After a light breakfast and little talk except for the stranger's orders, they both mounted Ta Chi's horse and rode for a mile to the end of the lake, where the stranger's horse was tethered. He mounted, and with the reins in his hands led Ta Chi's horse down the trail to Nimpo Lake.

It was an all-day ride, giving Noah time to size up his captor. He was very disciplined. He didn't smoke, only spoke when necessary and was alert to his surroundings. As a bushman he was almost comparable to Ta Chi. The difference was that she did effortlessly what he had to think about, and this gave her a few seconds' advantage when she rose up in front of the stranger's horse from what appeared to be a pile of leaves on the trail.

The stranger's horse reared and threw him. Ta Chi was on him, wielding the butt end of her .22 rifle, and clipped him on the side of his head. She signalled her horse to her, cut off Noah's ropes and removed his blindfold. She mounted the stranger's horse and they were away.

The stranger came to in time to sit up and watch them go. He walked the rest of the way to Nimpo Lake, where he found that Ta Chi had left his rented horse, and called his employer on their radiophone. "It's me. I found him. I questioned him. He wouldn't tell me anything. I think he knows who was on the lawn. I thought about bringing him to you, but decided against it."

There was a pause on the line before the major said, "That's too bad, Charlie. We can't have Noah implicating Belle. But we'll deal with him later. Here's what you'll do: get on the floatplane and return to Victoria. I need you for something else."

For the past two months Stan had been hibernating, gathering strength for what he believed would be his last stand. He had heard that Ta Chi had been seen at Anaham together with Justine, and that a special officer had followed her and been bushwhacked. Ta Chi had disappeared, swallowed by the huge landscape. The speculation was that Noah was with her. The word was out that the police wanted her for questioning. It was time for him to make his move onto the plateau. He phoned Belle.

"Belle, this is Stan."

"Stan. It's good to hear your voice." She said this as if she meant it. "How's everything with you?"

"I can't complain."

"You haven't sent me your bill for the work you did on Noah's trial."

"No, and I don't intend to. I wasn't satisfied with the result. But Belle, there is something you can do for me. You know how much I like fishing?"

There was a long pause. "Yes." She remembered the last time he had gone fishing on Tatlayoko Lake.

"I would like to spend some time at the ranch house and fish on the lake. You know my health isn't very good. I haven't been there in years and this would mean a lot to me. Your cook Feng is still there, and I won't bother you or your manager, Johnston." He didn't share with her his concerns about her involvement in Bordy's murder. He wanted to investigate his theory that she knew more than she had told him or the police and take the opportunity to confront her. He still thought of her as the kind woman who wouldn't say no to an old friend.

"All right, Stan, go ahead. I'll let the Johnstons know you're coming, and Feng will be pleased to cook for another person. Enjoy your stay."

She told the major about it later, and he asked, "Why would you let that man putter around the ranch?"

"Oh, he's harmless."

EXPEDITION

The team that the major assembled to survey the Homathko Canyon dam site was impressive on paper: twenty men led by Ian Richards, an engineer; a helicopter rented for four months to ferry men and supplies between camps; a boat to navigate Tatlayoko Lake from the north end where the road ended at Empire Ranch to the south end, the outfall of the Homathko River. The men gathered on a May morning in a Vancouver parking lot to begin their journey of six hundred road miles up the Fraser River valley and onto the Chilcotin plateau. The turnout didn't look impressive, however. They could easily have been mistaken for a line-up at an east-end soup kitchen. Fortunately, the major was not there to see them off. He intended to motor up Bute Inlet in his yacht and have the helicopter pick him up and take him to camp, where he could give encouragement to the men.

Charlie was there to make sure his crew survived in the wilds of the Chilcotin and to keep an eye on Ian Richards. The major had staked everything on the success of this survey and he was determined nothing would go wrong. He was aware of the failure of the Waddington survey that had attempted to build a road in Chilcotin territory many years ago. That had ended in a massacre. That was not going to happen to the Parmenter survey. He had personally sacrificed much and had made no compromises to realize this mission.

Ralph Richards had insisted that he be hired as a member of the survey. He would be on the alert for any sightings of his friend Noah. He listened to his father speak to the crew from the running-board of a truck.

"Men, we are heading out soon. I will have time to speak to each of you and to tell you what I expect from you on this survey. Our intention is to prove that the Homathko Canyon can be dammed for the benefit of the Vancouver Island Power Company and our customers. We will be surveying the dam site and roads so that work can begin next year on the construction of this grand project. Tonight our caravan will drive to Hope, then on to Williams Lake for more supplies, and from there to Empire Ranch, which will be the staging ground for our expedition."

While he was speaking, Charlie Rainbow—who was standing beside him—searched the face of each man as if he were weighing the man's value on his own scale. From the scowl on his face, they were all lacking; particularly Ralph Richards, who was self-conscious about his size.

Ian Richards intoned, "This is our chance, working as a team, to make a difference to this province and . . ."

He wasn't able to finish. A two-tone, blue-and-white Chevy Bel Air, chopped and channelled, turned off from a side street onto the lot with a rumble of exhaust and the squealing of brakes. It was driven by a dyed blonde as big as a crew cab. She jumped out of the car and held the door open for a twenty-five-year-old, gap-toothed draggle of a man with a coiled red-and-green cobra tattoo on his right arm. They embraced in a tangle of arms, legs, and lips. She jumped back in the car and laid rubber on a tight U-turn as someone in the back seat threw a duffle bag out the window that landed at the man's feet.

In the silence that followed he said, "Hi, I'm Aaron and I'm ready to roll."

The survey crew was complete.

*****

Justine looked up from her exam paper on the history of the Hudson's Bay Company in British Columbia to see the bowed heads of her focused classmates, and beyond them through the open windows the greening hills surrounding Williams Lake. She read the question: "Where did the Carrier Indians of Northern British Columbia get their name?" She knew the answer. It reminded her of Noah's favourite poet, Shelley, whose friends cremated his remains on the seashore. When his heart wouldn't burn, his wife, Mary Wollstonecraft Godwin, had it placed in a silk shroud. She wore it around her neck for the rest of her life.

Before Justine wrote the answer, she got caught up in a daydream about her father and mother at the range camp at the south end of Tatlayoko Lake. Her ten-year-old brother, Ben, was fishing in the Homathko River for rainbow trout; her mother, Maria, was scraping beaver skins stretched on their frames. And Noah Hanlon would soon be waiting patiently for her and thinking only of her in the meadow at the foot of Potato Mountain, where they had agreed to meet. They would recite Shelley's poems. All of her many daydreams ended this way.

"Time's up, girls," Sister Betty said from the front of the class. "No more writing, please."

Justine frantically scribbled, "Because the women carried . . ."

Sister Betty was suddenly beside her, taking the paper while Justine's pen was still scratching. "Justine, you know the rules."

"But I know the answer, Sister."

"Sorry, I've been watching you. You decided to daydream rather than answer the question."

It was the last answer on the last exam and she had worked hard. She had read Father Maurice's book The History of the Northern Interior of British Columbia. The answer was, "Because the widow of a deceased warrior picked up his charred bones from the funeral pyre and carried them on her back for years."

That afternoon her father picked her up from school and drove her to town, where they would stay overnight with friends before driving to the ranch.

After dinner, while they walked to the Rendezvous Café next to McKenzie's Department Store, Justine told her friend Sarah about Sister Betty refusing to let her write the answer. Justine was animated by the injustice of being denied a chance to answer the last exam question. The chill of the early June evening fired her temper: her chin jutted and her hands waved. "The old crow wouldn't give me a chance. She snatched my paper from me like it was a piece of garbage."

Her friend was more restrained. "Sister wouldn't snatch the paper. She is very strict about the rules. She didn't single you out."

"But I was working on a perfect score. I need the marks to get into nursing."

Changing the subject, which didn't interest her, Sarah said, "Will you be riding in the barrel races this year at the Williams Lake stampede?"

The stampede was at the end of June. Justine's horse Getaway hadn't been ridden since the fall. Every year at stampede time, her family came in from Tatlayoko and camped on the fairgrounds. Her father entered the bucking-horse, calf-roping, and steer-wrestling events, and for the last five years she had entered in the barrel races. She'd been runner-up last summer. "I'm going to enter and I'm going to win," she replied as they opened the door to the Rendezvous.

Charlie Rainbow sat in a booth with his back to the entrance. Opposite him and facing the entrance were Aaron and Ralph. The rest of the crew were in other booths eating their dinner. Aaron had not disappointed the crew by softening his first impression. All the way up the Fraser Canyon and onto the plateau he had acted as brazenly as when he first appeared. He drove the jeep fast but expertly, attempting to herd the other slower vehicles of the caravan by rushing to the front and then to the back of the line of trucks, scouting out stops ahead, and making sure there were no stragglers. This did not seem to disturb Ian Richards, the commander-in-chief of the expedition. Released from the shackles of his desk job, he felt it was only fitting that Aaron act the way Ian felt as the man in charge.

Aaron also hit on every girl he saw, including the one he had just spotted: Justine. "Would you look at that filly!"

Ralph looked but didn't say anything. Charlie turned around and noticed that the girl who had caught Aaron's attention was talking to a friend about horses as they both moved to a booth on the other side of the café. For his part, Charlie wasn't impressed; he liked a woman to be plump, with a forgiving nature and round, happy features, and he said so. Aaron said Justine looked as pretty as a wild mustang and as spirited. "I sure would like to ride that filly. Hey, Ralph, how about you and I go over there and talk up those two."

Ralph had manners. He wasn't going over without an introduction. The waitress brought the bill. Charlie settled up the account and the crew left the café in twos and threes. Aaron walked around the U-shaped counter to the booth on the other side where Justine and Sarah—unaware of any interest they had stirred in the crew—were sipping soft drinks.

"Hi," he said. "I heard you talking about horses. Are you going to the stampede?"

Their eyes remained fixed on their soft drinks.

"Hey, I'm talking to you. I'm going to be riding in the stampede. Maybe I'll see you. My name's Aaron, what's yours?"

Again, no response.

"Are you hard of hearing?" he yelled, and brought his hand down hard on the table.

The girls were startled, ready to bolt, but he blocked their way. Ralph came around the table and took Aaron by the arm. "Let the girls be."

Aaron shook himself free and spat at Ralph. "Leave me alone, mister. I'm breaking these Indians in my own way."

Justine looked up at Aaron. "I'm not an Indian; I'm a Chilcotin." She pointed at Charlie Rainbow: "He's an Indian."

Charlie called out, "Okay, boys, you've had your fun, so

let's go." The group left the café, but Aaron and Charlie parted from the crew returning to their hotel and headed to the Legion. They were settled at their table with a beer and Charlie said, "You know, Aaron, I hired you to drive and supply our camp. You're getting a good wage and the work isn't hard. It's better than living on welfare in Vancouver. The only other condition is that you take orders from me. Now, I want you to shape up and not cause trouble with the crew."

"That Richards kid gets under my skin," Aaron said.

"Lay off that boy," Charlie warned, and left after finishing his beer.

Aaron stayed for another round. He noticed at the table next to him a bulk of a man who knew his way around the bar. He introduced himself.

"Hi, I'm Aaron."

The bulk moved his lips in a menacing way. "What brings you to Williams Lake, Aaron?"

"I'm with a crew headed into the Chilcotin to survey Waddington Canyon."

There was an immediate change in the menace. "Well, glad to meet you. I'm Richard Snellgrove, That's great country you're going into. Come on over to my table, drinks on me."

The two men closed down the bar at the Legion on Aaron's promise that he would look up Snellgrove when he came to town for supplies and keep his eyes and ears open about Noah Hanlon.

*****

The potholed pavement on Highway 20 west from Williams Lake turned into washboard gravel at Hanceville. Billowing dust swallowed the survey caravan and the crew chewed grit and rubbed their eyes red. The truck hauling the boat trailer came to a grinding halt at Alexis Creek when the cabin cruiser shifted and tilted, breaking an axle on the trailer. The sight of the heavy V-hulled boat tilted at a dangerous angle drew a crowd of Chilcotins, who stood by and waited to see if the greenhorns would make a bad situation worse by shifting the boat so hard that it would topple over on the opposite side. Bets were being taken between a few of the crowd when Charlie arrived in the jeep and took charge. Here was something different: an Indian giving orders and dressing down the stumbling crew who, left on their own, would have created lots of fun for the onlookers. The local garage could not get the necessary part until the next day. The expedition was scheduled to be at the Empire Ranch that night to keep to the major's tight timetable. He would not be amused when they arrived late.

The crew cleared their throats of dust at the hotel beer parlour and propped their boots on the porch rail outside while talking to some young Chilcotins. Quietly whittling within earshot was an elder listening to the boasts of these young white men saying they were going to dam the Homathko River. Not to be outdone, a young Native pointed out Mount Tatlow in the distance amid a range of snow-capped mountains to the south. He gave it the Chilcotin name *Ts'yl-os.*

"He was the first chief, who with his three sons turned into stone, and he now guards our land. Better watch out."

After the young man left, the elder came up to the crew. "He's right about Ts'yl-os and Lendix'tcux and his sons. He prepared this land for the Chilcotin . . . but the young one points to the wrong mountain."

"Is that right, Pops?" Aaron said, winking at the others

to let them in on his joke. "Maybe you can point out the right one."

The elder took him seriously. "No. It is forbidden to point. I would then know his anger. It is enough for you to know that he is watching. What you do will not please him."

After a two-day delay the axle was repaired, and despite the elder's warning the crew travelled east past Redstone and on to Tatla Lake near the headwaters of the Chilcotin River. They turned south off the main road, taking the branch towards Empire Ranch. At about eight that evening they arrived at the ranch yard. A string of horses stood outside an open corral of beaten-down compacted dirt, with white-, blue-, and red-painted barrels set at each end. A couple of men were sitting on the rail.

Stan Hewitt turned and watched the crew emerge from their vehicles, but turned back when he heard a screech like a banshee from a young woman with curly chestnut hair riding a palomino horse at full gallop out of the barn and towards the far barrel. She made the turn around it and headed back. Flecks of foam and spittle flew from her horse's mouth as she stroked its flank with her crop. She passed the second barrel and brought the horse up to a quivering halt.

"Fifteen seconds," shouted another girl from the shadow of the barn. "Not bad, but it's not a winning time."

"You do better, if you can."

A pinto came out of the barn with its tail flying. Its sides were wrapped by the bare brown legs of a girl whose ponytail paralleled the horse's. A crop was between her teeth and the heels of her bare feet were raking the sides of the pinto, whose nose was aimed at the barrel. Coming opposite the barrel, Justine touched the horse's neck on the left side with the rein and pulled on the right rein. The horse responded by leaning to the right and digging his hooves into the soft earth, making a U-turn and grazing but not overturning the barrel. The crop came out of the Justine's mouth; she gave a wild war cry and used her free right hand to whip her horse over the finish line.

"Damn!" Sarah exploded. "You beat me by two seconds. You've been practising."

The survey crew was watching this race and shouting encouragement. The girls were too focused to hear them. The loudest was Aaron, who had taken off his hat and was waving it at Justine. "Hey, there! Remember me? I met you in town."

He jumped over the fence into the corral and sauntered over to the girls. Some of the crew who had heard him boast about riding in the rodeo urged him on: "Let's see you ride that pinto."

Aaron went right up to the girls standing beside their horses, not an inch of reserve in him, born of the arrogance of the city. He grasped the pinto's reins near the bit and tugged the loose end from Justine's hand. "I'll show you how it's done," he said, and vaulted bareback onto the horse.

Justine stepped back. She wasn't worried. Sarah reacted more directly: she brought her hand down hard on the pinto's rump and shouted, "Hyup!" The horse arched its back and flung its hind legs into the air, throwing Aaron high in the air. Then it came down on all four feet and blazed towards the far barrel, with Aaron a crumpled heap wheezing for breath on the ground. Justine whistled her horse into the barn, and the girls disappeared while Aaron dusted himself off to the jeers of the crew. Ralph watched from the edge and caught Justine's eye as she turned to go. Her look said, "You people are not welcome here."

Antoine had watched the exploration crew pull into

Empire Ranch from his son's cabin, just as he had watched Bordy and Belle arrive twenty years ago. He walked over to the corral just as Charlie Rainbow was shouting at the crew to gather for their orders. He had a long look at Charlie.

Stan, curious about Antoine's reaction and taken aback by the sudden arrival of visitors, asked, "What's this?"

"Midagh—white men come to destroy the waters of the Homathko."

"Did you know they were coming?"

"I was expecting them. Raven told me."

Stan muttered, "So they got their water licence. Bordy wouldn't have let that happen without a fight." Belle must have known that the Homathko waters would be dammed, Stan thought. She hadn't told him. She hadn't told him a lot of things. He had told Belle that he wanted to spend his time at the ranch fishing, which was true. He was fishing for fish, but he was also fishing for facts to prove Noah's innocence. Now Antoine had given him one more reason to suspect Belle Hanlon in the death of her husband.

"Antoine, I am looking for Ta Chi."

Antoine stretched out his right arm with his palm up and moved it in a full circle east to Potato Mountain, then south to Mount Ts'yl-os, and finally to the high mountains to the west. "She out there."

"Yes, but where?"

"Wait! She will come."

"Have you heard from Noah?"

Antoine trusted this lawyer. He had acted for Peter and Noah. He had acted for the Chilcotins.

"It is said Noah walks with Ta Chi. Are they all you look for?"

"If Noah had given evidence, he would have said that the

shot that killed Bordy came from the lawn near the lake. I'll look around a bit. It snowed after the shooting; perhaps the police missed something."

Antoine slowly got down from the fence and was starting to walk away when Stan said, "Say, Antoine?"

"Yeah."

"Do you know who killed Bordy?"

"A lot of people coulda killed Bordy."

PART III

Those who came to see us from below (Soda Creek) were on horseback. But tho' animals are plenty and the country in many places clear of wood, they do not use them to hunt, but use them to carry themselves and baggage, which is the chief cause of them not going much in canoes.

Simon Fraser's Journal, June 1808

QIYUS

After a long month's journey on foot and horseback through the back trails from Charlotte Lake, circling to the north of Anahim Lake and Tatla Lake, Noah and Ta Chi crossed the road to the west of the outfall of the Chilko River where it fed into the Chilcotin River and camped in the country known as the Brittany Triangle, named after a small lake in the centre of a pine forest and meadowland where wild stallions led their herds of mares and foals. The milky Taseko River to the east and the clear blue Chilko River to the west joined and emptied into the Chilcotin River, forming two sides to the triangle. The third side, to the south, was the Nemiah Valley.

They were fishing for suckers in the mouth of a small slow-moving stream at the edge of the Chilko River. Noah, who had trapped a fish and thrown it into a basket, said to Ta Chi, "I'm leaving you soon. I'll be meeting Justine in two weeks near Tatlayoko Lake. It's dangerous for me to be near the lake, but she's a friend. I'll need a horse."

Ta Chi stopped chasing a sucker. The day had come. She had taught him all she knew about survival. He was ready to survive in the Chilcotin on his own. There was no need for her. She continued to call him Wawant'x. She said the name suited him, and he had accepted it, along with his life, as a gift from her. How could he possibly repay her?

"Plenty qiyus in the Brittany."

"Those are wild horses. I have no horse to ride them down and rope them."

"That midagh way. Chilcotin finds stallion and her herd. Builds a small corral. Places good hay and salt in the corral and waits." While she explained, Ta Chi mimicked the movements of Noah and the horse, performing a little dance. "Qiyus goes into corral to lick salt, and Wawant'x shuts gate to corral. Wawant'x has qiyus."

Noah laughed and pretended he was on a bucking horse. "I will have a wild, unbroken horse. It would take me a month to break it. Or it will break me." He fell down.

For the first time, he heard Ta Chi laugh aloud.

"No," she said.

"Is there a Chilcotin way to break a horse?"

"Leave qiyus in corral with no food, no water. She is weak. Wawant'x give her a little water, a little hay, get to know her, give her a name. When qiyus still weak, Wawant'x slowly tame." And she demonstrated by gently riding a well-behaved pretend horse. "Take a week."

They were both laughing at the end of their pantomime.

*****

Ten miles east of Empire Ranch, Noah rode Chilko—his wild Appaloosa mare—out of the Brittany Triangle. Following Ta Chi's instructions, it had taken him three weeks to capture and tame his qiyus. He was heading back to the stream where Ta Chi was camped to show her what he had done.

Noah had been pushed by Belle to excel in school. He had. He had wanted to paint, which was also what Belle wanted for him. His drawings and paintings were displayed all over their Victoria house. Bordy had been as demanding as Belle. While Noah was growing up on the ranch, he had had to work as hard as Bordy, and Bordy criticized everything he did. Then, when he decided to give up his education and his painting to go back to the Chilcotin to ranch, Belle had fought him with logic and emotion. She had told that him he wasn't a rancher, that Bordy would not be impressed with his charity, and that Noah would be unhappy. Justine was the only person who had accepted him as he was, with no intention of shaping him into something that he wasn't, and she was the person he had turned to, to share his fears and dreams.

Belle had been right. He had soon discovered that he could not please Bordy. Unhappy and unappreciated at the ranch, he had also found that he didn't have time for painting. Running that huge operation and fighting with Bordy took all his waking hours and sapped his creative energy. Bordy's death had released him from his ordeal. He would have thought that running from the law would be worse; instead he found that he now had time to think and draw.

Thoreau's On Walden Pond was one of his favourite books. Thoreau equated freedom with lack of material possessions and living off the land. By that definition, Noah was free. Now he was riding a horse that he had tamed in order to meet up with Justine. He had time to draw with a new perspective—through the eyes of a Chilcotin, not of a rancher. His rough portfolio was full of drawings of wildlife that were influenced by Chilcotin motifs and symbols. He had begun drawing people, not as portraits, but as part of the landscape; not in a dominant role, but in a sharing perspective. One of his models was Ta Chi, but when he tried to draw her he couldn't capture her as a person. When she moved it was a sparrow's flight. When she rested, she blended into and became part of her surroundings. He had drawn and painted her as part of the landscape, something that gave the Chilcotin life.

Ta Chi could hear a raven caw a mile away or feel a horse gallop long before it came into view, giving her time to make herself invisible. But a boy from a family that was camped a distance away was playing and wandering along the river when, undetected by Ta Chi because of the noise of the rushing water of the Chilko, he saw her by her fire. He went back to his friends—all boys in their pre- and early teens, full of the devil and bored—who thought it would be a good idea to pester this nomad. They swooped down on her from all directions. She had nowhere to escape to. Their weapons were taunts and stones. They spent a half-hour amusing themselves in this way, taking her away from her bags of clothes and provisions. She tried to yell them off. She wouldn't fire her rifle at them, and it wasn't their intention to do her harm. They were baiting her. An errant stone struck her on the temple and she crumpled to the ground.

As he approached Ta Chi's encampment, Noah heard a commotion and urged Chilko to a gallop. The horse was fresh and excitable. It plunged and reared as Noah thundered down on the boys, lashing out at them with a willow whip.

He hounded them across the stream and into the woods and watched them scatter over the next rise. Their story that night around their parents' fire was not of their mischief but of being chased by a Chilcotin stranger on horseback who threatened to kill them. Their parents made the connection: it was Noah, and this sighting came to the attention of the police.

He had intended to ride the next day for Tatlayoko Lake and his meeting with Justine, but Ta Chi was disoriented and couldn't move; he had to look after her. It was his turn to help her now, and he used the same method that she had used. He fashioned a travois, attached it to his half-wild horse, moved her a few miles west towards Potato Mountain out of harm's way, and nursed her for a week. He would be late for his rendezvous with Justine.

Potato Mountain wasn't the only obstacle in the way of the two lovers. Sergeant Boyd had been tipped off that both Ta Chi and Noah were in this vicinity and he had formed a special patrol to track them down. Nor had Richard Snellgrove given up the thought of the reward; but now a more powerful incentive was his thirst for revenge. Aaron kept his promise to Snellgrove, and on his supply run to Williams Lake told him of the rumours that Noah had been sighted in the vicinity of Tatlayoko Lake.

Ian Richards had foregone his usual pleasures of a summer in Victoria—sailing, playing golf, and occasionally giving some thought to his desk job. He had taken the Homathko field assignment because the major had asked him to and to advance himself in the company. He also pretended that he was inconveniencing himself for the good of his family; had he refused, he probably would have been declared redundant. Whether he was suited for the job was another question. His idea of heading up the survey was to be chauffeured about by Aaron, who had been hired because he was a taxi driver; to have Charlie build him a fancy office and living quarters in a tent with a wooden floor; and to order the cook to prepare meals he preferred. His job was to oversee the compiling and the charting of the information collected by the field crews and to be in constant contact with the major, and cater to him when he showed up on site. In his frequent letters home to Enid, he dwelt on the hardships that he was enduring.

For Ralph Richards, life was raw. Overriding Ian's objections, the major had insisted that the boy be on the survey as another character-building exercise. He was assigned by his father to one of the field crews. As the son of an unpopular boss, he had to hear all the gripes and snipes directed at Ian. He was not inclined to defend him and asked for no favours; nor were any given. Ian felt that the best way to treat his son was to give him the hardest jobs, not the cushiest; to send him off to the field camp out of his sight, far from fine cooking and permanent quarters. This suited Ralph, whose main threat was Aaron. Since the time Ralph had crossed Aaron over his harassment of Justine, Aaron had treated him as an enemy. Ralph believed Aaron to be a psychopath, or at least a very dangerous person, and he thought that for good reason.

The day following the crew's arrival at Empire Ranch they travelled the fourteen miles down-lake from the ranch in the cabin cruiser they had taken so much trouble to haul from Vancouver. They were now in the heart of the Chilcotin and spent their first working day setting up camp under the direction of Charlie Rainbow. At the end of the day they were exhausted. The cook prepared a makeshift meal on gas burners as the cast-iron cook stove had yet to be lifted in by helicopter from the other end of the lake.

They had finished their hotdogs and Charlie was amusing them by demonstrating the art of axe-throwing. He was able to impale a tree trunk with a single-bladed axe at thirty feet and then throw another axe to strike the first axe with its blunt end and drive it farther into the tree. The whole crew wanted a try, and Aaron was at the head of the line. There were only so many axes to go around and of course the thrown axes had to be retrieved. Ralph was at the target pulling an axe out. It was well-imbedded. Aaron was primed and ready to throw at the target.

"Get out of the way, Shorty, or I'll stick you."

Ralph ignored him and gave another tug. The axe resisted, but was loosening when he heard a shout from another crew member and ducked. Aaron's axe hit the tree where he had been standing and clattered to the ground.

"Shorty, I told you to move. I gave you fair warning."

Ralph charged Aaron with an axe and Charlie, who had not seen the near miss, intervened. Ralph refused to say why he had taken an axe to Aaron, who slunk off to his tent. Within ten minutes everyone was jolted by the discharge of a gun. Aaron, rifle in hand, was shouting and pointing into the bush. "Did you see that buck? It was huge. I think I hit him."

Aaron pointed towards the lake, where a deer was staggering towards the underbrush. He ran after it with the camp's rifle, stopped, and fired again. The deer was still on its feet. It crashed into the willows and was lost to sight.

Charlie pursued Aaron. "What the hell are you doing?" He caught up to Aaron and yanked the gun from his hands.

Aaron said, "All right! You can have the damn gun. The deer's gone, but you saw me hit it."

"You wounded it in the stomach. It'll die a painful death."

"What the hell! It's just a deer."

"The deer is sacred to the Natives. You don't shoot deer for fun. Now we have to track it and kill it before it suffers more. All of you fan out and find that deer."

The deer had taken cover about two hundred yards into the thicket. It tried to rise. Charlie came up to it and shot it in the head. The crew stood around the carcass while Charlie cut it open. It was a white-tail, a doe, and it was carrying twins. Charlie had difficulty controlling himself. "The Creator placed these creatures here for a purpose," he said. "You killed them for no reason. You have to respect what you kill. Even animals know that."

"Whatever," Aaron said with a scowl.

Ian was in his tent drinking scotch with his head draughtsman when Charlie told him about the killing of the pregnant doe. Ian wanted Aaron fired, but Charlie recommended that Aaron be told that he was on probation and said he would make sure that Aaron behaved. The gun was returned to Ian's tent for safekeeping.

Maria Paul had sat up on hearing the first report of a rifle, and the second shot confirmed that it had come from the survey camp. The sun had gone behind the coastal mountains, yet it was still light. She had noticed the activity during the day as the crew set up its camp. The gunshot was a surprise. Alec, her husband, would have investigated, but he was up on Potato Mountain with Justine riding herd on the cattle. She took her young son, Ben, with her to find out what they were shooting at. She was on the trail to the survey camp when a second shot echoed down the lake. She motioned Ben to stay behind and left the trail, using the cover of the brush and trees to get closer.

Ben followed his mother until she came to the edge of

a clearing. A pregnant doe was stumbling into a thicket, a stone's throw from where she was hiding. It had been around her cabin for the last few weeks, and she had been looking forward to seeing it fawn soon. Across the clearing she saw a Native, not a Chilcotin, a heavy-set, powerful man who was taking a rifle from the hands of a young white man and shouting at him about slaughtering deer out of season.

The deer was mortally wounded and the Native ordered the crew to find it. The woods were full of young men trying to flush out the doe. She turned and stumbled over Ben, who was right behind her. They retreated and heard the finishing gun shot. On their way back to the cabin he asked, "What will happen to the man who shot the deer, Mommy?"

"Your father will speak to him."

CONFESSION

It took Stan a few days to settle into the routine of the ranch, to get his bearings and to begin his investigations. Within the week he was ready. He began by sitting in a chair in the great hall where Bordy's body had slumped to the floor after he was shot. Looking out the double doors to the lawn and the lake, he took in the scene and—aided by the sketch of a police expert showing the trajectory of the bullet that had killed Bordy—narrowed down the area of his search. The police expert had said that the shot must have come from someone firing in the room by the double doors, which would account for the shell casing found in the room.

Stan had urged Sergeant Boyd to search outside the room for another shell casing, and was told that there had been a search and nothing was found. But there had been six inches of snow on the ground at the time and a lot of ground to cover. Stan started with the porch, going over every inch and even pulling up the floor boards. Finding nothing, he extended the search over the next few days to the lawn itself. He did this methodically by stretching string from the spot where Bordy had fallen along the sightlines through the door opening to the lawn and then laying out gridlines on the lawn. He combed every inch of lawn within those lines, starting from close to the house. All that day and till noon of the next day he searched and found nothing: no cigarette butts, no candy wrappers, no shell casing. In the heat of the afternoon of the second day of his search, he was running out of lawn and was a fair distance from the house. The shooter would have to have been a good marksman to kill Bordy with one shot from this distance.

He began thinking as he got further out from the house that even if he found nothing it wouldn't prove that there was no killer on the lawn. He or she may not have ejected the shell from the gun. He was on his hands and knees behind a small lilac bush when he lifted a branch and saw a glint of metal. He didn't disturb it. He looked closer. It was a shell casing. There were some dead leaves half-covering it. He got up looked around him. There was no one about. He walked to the house, got on the radiophone and phoned Sergeant Boyd.

"I've found something that you must see."

"What is it, Stan?"

"It's 3:00 o'clock. You can be here in four hours. Bring a camera and an exhibit bag."

"Okay, I'll be there, but it better be worth my while."

The police officer arrived at the ranch tired from his journey. Stan brought him to his find. The shell was photographed and bagged. It was now part of police evidence.

Belle arrived at the ranch at the end of June. Stan was still there convalescing. The day after her arrival she was sitting in front of the open double doors of the great hall, watching the moon glitter on Tatlayoko Lake. The room designed to house her Bechstein now looked empty without it. This room had been the centrepiece of the "log cabin" based on a Scottish hunting lodge that she had planned and built in happier years. Made from massive peeled and polished pine logs, the great room itself measured thirty by sixty feet and seemed even larger since it was open to the second-floor ceiling and surrounded by a balcony on three sides. The building dwarfed the old ranch house, which was now used as a guesthouse. Belle was alone; her guests and the major had retired. Since following the major's advice of being quiet about what she believed was her incidental involvement in Bordy's murder, her mind was at ease. The new lawyer assured her that her son's chances of having the verdict against him set aside were good. She was sure that this would lead to his ultimate acquittal. Rumour had it that Noah was in the area. She hoped that he would contact her. She would do everything in her power to see that he was acquitted.

The survey was apparently going well. The major had arrived at the ranch by helicopter that evening and was leaving before breakfast to inspect the crews and their progress. From there he would return to Victoria. Her bridge group, who were all involved in the project, were expected in the next few days and she was looking forward to their company. This summer would be her last look at the Chilcotin pioneer landmark before construction started on the dam and the floodwaters claimed it.

She heard Stan shuffle in.

"Oh! Stan, you startled me. I'm having a nightcap and

thinking about happier times in the Chilcotin. You know I haven't been here for ten years."

Stan sat in the chair opposite. He could see her quite clearly in the moonlight. He got comfortable and said, "Yes, Belle, if you don't count last Thanksgiving."

"What do you mean?"

"After you took me off the case, I visited the 122 Mile and was told by Dorothy Barton that you stayed at Molly's place for two nights last fall. On Thanksgiving Sunday, the day Bordy died, you were gone from early morning to late evening. You told them you had gone to Quesnel to see Hetty Southin. I know Hetty, and she told me you weren't there. Then there was another little fact that you didn't tell me: you are a silent stakeholder in Vancouver Island Power Company. Bordy hired me to prevent the company from getting the licence. I'm sure that you were here that day. You argued with Bordy and something happened that you regret. Do you want to tell me about it?"

"You must think I'm an evil woman."

"No. I think you are confused and worried, and you want to do the right thing for Noah."

Belle knew that she shouldn't say anything and that the major would be furious with her, but Stan Hewitt now knew what had happened and she couldn't keep up the months of sham any longer. Words began coming out of her without her thinking about them. She was so relieved to be finally telling her story.

"I was here in this room on Thanksgiving at about six o'clock. I had returned to the ranch for the first time since I had left with Noah for Victoria. I had to speak to Bordy about many things. Bordy was charming when we were first married and we were very happy. I had money and he had drive—the ambition to create Empire Ranch, which grew into his obsession. But in our last years together, we quarrelled about everything. He wouldn't take vacations and he grew distant from Noah, treating him like a ranch hand. Finally, his infidelities drove me away. You know I caught him in our bedroom with a woman from Williams Lake. . . . I found a new life in Victoria. Noah flourished and I had the arts and culture and my music. As you know, I also found a new man. I'm Catholic, and I didn't divorce Bordy.

"I came back last Thanksgiving to tell him to let Noah go because he was destroying his life. I also came back to tell him that I wanted to sell the ranch and if he didn't agree I would force him to sell. Bordy's stroke had made him even more bitter than he was when I left. He yelled at me; accused me of being a whore. I told him that he had been sleeping with the whole Chilcotin. He didn't deny it. Then a sly look came over his drunken face. He asked, 'Who would buy this ranch knowing that it could be flooded in the next few years?' I said, 'I'll buy out your share and agree to the flooding.' He started to shake with anger. He said, 'This ranch, this land is my whole life and you're going to drown it. I'll never give it up.' As he said this he moved towards his gun cabinet. I rose from my chair and asked him what he was doing. He answered, 'You've done enough talking. I know how to end this.' His rifle was in his hands when I ran out the doors and to my car, which I had hidden in the bush. Before I got to the car I heard a muffled sound; it could have been a gunshot. Then at the car I heard a distinct gunshot. I didn't think that he was firing the rifle at me. I thought at the time he was firing into the air. I drove away. I thought that once I was gone Bordy would cool down."

She ran out of breath and took a sip from her glass. Stan inhaled deeply on his cigarette, secure in its holder. Since his cancer scare, he had been trying to cut down on his smoking. The smoke didn't bother his lungs during the day. It was when he got up at five in the morning that he would cough from his guts for ten minutes.

"Now you know what a terrible mother I am," Belle continued. "I believed Noah would be acquitted if he took the stand. And had I come forward the company would not have been granted a water licence because people in Victoria knew my close connections to it and the major. And if I had come forward, my son might still have been convicted because I don't know who fired the shot that killed Bordy. But at the time, my judgement was impaired, and I jeopardized Noah's life by being selfish."

Stan could understand her reasoning, but he had found that when one's children were involved, reason and justice usually took second place to a parent's protective instincts. He couldn't be hard on her now.

"Don't punish yourself," he said. "You can make it right by signing a statement, which I will draft."

"Please! Please. I will sign it."

"I have found an additional piece of evidence that may help convince the Court of Appeal to set aside the verdict and grant a new trial. I have searched the ground outside these doors and I found a shell casing from a rifle near the lilac to the left of the lawn. You can see its moon shadow from here. I believe the shooter was kneeling there and would have had a clear sight of Bordy in the lighted room."

"Who do you think the shooter was?"

"I don't know for sure."

"Have you matched the shell casing to a gun on the ranch?"

"Sergeant Boyd has the casing and he gave me a photograph of it. The casing doesn't match Bordy's rifle, and I haven't found a match with a rifle on the ranch."

"Could it have been Noah?"

"He thinks it was you."

Noah hadn't told Stan his reason for refusing to testify, but Stan was sure that he was right.

Belle was a suspect. She had not confessed to the murder, nor had she given him a clue as to who could have done it. Could he believe her now after such a cover-up? He wanted to.

She took her time replying, then pleaded with Stan, "What shall I do to make it right?"

"Noah is out there tonight and probably not too far away. The RCMP has a special patrol in the area to find him, and Snellgrove, the former deputy sheriff, is looking for him too. I'm afraid your husband's killer is still on the loose, and we don't know who or what his or her motive was. All you can do now is pray and tell Noah the truth when you see him."

Belle remained in the room when Stan left. She now had the dreaded task of telling the major that his project to tame the Chilcotin was in jeopardy because of her.

That night on the western slope of Potato Mountain, halfway down Tatlayoko Lake, Noah could see the fires of the survey base camp to the south and the lights of the ranch house to the north. He was waiting at the meadow where he was to meet Justine. He was a month late. Ta Chi and he had parted a few days ago. She had moved towards the outfall of the lake and on to Waddington Canyon and would return to dig wild potatoes on the mountain. Chilko, Noah's newly tamed wild horse, was tethered further up the mountain. A horse whinnied. Noah heard hoofs on rock. He took cover, becoming part of the moonscape as Ta Chi had taught him. A horse and rider passed almost within touching distance and continued on another fifty paces to a small clearing, then stopped.

The rider whispered, "Wawant'x. It's Justine."

He didn't move or reply. After a few very slow minutes, he heard a rustle in the brush thirty paces down the trail. She had been followed. She whispered again as she had done at intervals at this clearing for the last month, hoping that he had come.

"Wawant'x. It's me."

There was still no answer. He wanted to reach out to her, to call her, to touch her. He couldn't. To reveal his presence would jeopardize her. She turned her horse and retraced her steps back to her father's range camp near the base of Potato Mountain. Her trackers didn't reveal themselves as she walked her horse by them. Noah waited to make sure they were not coming to the clearing. She was now well away and he overheard them as they talked openly.

"This is their meeting spot. She's been here twice since we've been watching her. We'll speak to the sergeant and have someone posted here for the next week or two. Let's get back to the ranch."

They headed off on foot in the opposite direction from Justine.

Justine had suffered yet another setback since she'd helped Noah escape from the courthouse. In April at school break she had expected to see him for more than a fleeting moment, but Snellgrove and the police officer had interfered. In the last few weeks, she had been to the clearing a half-dozen times and Noah had not been there. Where was he? Was he injured? Was he dead? She was feeling beaten. Surely no lover had ever been as tested as she was. She was so completely caught up in her thoughts as she approached the range camp that at first she didn't hear anything; then she heard a horse galloping behind her and closing fast. She stopped and looked back over her shoulder, thinking it might be Noah. In the bright moonlight, she could see it was Snellgrove.

Snellgrove and one of his posse were camped near the Pauls' range camp to keep an eye on her. Earlier that evening she had given him the slip. Snellgrove had gone out on horseback to locate her.

Snellgrove had been drinking. He had been made to look a fool again by Justine. He threw aside any control over his quick temper. He would show her how he treated Native women, especially when they embarrassed him publicly and got him fired. When Justine turned her horse to confront him, he rode up to her and attempted to sweep her off her horse by circling her with one arm. He succeeded, but her horse reared. Snellgrove lost his balance and both were unhorsed.

As he was a corpulent man, Snellgrove's bulk winded him when he hit the ground and he loosened his grip on her. Justine used the chance to break free of his arm, but when she rolled away he grabbed her ankle. He held her hard, and all her kicking and stamping on his head with her free foot meant nothing to him as he formed an idea to assault her. This would be part of his revenge against the breed, and if Noah felt anything for Justine, Snellgrove would not have to look for him: Noah would seek him out, and Snellgrove would be ready.

Snellgrove's evil strategy might have worked, but he was fatally off on his timing. He had Justine on the ground, choking her with one hand while the other ripped off her blouse and stripped her jeans. She couldn't scream—she could hardly breathe. He was so intent on his task, so inflamed that he was unaware that Noah stood behind him with a stone. It came down on his head with enough force to knock him out.

When Snellgrove came to it was still dark, he had a lump and a cut on the back of his throbbing head, and Justine was gone. He didn't know how he had received the injury. Perhaps Justine had been able to strike him with a rock. He had enough sense to know that he was now in danger. Dazed and with no firearm, he could not go back to his camp near the Pauls', from where he had tried to keep Justine under surveillance. She must have returned and told her story, and there would be retaliation. He had to seek help, and he chose to find it at the survey base camp at the end of the lake with his drinking buddy, Aaron. He rode into the camp at about two that morning and asked for protection. He claimed that Noah Hanlon, the fugitive, was in the area, and that he had attacked him. He showed everyone a poster of Noah, who he said was probably tracking him.

After he had knocked out Snellgrove, Noah had calmed Justine, dressed her, and taken her to the safety of her father's camp. She was lying on the couch and coming out of shock when she said to Noah, "Come and hold me." He held her until she stopped shivering.

"What happened?" she asked.

"I knocked Snellgrove out with a rock and left him there. Alec is out looking for him now."

After that, she fell asleep in his arms. He remained with her until morning when Alec took him aside. "Snellgrove has been injured and the RCMP may soon be around asking questions. You go to the top of Potato Mountain. We Chilcotin will be there soon for our jamboree."

Since Peter's death in Vancouver, Alec and Maria Paul

had feared for their daughter's safety. Alec had worked under Bordy's whip hand for years. Where other men had given up, fought or cursed Bordy, Alec had watched, obeyed, taken the abuse and learned. But where Alec was submissive and silent, his daughter was headstrong and vocal, and although he was proud of how she stood up for herself, took the lead, and exercised her free will, he feared for her.

PART IV

In the morning of July 17th, 1864, McLean—who pooh-poohed all warnings of danger and declared to whites and Indians that when the Chilcotins would see him they would "bend down their heads" and he would "kill them with a club"—went reconnoitering in company of a single Indian, Jack of Alexandria. After having crossed a prairie where they were observed by several pairs of unfriendly eyes they climbed a rocky hill, the top of which they were just nearing when Jack thought that he heard a gun snap. "Pshaw!" exclaimed McLean contemptuously in answer to the Indian's remark, "they would not shoot us. They are too much afraid of me." He had scarcely finished the sentence when he fell dead, shot by Anaukatlh—a Chilcotin who was never apprehended, so the death of him who had ill-treated and slain so many natives remained unavenged.

The History of the Northern Interior of BC,
A. G. Morice, page 17

SNELLGROVE

Ian Richards wasn't prepared for the change in the routine of his base camp brought about by Snellgrove's sudden night-time appearance. He turned Snellgrove over to Charlie Rainbow, who said he would deal with him in the morning. Charlie had Snellgrove bunk in with Aaron, reasoning that he would then know where the two troublemakers were. He assumed sentry duty and sat hidden under a tree near the perimeter to keep an eye on the camp sleeping under the shadow of Lendix'tcux. During the night he heard only the movement and sounds of wildlife.

In Chilcotin, Tatlayoko means "windy lake," and the camp was at the windiest end, where the narrow Homathko Valley funnelled the heavy weather in from the coast. The wind came up as dawn was breaking. It stirred the treetops and rippled the water. The men would soon be up. Charlie knew from his army service that the half-light of dawn when one's guard was down was when enemy raids could be expected. He shook off his drowsiness and watched the cooks, who were up to light the fire in the big cook stove and check on their hidden home brew, which everybody in camp except Ian Richards knew about.

A twig broke. To an untrained ear, like those of all the whites around him, it would've meant nothing. To Charlie, it was out of place and much too close to camp to be an animal. Immediately and farther away, a coyote yipped twice, and then came a responding howl from the opposite direction. The coyotes' noise woke up a few men. Snellgrove, whose head still rang from the stone's blow, stumbled out of his tent. Before Charlie could shout a warning, the morning was disturbed by a swishing sound as an axe parted the air and struck Snellgrove on his left abdomen. He took two steps and fell. When Charlie reached him he was alive and howling. The cooks scrambled for cover, not knowing where the attack was coming from. Charlie circled the area from where the axe would have been thrown. He found no one. Whoever had thrown the axe was familiar with the bush and the terrain and had melted into the underbrush; there was no sense in chasing a shadow. He turned his attention to the men, now emerged from their tents, to assure them that the danger had passed, and then he bandaged the yelping Snellgrove's wound. Had the assailant wanted to kill Snellgrove, he could have, Charlie thought, but the intent was obviously not to kill. The axe was single-headed and thrown so that the blunt end struck Snellgrove, breaking several ribs. It appeared to Charlie to be a warning.

Aaron went to Snellgrove's camp near the Pauls' range camp to collect the ex-deputy's belongings, but when he got there he found them scattered about and Snellgrove's man gone. Aaron gathered what he could find of Snellgrove's possessions, brought them back to the base camp, and set up the other's tent on the perimeter.

In camp, Aaron seemed to be under Snellgrove's spell. He was quite happy to act as his servant, yet Charlie and Ian had difficulty getting Aaron to do his job of supplying the camp. Ian had agreed to feed Snellgrove until his ribs healed and he could move. Aaron brought him his meals, and they weren't all that he brought. It had not taken Aaron long to discover the cook's still. He had been siphoning off small quantities for his own use. He didn't like drinking alone, so when Snellgrove showed up Aaron shared it with him. The two of them sat for hours each night polishing their grievances against Noah and Justine and plotting revenge.

"I know Noah's around here," Snellgrove said one night. "When I can move, I'll get my posse together and we'll ride down that fugitive."

"What about Justine?" Aaron still had dreams about her.

"Those two have destroyed me. If I see him, I won't talk. I'll shoot. That bastard is outside the law. And if she's there, I'll shoot her too." He shifted his weight and grimaced in pain, a fresh reminder of what Noah and Justine had done to him.

Aaron topped up Snellgrove's glass with more home brew. Fawning over him, he said, "These cooks know what they're doing. The food is garbage but the hooch is not bad. They make it from raisins."

Snellgrove still had his mind on revenge. "Noah's outside the law. I'll call it self-defence and I'll get a reward for it."

"A ree-ward?" Aaron's eyes grew bigger. "You mean for killing him? How much?"

"Twenty-five thousand dollars!"

"What's my share?"

"What have you done?"

"Waited on you hand and foot and saved your life. Where would you be if I wasn't in this camp?"

"I'll think about it."

"I don't think you should shoot Justine," Aaron said. "You leave her to me. I think she's sweet on me."

"Ha! You can have her. That one's a she-wolf." But later Snellgrove said, "We can't have any witnesses."

In the early hours of the next morning, an animal's scream echoed through Waddington Canyon, shattering everyone's sleep. The survey crew, housed in their own small camp on a sandbar downstream, jumped out of their bedrolls and tents and peered into the blackness. They heard the heavy raspy breathing of a grizzly. These sounds died down only to be followed by the whimpers of a child. When these ceased, no one could get back to sleep.

Charlie Rainbow was dispatched from the main camp at Tatlayoko Lake the next day to calm the crew, who refused to go into the bush to cut lines and take levels and transit sightings with a wild animal on the loose and stalking them. Ralph was part of the crew. His transit man was not moving from the camp and so he was there when the helicopter brought Charlie with the camp's rifle. The Native's presence calmed the crew, and after lunch they went into the woods with Charlie patrolling and on guard. He stayed overnight.

That night after midnight, a deep guttural throaty sound like that of a rutting bull moose came echoing down the canyon. Charlie would have welcomed that explanation. Even a grizzly lured by the smell of the cache of food in the camp would have been more acceptable than what he now figured had made the sound: a human probably—a creature more deadly than a grizzly, especially since the camp was forty miles from the nearest road. Charlie thought it was a human who didn't welcome the presence of the camp in the Chilcotin. He didn't share his fears with the camp, nor did he tell them of the axe attack on Snellgrove, but he did remain with them for several days until the night sounds receded farther away and on the fourth night stopped altogether. Charlie returned to the base camp with the rifle and Ralph on orders from Ian.

As Snellgrove improved, he became more impatient and nasty to his servant. He was able to walk a bit in the second week and started to make a nuisance of himself to the crew. Ralph had returned to the base camp to accompany and assist the geologist every day in the helicopter. The pilot would leave them on a sandbar in the morning and pick them up in the evening. They would climb the canyon walls examining the rock formations at the proposed dam site.

In the evenings after dinner Ralph practised axe-throwing. He had learned everything that Charlie could teach him and was becoming an expert. At thirty paces he could light a match with a thrown axe seven times out of ten. Snellgrove and Aaron watched him practise for a few minutes, then Snellgrove—who recognized Ralph from Ralph's visit to the jail at Christmas—asked Aaron in a loud voice overheard by Ralph, "Who is that little snot? And why is he wasting his time throwing axes?"

Aaron snickered and looked around to see if Charlie was nearby.

"He's the chief's kid. I don't think he likes me. I almost stuck him early on at this camp. If I hadn't been hired directly by the major and Charlie hadn't stuck up for me, the chief would have fired me."

Ian refused to allow Snellgrove to eat with the crew. He

had to eat in his own tent. Ian told him that if he didn't like that, he could mount up on his horse—which Aaron was also looking after—and leave. Snellgrove wasn't fit enough to do that, so he backed down but let it be known that he didn't enjoy being talked to that way.

CIRCLE

The annual Potato Mountain potato harvest was a time for the people of the Chilcotin to gather on summer days in July to dig the wild root, roast and eat it on the spot, and store the rest for winter. The men gambled on horse races down the mountain or on *lahal*, a game played by Natives in the coastal and plateau regions of British Columbia. It was as simple as craps and as addictive. Men could leave the game stripped of all their possessions, including their wives. It was also a social occasion and was played to the accompaniment of songs and drumming. The play was usually done with five sets of sticks for each team and male and female bones. It was a guessing game where one team must guess where the male bones were hidden by the other team. The team that guessed correctly got some of the other team's sticks. The first team to win all of the other team's sticks and to ensure that all the sticks were dead won the game.

The two-week-long celebration on the mountain drew people from all over the plateau and beyond. It was not for whites. Noah had never been to Potato Mountain during the harvest.

It was a hard climb up the mountain. For that reason many of the old people didn't come. Old Antoine was there, though. His son, Alec, mounted him on a quiet horse and shepherded him up to the flat ridge while Justine rode beside him. Antoine had lost count of his years riding up Potato Mountain at harvest, where he gained spiritual strength from the land that stretched before him and ate the traditional potato, which sustained him. A woman could dig fifty pounds of potatoes in a day using a piece of metal from a rake tooth or an old metal spring leaf. He could see the women now on the mountain in the midst of the plants, bending over them, grubbing for the small tubers and placing them in a woven bark basket. His rheumy eyes stopped at a familiar figure wearing a cloth headband, denim jacket, print skirt, and moccasins. He walked towards her. She was smiling. She always smiled now.

"I hear you are not travelling alone," he said. Ta Chi looked up at him standing over her. "A while ago near Chilko River," he added, "I hear a man chased away some boys who bother you."

"Damn near killed me," she said, and then, after a few more potatoes, "I need help."

He had never heard her ask for anything from anyone for herself except maybe a ride to the store for supplies. He sat down beside her. After five minutes she said, "I know where Wawant'x is. She can't live like me. She don't kill her father."

"I was at the trial. The jury said he did."

"What do you say?"

"Tell your son to attend our circle of elders tonight. He can tell his story to us."

"When?"

"Tonight at my son's tent."

"You tell her. You tell her about Lendix'tcux. It's your story to tell. Tell her more of our stories."

"Have Wawant'x meet me before tonight. I will be on the rise over there where we can see Lendix'tcux."

She had not stopped grubbing potatoes while they talked. He left her and wandered up the hill.

The casual meeting of Ta Chi and Antoine had not gone unnoticed. Two RCMP officers had the camps under surveillance. They were ordered not to make a move or show themselves until they were sure Noah was in the camp, and then to radio for assistance. They had an informant in the camp who reported to them twice a day and was told to tell them when he saw Noah. After they had spotted Ta Chi talking with Antoine, they told the informant to follow her. This proved impossible. He lost her in the first stand of trees, which seemed to swallow her. He abandoned the job to go back to the camp to drink and gamble with his friends with the money the RCMP paid him.

Later that day, Antoine met Noah on a knoll above the flat ridges of the Potato Range, in sight of the mountain Ts'yl-os to the south and overlooking Chilko Lake to the east. Antoine and Noah could see Lendix'tcux and his three sons cast in stone on the northern slope of the mountain.

Antoine said, "When in your cabin near Charlotte Lake I see drawings. Since you catch and tame wild horse, I want to tell you story my grandfather told me about boy and his drawings and his magic horse. Do you have time to hear?"

"Yes, Antoine," Noah answered. "I have time to hear it."

Long ago before my time there lived a chief with many sons. In those days wind used to blow furiously all time, and chief told one son to try to capture wind. So young man make snare and place it in tree; and the next day, he go to examine it, he find small boy with potbelly and streaming hair caught fast in snare. Now, this boy was Wind; chief's son keep him for some time, but finally agree to let him go if he not blow so hard, and only once in a while. The wind boy agree, and was set free.

Now, chief have garden where he grow many potatoes, and someone constantly stealing them, so he tell son to try to catch thief. So one night young man sit up to watch, and when hear someone among potatoes he throw spear and break thief's leg. But young man not see him plainly, and thief escape and disappear in ground. Young man follow him underground, and finally come to big village. Going up to central house of village, which belong to chief, he find chicken living there and he feel sure it is chicken that stole father's potatoes; but no way to prove it. When young man try to come back to surface of the ground, he cannot, and ask chicken to help. The chicken refuse. Now, young man have under blanket a magic picture of horse which a chief up above, his father-in-law, give him when he give him his two daughters as wives. Young man take picture, whip it, and it become horse with fine harness and spurs. He ride horse back to surface of earth and to father's house.

Now, young man gone for some time and his father give him up for lost, so he make long spear and stick it in ground slanting towards the people and say that any man who ride horse at full speed straight onto spear win the two wives of his son. Now, when young man return, he is very thin and haggard, and his clothes is worn and ragged and no one recognize him, not even his own father the chief, who treat him roughly and make him fetch wood and water for cooking. Every day young men of the village gather and try to ride horses onto spear, but no one succeed.

One day young man watch trials for short time and then start to fetch water, but leaving water-basket at stream, he go into brush and take out magic picture, whip it, and it become a horse. He then mount and ride around. Suddenly he appear among young men and ride his horse at full run straight onto spear and disappear beyond in brush. Then, turning horse back into picture, he take up water and come quietly back to village. Everybody wonder who strange rider is and what become of him, but nobody guess.

Another day young man does same thing, but still nobody know him. Now, his two wives are watching from window of house, and when they see strange rider and what he does they think, "Surely this must be our husband who comes back," for they know about magic picture. So two women begin to search all the men to see who has picture, but they find no trace. All this time Raven keep saying that it is he who ride onto spear, but everybody laugh at him.

Noah laughed out loud and Antoine couldn't help but laugh as well. Then he took up the thread of his story again.

Finally women tell chief about matter, and he direct a man to search everyone's clothes for picture, but it is nowhere to be found. When man search everyone else, he come to young man and about to pass him over, for he think it impossible that so poor and miserable a person could have any such thing as magic picture. But chief tell him to look and when he does, sure enough, there it is. Then, to prove that he is the strange rider, young man whip the picture and it become horse, and he ride straight onto spear and back again to chief's house; then, whipping the horse, it become picture. He put it under his blanket. Then chief recognize his son and give him back his wives.

"I been saving that story to tell to the right man. Now you ride your horse onto spear and you tell your story this evening to a circle of elders so that they may know what happen last Thanksgiving."

Noah didn't reply.

"Will you come?" Antoine asked.

"Yes, I will come and tell my story to them." . . .

Snellgrove's attack on Justine had made Noah believe that Justine was in more danger than he was. He was prepared to submit to the judgement of the elders. If they decided that he should turn himself in to the RCMP, he would accept their decision. He hadn't confronted Belle, whom he believed knew the person who shot Bordy, but he couldn't continue being an outlaw without the support of the Chilcotins. There was no mercy for outlaws.

A young, strong Chilcotin had approached Stan that day while he was sitting in a chair resting at the ranch and told him that Noah was appearing before the circle of elders that evening and that he and his friends—he motioned to six Natives standing nearby—had been sent by Antoine to escort him up the mountain.

Stan was recovering from his latest chemotherapy treatment and was quite weak. He had not left the guesthouse since his confrontation with Belle, but he could no more have resisted the call to trial than his dying black lab, Oscar, could have failed to slowly and painfully scrabble to its feet for a last walk with its master in the hope that it could be of further service. Every instinct bred into Stan and practised by him over the years dictated that he be there. They loaded him onto a Bennett wagon, which he rode until the trail became too steep. Then the Chilcotins placed two poles through the bottom rungs of the chair Stan was sitting on. Four Natives each took an end of a pole, lifted his chair, and in this way moved him to the top of Potato Mountain and the circle of elders.

An afternoon wind blowing from the coast up the Homathko through the canyon and onto the plateau swept the drizzling clouds from Potato Mountain and brought the warm July sun, drying the underbrush and making the rocks steam. The evening remained warm. The eastern moon lit the way as Noah picked his way through the tents to Alec Paul's, where he saw eight men sitting in a circle around a fire. He knew them.

They were the Chilcotin elders: Willieboy, old Antoine, Alec Paul, Jimmy John, Harry Sepia, Tom Lupa, Jack Loneman, and Harry Patrick. Noah was surprised to see Stan Hewitt sitting slightly apart from the circle. He also knew that Justine and her mother were listening in the tent. He took his place beside his lawyer.

Antoine began. "Wawant'x will tell you about the death of Bordy. Most of you were at courthouse in Williams Lake. You heard others talk, what they saw and didn't see. We not the jury. We sit in courtroom and listen. Wawant'x decided not to tell his story to white jury. He now tell us and we judge him."

Noah looked about him. The elders were waiting and attentive.

"You have known me as Noah Hanlon, adopted son of Bordy and Belle Hanlon and brought up white," he began. "I don't know my blood father. My mother is Ta Chi. I knew little of my Native heritage until five months ago when I was exposed to the land, and since then I have lived as an outlaw from the white society. I survived because I had someone to interpret the land for me. I have been told that in our land the stones speak to us. I now know that to be true.

"Many of you were at the trial and heard the evidence that the Crown brought against me—the fingerprints, the hired hands, the gun expert—but no witnesses came forward to say that I held the gun in my hands that shot and killed Bordy.

"Bordy and I quarrelled on the range near Eagle Lake in the presence of Alec Paul and some ranch hands. Justine was not there. She had returned to the ranch a day early because her mother was not well. It was not the first time Bordy and I had quarrelled. The next day was Thanksgiving, and by that afternoon we had the cattle in the home fields. Alec was the first to leave to check on Maria, his wife. I stayed another half-hour to make sure the cattle were secure. Justine found me there by the barn and told me that Bordy had assaulted her. I went to the house about dusk to warn Bordy off. He was in the great hall by the fire and the first winter snow was falling. We quarrelled, and he grabbed his gun and would have shot me if I hadn't taken it from him. I had the gun in my hands. Bordy lunged at me in a drunken rage and the gun fired accidentally. The slug must have gone through the open doors, as the RCMP found only one slug in the fireplace. I left him in the room without looking back and as I got near the doors I heard a scream and a shot fired from outside the house. I turned back and Bordy was on the floor, shot through the chest."

While Noah talked in the dark with the fire lighting his face, the eight elders listened as they would to a young hunter who had returned from the hunt to tell of his adventure, perhaps to explain that he had no game for the fire and that they would have to dine on his story instead. Willieboy, who should have been on the jury, asked, "You jumped off my truck at Riske Creek, didn't you? The old truck was wheezing up those hills. I thought the wife and the rest of them in there ate too well at Williams Lake, till you lightened the load. Did you see who fired the shot or in what direction it came from?"

"The shot came from the lawn in front of the house. It was dusk and snowing; I thought I saw a figure out there. At first I didn't know who it was, although I thought I heard an animal scream. Then in the courtroom, I came to believe that the person was my mother, Belle.

Johnny Setah asked, "Why did you run away from court?"

"You were there. You saw the Queen's coat of arms on the wall above the judge. Two beasts: the one on the right was mythical, a unicorn in chains; the other on the left was a crowned lion, and both supported a crest with the motto in Norman French DIEU ET MON DROIT, 'God and My Right.' Beneath these splendid displays, and busy deciding my fate, were the white judge, jury, and prosecutor. The newspaper reporters and the court clerk were also white. When I turned around there were no whites in the public area. That's where you Natives sat: the Chilcotins, Shuswaps, and Carriers. I was raised by Belle to be white. I thought, prayed and painted as a white person. I love my mother, but for the first time in my life I understood what it was like to be a Chilcotin, to be part of a community of people who cared for me in good times and in bad."

"That's not a reason for running away."

"Yes, there were other reasons. I wanted to confront my mother."

Before anyone in the circle could ask the question, "Is Belle the killer?" Stan cleared his throat. "I wonder if I could say something. I think it will help."

Antoine looked around him. The elders were nodding their heads.

"Speak."

"Thank you for bringing me here. I appreciate your trust. I haven't seen Noah—or Wawant'x, as you call him—since he left the courtroom at Williams Lake. I have continued to represent him and I have done some investigations to try and clear his name. Belle Hanlon—Noah's mother—has admitted to me and given me a sworn statement that she was present in the great hall last Thanksgiving and argued with Bordy. After some name-calling, Bordy went for his gun and Belle ran through the open doors and onto the lawn. Running towards her car, she heard a muffled bang that could have been gunfire. When she got to her car she heard a loud gunshot. She headed immediately back to Williams Lake. She spoke to no one about this, believing that to do so would jeopardize the power company's application to dam the Homathko River. She also believed that Noah would be acquitted, and that is another reason she told no one about her involvement."

Noah—sitting beside Stan—turned, looked at him and shook his head. It was Belle he suspected had been on the lawn and fired the shot that killed Bordy. It was his intention to confront her with his suspicions at the ranch, and then they would decide what to do, because he believed that she would not let him take the blame unless there was someone forcing her hand. He had already made excuses for her in his mind in that Bordy was going for his gun and could have killed him as he left the room. But she was not admitting to the shooting. Could he believe her?

Stan continued, "My theory of the crime, as I put it to the jury without any proof, is exactly what Noah has just told you: that someone hidden in the shrubbery outside fired at Bordy. How else could the ranch hands have heard the gun so clearly? Had there been only one gunshot from the house, it would have been muffled—that is what Belle probably heard. Recently I spent a week searching the ground in front of the house for clues. You will recall that on the night of the shooting there was a large snowfall in the valley that covered the lawn, and even if the police had wanted to look it was impossible to find anything with a foot of snow on the ground. My search was rewarded: I found a cartridge by a lilac to the right of the double doors. A person kneeling in that position would have had a clear view into the lighted hall and a clear shot at Bordy."

Maria came out of the tent. She took a place at the fire. She spoke, not to anyone in particular, but to the night, lifting her eyes to the stars. There was noise from a tent some distance away, where a lahal game was being played to the constant beating of drums. "This has gone too far. We stay back and don't speak about what happened and see Wawant'x found guilty when we all know he didn't shoot Mr. Hanlon. I tell you on the day of the shooting, I was sick and Justine came back early from the roundup to look after me. After lunch Mr. Hanlon came round to our cabin. This is not usual. If he wants to speak to Alec they go outside. He never comes in, and he knows Alec is not there. He is drunk and says he wants to know how I am feeling. He is not looking at me when he says this, he is looking at Justine. We have two rooms. Justine is embarrassed, so she leaves the room. Mr. Hanlon waits a minute and he follows her. He is whispering something and she is saying no. Then the kitchen table is overturned. I call out and Justine says Mr. Hanlon is going now.

"Ben then comes into the house and goes into the kitchen. He screams at Mr. Hanlon, 'Stop hurting my sister.' I hear him being struck. He land on floor, then sounds of a struggle. Justine break free and run through the room and out the door with her blouse torn. Mr. Hanlon come out of the room as if nothing had happened, says 'I hope you're feeling better tomorrow.' I could hardly get up. I struggled to the kitchen. Ben was whimpering in a corner with a welt on his face. I told Ben to hide gun before his father come home. Later Justine come back and treated him and got me back to bed. She told me not to tell Alec, as he would be mad. Then my husband come, I told him what happened. He went looking for his gun."

Maria went back into the tent.

Stan said, "I haven't been able to match the casing to any gun on the ranch. It's a .30-06 cartridge from a Lee Enfield. I gave the casing to Sergeant Boyd for evidence, but I have a photograph of the casing with the firing-pin mark on it."

He put his hand in his pocket and pulled out the photo. It was passed among the elders to be examined. They all owned rifles and each was familiar with the mark that the firing pin makes on the casing when it is fired. Antoine did not examine it; he passed it on to his son Alec, who looked at it closely in the firelight before passing it on to Willieboy. The photo came back to Stan, who put it in his pocket.

Alec said, "I seen a spent .30-06 shell casing like that

with the same firing pin markings."

Stan raised his hand, "Before you say whose it is I want you all to know that the owner may not be the person who fired the gun."

Alec stroked his chin with his hand. "I found the casing near where the surveyors shot the pregnant doe. Maria told me about the kill and it upset me. The doe was pregnant with twins. Maria told me where it was and I went there. The bears and coyotes had eaten most of the carcass. I looked around and found a casing. I figure they wounded it and that was the kill shot."

The focus was off Noah. Alec was a steady influence amongst them. He usually spoke rationally and acted moderately. Johnny Setah asked him, "Why were you looking for your gun that day?"

Alec didn't respond right away. But this was a time to speak the truth.

"When I went back to my cabin on the ranch that day I looked for my gun and it was missing. The next day it was back in my cabin. I thought that I had misplaced it. Maria thinks I killed him. If I had the gun I probably would have."

Antoine asked, "Have you heard enough?"

Each one in turn nodded and Antoine said to Noah, "You may go into the tent and wait while we talk."

Inside the large tent, Maria and Ben sat near the front so they could hear the elders. Justine, who had recovered from Snellgrove's attack, was sitting by herself at the far end. She was dressed in a white doeskin vest and skirt. Noah sat beside her on a bearskin spread on the ground and held her hand. For the first time since his arrest, he searched her face free from capture or the threat of immediate capture. Even after the Snellgrove attack, he had only been able to comfort her and assure her she was safe before fleeing once again. He forgot why he was here, for all he could think about was Justine.

"You look beautiful in white."

"I've waited so long. I hope I don't disappoint you." They embraced and Justine continued, "You don't know how hard it has been on me to know you were being hunted and I was not there to help."

Stan, who had remained with the elders, clutched his jacket and crossed his arms. It was mid-July, but on Potato Mountain the temperature was dipping. He was so close to an acquittal of his client that nothing would move him from this spot until he heard what the elders had to say. He was so passionately involved in his brief to defend Noah that he had caught himself praying in the last week—not for his own soul or for an afterlife, but for the strength to see this case, his last case, through to a successful end.

While Alec and Maria spoke around the fire he had written down their words. He would have them swear their statements. They hadn't told their story to an RCMP officer because they weren't asked, and had they been asked they might well have remained silent. They had told it tonight to their own people, their equals, who would not look down on them.

Stan was no closer to finding out who had killed Bordy, yet he was confident that he had enough evidence to convince the Court of Appeal that Noah's guilty verdict should be set aside, and he would stake his thirty-five years as a lawyer that the Crown would stay the charges and Noah would be a free man.

The elders were talking. Willieboy summed up their conversation.

"If Noah is the murderer he has to have the Lee Enfield. How does it end up with the survey crew? Find who owns the gun, maybe find the killer."

Antoine asked, "Does anyone believe that Noah killed Bordy?"

They all shook their heads.

"Mr. Hewitt, we say Noah didn't shoot Bordy. What happens now?"

Stan had the next steps worked out in his mind. "I will go down the mountain to the ranch tomorrow and tell Sergeant Boyd that Noah will turn himself in at the ranch in a week. I think he will agree. I will give him the sworn statements from Maria and Alec and Belle. Noah may have to spend a few weeks in jail after he turns himself in. The Court of Appeal will be hearing his appeal in two weeks and this evidence will be before them. It should set aside the guilty verdict, and the prosecutor, Mr. Bates, should drop the charges."

Antoine signalled Maria to have Noah come back to the circle. He stood in front of the elders with Justine by his side. "Wawant'x, we have decided that you did not kill your father. Amongst your people you are free. Mr. Hewitt says that you have to face the Queen's justice, and he will arrange a time and place for you to turn yourself in. For now, up here on the mountain, you will be safe amongst your people."

Noah looked up beyond his fire to the many fires on the flat of Potato Mountain. They mirrored the stars overhead and gave Noah a sense of earth meeting the cosmos. This was the time to tell the camp. He had not spoken to Justine about marriage. There was no need. They had spent a lifetime in the last nine months trying to be together. He had searched her face: it told him that this was what she wanted. He said to the Chilcotins—including Justine's mother, father and grandfather—"Now that I am free I want to bind myself to Justine. We will live together as husband and wife. We have been apart long enough."

The news spread through the camps, and the cheers could be heard in the night as runners told it to each fire.

Stan caught a chill on the mountain. The morning after the hearing before the elders he coughed long and hard enough to bring Maria to him with a tonic, which seemed to soothe him. He had a smoke and some coffee but wasn't able to eat breakfast. He also wasn't able to leave the mountain in that condition, but did have enough strength to write a note to Sergeant Boyd saying that Noah was in the camp and would turn himself in at the ranch in a week's time—on Saturday, August first—on the condition that he not be hunted and be given safe passage. Stan also said that he now had enough evidence to prove that Noah did not murder Bordy and that he would bring that evidence with him when he recovered from his illness. Stan wrote a separate note for Belle telling her of the marriage of Noah and Justine and that—in his opinion—with the evidence that would be soon in the hands of the law, Noah's appeal was assured of being successful, that the Crown would probably stay the charges against him.

On receiving Stan's note, Belle asked the young Chilcotin men to wait till the morning to deliver her note to Noah on top of Potato Mountain. It took her some time to compose, for she had much forgiveness to ask of her son, and some advice to give.

POTATO MOUNTAIN

If there was such a place as paradise on earth, or Heaven as Dante had described and as Noah's Catholic upbringing had taught him, then he and Justine found it in the week they were together on Potato Mountain. In the early hours of the morning, after his trial before the elders, Noah and Justine walked towards their tent on Echo Lake, which was set apart from the others. They had visited most fires on the mountain and were offered congratulations, food, and drink. At one fire, the lahal game stopped for a few minutes and one of the winners, Johnny Setah, insisted on giving half his winnings to Justine, while his cousin Clarence yelled at Noah, "Come and join the game. You can bet your bride."

The gamblers enjoyed his humour while envying Noah.

Maria had prepared a bed of spruce boughs that were as springy as a mattress and more fragrant. They undressed as the eastern sky was brightening, fell into bed in each other's arms and immediately fell asleep.

Justine was awakened a few hours later by what sounded like rain on the canvas tent. She opened a flap and looked into the face of one her little friends from Anaham, who asked her to play with them while the other children threw wild alpine flowers onto the tent. She dressed, leaving Noah asleep, and stepped out onto the dew of a new day. She motioned them away from the tent, and with her finger on her mouth for silence she brought them to her mother's camp.

Noah slept till noon. He woke to find her gone and called, "Justine?" There was no response. He went outside and called again, louder now: "Justine!" There was no one in sight. Then he saw her running towards him. She jumped into his arms and they kissed. He needed her there. She had come to fill the void in his life and his heart. For the first time since Bordy had strapped him for being late he discovered that life could include happiness.

That evening, Alec and Maria had a feast for the couple. The guests ate roast venison, wild potatoes, husham berries whisked into froth, and dried Saskatoon berries, which the Chilcotins call *dik*. They didn't stay for the drinking. Silently, walking hand-in-hand, they entered their tent. He undressed her slowly, touching the curve of her face with his hand, tracing the line of her shoulder and caressing her while she stood, still as a fawn, her wide eyes willing him to continue.

He undid her dress, which was tied at the back, and it fell to her feet while his hands rested on her hips and gently pressed her to him. A man had never treated her this way, nor had her friends told her that lovemaking was something to enjoy. She had never given herself to a man, although a number had tried to take her by force. She was in love with

Noah, and if he had been violent she would have accepted that, but he wasn't. She undid his belt and his pants joined her skirt. She felt him, very hard against her. She sank to her knees, pulling him down with her. On their bed of spruce boughs she slid under him, and they looked at each other until they kissed; and coming up for breath, he told her that he loved her, which she repeated. They joined in an embrace which nothing could break apart. . . .

In the morning they woke early and jumped into cold Echo Lake, screaming and yelling the names of saints, cherubim and Lendix'tcux and hearing their voices thrown back at them. Then it was back to their bed, where Justine asked, "You were out on the plateau from March to June with no company except coyote, raven, wolf and Ta Chi. How did you survive?"

"I had to go through all of this just to meet you. It was a test to show that I was worthy of your love."

"Well, then I should mark you to see if you passed."

"There were some low points. I almost starved to death. I broke my leg. I was trussed up like a papoose for a week. There were many times I thought of giving up and turning myself in."

"What kept you going?"

"Besides you? I kept a diary. Not the written kind, but a portfolio of drawings of the Chilcotin."

"I want to see it."

"Of course you'll see it, but it will take me days to explain it to you because it's the story of my journey to find you and to find myself. First you must tell me how you avoided taking my place in jail after I escaped."

"That'll wait. You must be hungry after last night. I'll make breakfast."

She built a fire, boiled water and soon gave him his usual

fare of oatmeal, sugared tea and cold venison. After that simple meal they rode Getaway and Chilko over the Potato Range. There was a horse race every day down the steep slopes of the mountain, and they stopped and watched the riders launch themselves off a precipice in a test of man and beast against the mountain. The rules were that horse and rider had to finish the race together, and few contestants met the rules. They were on their horses when Joe Willieboy came up to Noah with a sealed letter from Belle. Noah put it in his pocket and didn't look at it until he and Justine returned to their tent, where seated on the ground with his arm around Justine, he read it out loud.

My dearest son,

This is my first contact with you since the trial, and I am overjoyed to write you knowing that you are safe and well. It's ironic that you are five miles away on Potato Mountain, yet it seems like leagues and centuries to me.

Stan Hewitt has told me of the arrangement he made with the RCMP that you will give yourself up in a week at the ranch. He has worked very hard on your behalf and because of him you will be cleared of these charges. I hope you will find it in your heart to forgive me for not telling the court and the police of my being at the ranch at the time of Bordy's death. There is really no excuse for my conduct, but I will try to explain.

I went to the ranch to persuade Bordy to sell to the power company. The dam would flood the ranch, which he couldn't manage after his stroke, and you are a painter, not a rancher. He threatened me and I ran from the house. I wasn't there when the shooting started and I didn't think my evidence would help you. Stan has since told me I was wrong. My evidence would have explained why Bordy was so angry after I left the great room that he threatened you with his gun. It would also verify that there were two shots fired at the ranch house. I didn't come forward about my involvement because I was thinking about my attachment to Jack Parmenter.

I have been unlucky with men. My first husband died. It took me a dozen years to find out that Bordy didn't love me, and so I was determined to make a success with Jack. That's why I risked confronting Bordy to get him to see reason, to get him to see that he was not well enough to run a large cattle ranch and to get him to drop his opposition to the water licence. When everything went so terribly wrong at the ranch, I believed that if I came forward the knowledge of my involvement would have meant the end of Jack's plan to dam the Homathko. The government wouldn't want to grant Jack's company a water licence in those circumstances. Jack thought so too.

Jack offered to send Charlie Rainbow out to find you and to bring you to me. Before I came up to the ranch this summer Jack told me that Charlie was unable to locate you, and if Charlie couldn't find you in the Chilcotin wilderness then no one could. I have given my statement to Stan. I hope it's not too late.

When he read the part where Belle wrote about Charlie being sent out to look for him, he stiffened and Justine said, "What's wrong?"

He asked her, "Who is Charlie Rainbow?"

"He's an Iroquois working for the survey crew. Why?"

He shrugged, "Just wondering."

He continued reading the letter in a monotone, for his mind was back at Charlotte Lake.

Stan also told me that you and Justine are living together as man and wife in the Native way. I am pleased that you are happy. I saw Justine at the trial and she is a lovely woman. Everyone speaks well of her. I do hope that you will have your marriage blessed by the church.

All my love,
Mother

So it had been Charlie who had questioned him, had held him prisoner, and had tried to abduct him from the cabin, and that meant that Charlie and/or the major had lied to Belle about not being able to locate him. His fears about his and Belle's safety returned. He didn't want to alarm Justine, so he said nothing.

During the young couple's week together, Belle came to Potato Mountain at Noah's invitation. She arrived at the top of Potato Mountain by helicopter. Noah and his bride waited arm-in-arm by their tent, their clothes whipped by the wash of the rotor blades until the pilot helped Belle out of the cockpit.

Belle walked slowly forward. She hadn't seen Noah since the trial. He looked different now, more like a Chilcotin than the boy she had raised as her own son. He was very lean. His hair was long and cut off at his shoulders and he wore a headband. Justine was holding on to him. When Belle had left the Chilcotin, Justine had been a slip of a girl. Now she was a beautiful woman and, from what she had been told, had a lot of spirit. Still, she couldn't help thinking that

Noah could have done so much better; she was particularly fond of Emily. She suppressed those thoughts. She didn't know how Noah would react to her failure to tell the whole truth at his trial. She was also in no position to judge him, having betrayed him and set a bad example by living with the major while still married to Bordy. Her church didn't condone that arrangement, but would excommunicate her if she divorced Bordy to marry the major.

Noah took a step towards her with outstretched arms. That broke the ice between them. He hugged her and said, "Mother, I would like you to meet my wife, Justine. She has saved my life and made me the happiest man alive."

The two women embraced and Belle said, "Thank you, Justine."

Noah added, "I wanted to introduce you to Ta Chi, but she is shy. She could be in that thicket over there watching us. If you want to be friends with her, all you have to do is to love and respect the Chilcotin."

Belle remembered that Bordy had said the very same words when he was courting her. She said, "I would have brought Jack up here with me, but he had to go back to Victoria for some important meetings."

Near the end of their week together, Noah and Justine began to plan for the future. Justine wanted to go to nursing school in Vancouver. Noah wanted to apprentice to a Native artist, also in Vancouver. After completing their training they could move back to the Chilcotin. Justine would nurse and Noah would run a small ranch and paint in his spare time.

One night after making love, he talked about his idea for a mural. He had shown her his sketches and drawings. The master drawing was to-scale on white paper measuring one by four feet. He explained to her that it would be enlarged ten times, painted on three panels, and mounted on a wall. The wall Noah had in mind was the west wall in the great hall at Empire Ranch. He was excited as he told Justine, and she was amazed at the scope and breadth of his vision. What he saw was the whole of the Chilcotin territory, from the curve of the mountains to the mighty Fraser, an ovoid shape with the Chilcotin River as the umbilical cord to the Fraser River itself. Within was the circle of migration and life of the people of the azure water, both white and Native, nourished by their myths and religion, encouraged by their heroes and heroines, sustained by nature's bounty and chastened by its laws. Justine fell asleep listening to his dream.

When she woke in the morning, he was outside their tent sketching Lendix'tcux and his sons outlined on Mount Tatlow as the rising eastern sun highlighted their features. When he was finished, he spent the rest of the morning sketching Potato Mountain, which he said would be the centre of his mural.

Pointing to the sketch, she asked, "Is that a bush with sparrows, or is it a figure of a woman in the foreground bent over with a sack on her shoulder?"

"That's Ta Chi. I can't seem to capture her in my painting without making her part of the land and the sparrow."

Having rested on Potato Mountain under the care of Maria, Stan felt well enough to travel down to the ranch and deliver the statements to Sergeant Boyd. He arrived the day before Noah was to give himself up. He spent a few hours with the sergeant in the den and provided him with all four affidavits: Belle's, Maria's, Alec's, and finally, Noah's.

The bridge club had been at the ranch for a week and they had played every afternoon. On the day she returned from Potato Mountain, Belle decided to tell them her secrets, her lies, and her frailties, for they had followed and invested in the Homathko project and should hear her confession first. For years, the four women had shuffled their way through the cards, exchanged bids, followed convention and taken chances together on the game and on the lives of those around them.

When Belle came to the table with her secret, it took them only a few hands to know that she was waiting to unburden herself. It was Samantha who voiced their concerns. "The Chilcotin has a negative effect on your bridge. What's on your mind?"

"I am not what I seem," was Belle's enigmatic reply.

They waited for a revelation from their sister gambler.

"I have not been open with you."

She was stalling for time to gain the courage to tell them. Adele, Emily, and Samantha remained silent. Then it came out.

"When Bordy was shot last Thanksgiving, I was at the ranch. I didn't witness the shooting, but I saw him, and he threatened me with a gun before I left. I didn't tell the court because if I were implicated in any way, the major's company would probably not have received the water licence."

There was a chorus of sympathy from Adele and Emily, but Samantha didn't join in.

"Why are you telling us this now?" she asked.

"Because,"—and Belle drew that word out slowly—"I have given Stan Hewitt a statement, and it will be made public. I thought you should know before it is."

"Have you told the major?" was her next question.

"He knows my lie, but he is not aware that I have corrected it. He's been away in Victoria for over a week. I will tell him tonight when he returns."

The game of bridge was forgotten as each woman

considered how to best deal with the consequences of Belle's revelation, and how to advise her own clique to turn Belle's personal anguish and defeat to an advantage, or at least to lessen the political and financial fallout. They all agreed in the end that it was possible for the Homathko project to proceed, based on Belle's assurance that she was not connected to the shooting and that Belle would tell the major that evening.

Exhausted, yet elated from his strenuous physical and mental workout over the last few days, Stan fell into his bed at Empire Ranch, the scene of his many drunken binges and now his most successful defence. He had his last smoke for the day in bed before turning off the light, and thought about how strange it was that his last acquittal was not from a traditional jury but from a Native circle of elders. Before the elders, the evidence was not squeezed out of witnesses by heavy cross-examination with each side covering up as many of the facts as possible to make their client appear honest, and trying to throw as much mud as possible on their opponent's witnesses to make them appear bold liars. His ever-active mind thought that this would make a good comparative law article for the Advocate or the Canadian Bar Journal. On that pleasant thought, he turned off the light and fell into a deep sleep.

Stan dreamed that he and his fishing friends were on a Chilcotin lake when he hooked a beauty that bent the rod and flashed silver until exhausted. It was brought to the surface near the boat. Bending over the gunwale to net the big rainbow trout, he realized that he was netting Belle.

He woke with a start. It was late morning, the sun was shining in the window and Belle was leaning over him.

"Are you all right?"

"Yes. Yes, I just had the most uplifting dream in my whole

life. I've never felt better."

"When you didn't come down to breakfast, I worried."

"Thank you for worrying. You know, I think I can beat this cancer."

She smiled and said, "I know you can."

"Belle, have you told the major about your confession?"

She looked surprised and thought of dissembling, but this was the new Belle, so she answered truthfully: "No."

"The sergeant has your written affidavit. I thought it best that the major hear it from you."

She turned away and walked to the door, then stopped. "Come down for breakfast now."

The previous afternoon, Belle had promised her bridge coven that she would tell the major that evening, but he hadn't arrived at the ranch until now. When she left Stan, she went to the main house and found the major in the kitchen having a cup of coffee. Belle took him upstairs to her bedroom for privacy and sat him down. He had not stopped moving the whole summer. He was monitoring the progress of the survey crew and the geologist. He had secured the right-of-way for the transmission line down Bute Inlet and across the Redonda islands to hook up with the Island grid at Campbell River, and he ran the day-to-day business of the company. In his consuming assault on the stored energy of the Chilcotin, he could taste victory and visualized thousands of kilowatts of electricity being generated and distributed. Belle's attention at this time was unwelcome.

"As you may know," she began, "Noah is surrendering himself at the ranch at noon. Sergeant Boyd is here, waiting to take him into custody."

He sat there motionless, waiting for her to proceed.

"To make sure he gets every chance to prove his

innocence, I've sworn an affidavit Stan Hewitt prepared saying I was at the ranch at the time of Bordy's death."

The major laughed out loud. He laughed long and hard, almost maniacally. Finally controlling himself, he said, "Belle, Belle, Belle, you foolish woman. You came to me for advice and help. I gave you advice and now that I am giving you that help, you change your mind."

She felt a chill. "What do you mean, you're giving me help? What help are you giving me? You can stop that help right now because I don't need it."

"Never mind, my dear. It's too late now! We shall try to make the best of it." He left her to puzzle on what he had said.

VENGEANCE

Potato Mountain had another visitor on the day before the breakup of the Chilcotin Jamboree: Charlie Rainbow arrived to talk to Alec about the deer shooting. Over the summer, Alec had told Charlie that he was aware a pregnant doe had been shot out of season by someone at his camp. Charlie had told him it wouldn't happen again, and Alec said the person who did it should be punished. Charlie hadn't responded, and they had gone their separate ways.

Up on Potato Mountain Charlie again brought up the dead doe to Alec. "The chief engineer has punished the guy who killed the deer."

Alec said nothing.

"It was a bad kill, I know."

Again Alec remained silent.

"A few days ago our camp at Mosely Creek was upset by the wailings of a person in pain. Do you know anything about that?"

"No."

"Is your jamboree finished?"

"Yeah, the last of us will be moving out tomorrow morning."

"Okay, see you around."

Charlie headed off down the mountain and arrived back at the survey camp in time for dinner. He knew about the cook's still, and because he virtually ran the camp he was given a glass from time to time. He checked in on Snellgrove and noticed that his ribs had healed enough that he could move about.

After dinner, Snellgrove told Aaron that he was tired of sipping booze. He wanted a real drink. Aaron came back with a bottle of the cook's hooch. Their drunken shouts after midnight when they attempted to get their hands on more woke the cooks, who defended their cache. The ensuing brawl brought out Ian, Charlie, and the head draughtsman, who had to break up the fight.

Charlie—without speaking to Ian, who would probably have contradicted him—told Snellgrove to leave the camp in the morning. He told Aaron that he was fired and could leave with him. When morning came, Charlie saw to it that they were packed and ready. He took Snellgrove aside and spoke to him. It appeared to Ralph—the only one who noticed this exchange—that Charlie was doing more than just pointing out a direction.

Snellgrove was hung over and still in some pain when Aaron got him on his horse along with their gear. The sorry pair walked out of camp with Aaron on foot leading Snellgrove's horse. Ralph watched them go. He had survived their presence in camp and could now breathe easier. But within the hour Charlie discovered that the camp's rifle was missing. He told Ian that he would run Snellgrove and Aaron down and retrieve it. Ralph was still in the camp. When Charlie started off jogging down the trail armed with a double-bitted axe, Ralph followed him with his own axe in hand, on what was going to be a long run along the eastern shore of Tatlayoko Lake. With Aaron walking beside Snellgrove and Snellgrove still hurting, they would likely catch them up about halfway down the lake—before they could do any harm. . . .

The Natives on Potato Mountain broke camp in the morning. Some had left the day before for Anahim Lake, Nemiah Valley, and Farwell Canyon. They took a number of trails off the mountain. In the morning, Noah and Justine travelled down the western slope with Antoine, Alec, and Maria. The couple separated from the family at the Pauls' range camp and rode towards Tatlayoko Lake at its halfway point on the way to the ranch house, where they were expected in the early afternoon. It was eleven o'clock. They were early.

They walked their horses side-by-side, Noah on Justine's left. They felt safe because they were only a few miles from the ranch where Noah would be arrested and they would be parted. Even a week away from each other would be too long. As they approached the lake, the land flattened and the trees thinned to a small clearing where the mountain trail joined the lake trail that would lead them to the ranch. At that moment, Justine was very happy with the promise of living the rest of her life riding beside the man she loved. He turned to her and said, "I'm sorry Ta Chi hasn't shown up to congratulate us.

She said, "Don't worry. She will appear when we least expect it."

It appeared to Ralph when he followed Charlie Rainbow

out of the survey camp that Charlie was quickening his pace to outrun him. But it wasn't possible to leave Ralph behind; he could have run all day, for he had spent the last two months climbing up and down mountains. He was also driven by the fear of what might happen with the gun in the hands of those two men. Rainbow Charlie couldn't keep up the pace that he had set and Ralph, barely winded, passed the older man without exchanging a word. This marathon continued, each man holding an axe in his hand like a baton, as they headed for the encounter.

The lovers could hear the lake waves striking the beach before they saw the meadow and the shoreline. It was a peaceful morning scene. There was a flurry of sparrow calls and then a fluster of movement in a bush about fifty yards to their left. Noah felt a cold hand on his heart. He turned Chilko's head towards the bush.

Ralph ran by a pile of steaming horse dung. Snellgrove and Aaron were not far ahead. He came to a rise in the trail where he saw below him a picture so clear and ominous that his mind seemed to become detached from his body. Part of him was looking down from a height watching a scene play out, and at the same time he was physically part of the action: shouting and running hard towards the ambush.

Noah and Justine were riding slowly down the trail. To their left was Snellgrove, impatiently waiting crouched behind a bush with Aaron lying beside him. Snellgrove was aiming the rifle at the advancing, laughing couple and Ralph, running and breathing hard, raised his axe for the throw.

Chilko responded to Noah's rein and immediately, without any urging from Noah, charged the bush. Noah drew Ta Chi's small axe from his belt and in one motion hurled it at the bush, which belched a tongue of flame. The gun snapped. Noah fell from his horse.

Ralph ran on.

On the ground, Noah felt a searing pain in his right side. Justine flung herself from her saddle and fell beside him on the ground, cradling him in her arms.

Aaron, lying next to Snellgrove with his eyes fixed on Justine, shouted, "Now! Shoot the bitch!" Richard Snellgrove didn't answer. Aaron looked at his master and saw Ta Chi's axe imbedded in his forehead.

Justine was on the ground beside Noah. She took no notice of what was happening around her. She only knew that Noah was badly wounded, perhaps mortally. She wept and frantically said, "Dearest, don't leave me."

With a rasping breath he whispered, "I'm hit in the side. You must stop the bleeding."

Ralph, in full flight, had raised his axe. Had Aaron attempted to reach for the gun, he would have thrown it. Aaron didn't move. He was in shock, and when Ralph picked up the gun, Aaron cried, "Don't kill me! I didn't do it. We were set up."

Ralph ignored Aaron. He grabbed the gun and ran to his bleeding friend Noah. Aaron came to his senses, and seeing Ralph tending to Noah, took flight. Charlie Rainbow crested the hill, axe in hand, surveyed the scene, then retreated to the other side of the hill out of sight of the young people fighting for Noah's life and followed Aaron.

It took some time to stop the bleeding. Noah was alive but needed a doctor. It wasn't until then that Rainbow came forward and asked, "How is he?"

"He'll live, but he needs a doctor."

"I'll ride to the ranch house and they can radio for a float plane to take him to Williams Lake."

Ralph asked, "Where is Aaron?"

"He had an accident. He won't be bothering you."

At eleven-thirty, the sergeant ordered two of his officers to head out on horseback to escort Noah from the trail off the mountain to the ranch house, as arranged. At noon the sergeant, Stan, the major and Belle were waiting for Noah when Charlie Rainbow rode up with one of the officers at a gallop, shouting that Noah had been shot. The major ran towards Charlie to help him from his horse, and Stan watched as the two of them had private words together. The major spoke to the sergeant.

"I'll call my base camp and have them send the helicopter to pick Noah up and fly him and Justine directly to Williams Lake Hospital."

Sergeant Boyd mounted his horse. "I'm going to the scene of the shooting with Corporal Tate and Charlie. I'm ordering all of you to remain here until I return.

Belle refused the order. "My son is injured. I'm going with you."

Stan took the sergeant aside before they left and said, "Would you time your ride from here to Noah at full gallop?"

REVELATION

It was after six when the sergeant returned with Snellgrove's body in the wagon and Aaron, head-bandaged and in cuffs, sitting beside the dead man. Ralph was mounted on Justine's horse. Riding with them were Belle, Alec, and Maria. Sergeant Boyd told the others that Noah's wound was not fatal and that the helicopter had taken him to the hospital with Justine. He talked to Charlie Rainbow and Ralph separately in the den.

After dinner, the sergeant gathered everyone in the great hall. Belle insisted that he tell them what he knew of the shooting before she and the major flew to Noah's bedside. Stan approved of her taking responsibility when she said to Sergeant Boyd, "I have been guilty of a cover-up, and I want you to lay your cards on the table. The major is here to answer any questions and so is Charlie."

The major, looking cautious and wondering where this

was all leading, seemed concerned for his men. "You've finished with Charlie. I would like him to get back to the camp to tell the men first hand what has happened."

The sergeant brushed that aside. "This shouldn't take long. I would like him to stay." Then he began his review.

"When Bordy was killed in this room last Thanksgiving, we now believe that the killer was outside the house on the lawn, and the shot that killed Bordy came through the open French doors.

"Stan found a shell casing by the lilac on the lawn, where the shooter must have knelt. The casing was from a .30-06 Lee Enfield rifle. Mrs. Hanlon has admitted to seeing Bordy minutes before the shooting, but claims to have left him alive. Within minutes of her leaving and without knowing that his mother was in the Chilcotin, Noah entered the room and quarrelled with Bordy. They fought over a gun and it discharged without harming anyone. Noah left, and as he neared the door a shot was fired from the lawn where the casing was found. We have eliminated Noah as the person who fired the shot. We cannot eliminate Mrs. Hanlon at this point because Major Parmenter owns that gun, and as she is a friend of the major, she would have had access to the gun."

The major sputtered, "What?"

"Here's the evidence." The officer produced the spent shell.

"It's from the gun that Snellgrove used to shoot Noah. Fortunately—according to his wife, Justine, who was riding beside her husband—Ta Chi's sparrows alerted Noah to the ambush. The bullet struck Noah in the right side as he threw the axe. The axe struck Snellgrove on the head and killed him. Aaron, his accomplice, who was waiting in the bushes with him, tried to escape. Mr. Rainbow caught him. That is the reason I spoke to Mr. Rainbow earlier."

The major interrupted. "Charlie should be congratulated."

"Save your applause."

The major, not used to being spoken to in this way by a non-commissioned officer, became cool and calculating. "I asked Charlie to buy a gun in the Chilcotin to protect the camp and the surveyors from bears, so if that is the gun, it could not have been used by Belle to shoot her husband. She is in the clear."

"No. Somebody remembers seeing that gun."

He went to the door and called out, "Ralph, will you come in and tell us what you saw at the major's house?"

Ralph Richards entered the room and stood by the door looking at the gathering. He drew a breath and said, "I was in the major's home a few years back, and in his den where he kept his gun collection I noticed this Lee Enfield bolt-action rifle that seemed out of place in a cabinet of beautiful guns. It had particular markings on its butt: three notches. This was the camp gun, and it was the same gun that Snellgrove had in his hand when I saw him shoot my friend Noah."

The major's pink face reddened. He turned to Belle and asked, "How were you able to get that gun out of my house without me noticing?"

She appeared confused, but before she could say anything the sergeant continued.

"Mrs. Hanlon, Mr. Hewitt has provided us with your sworn statement saying that you were at the ranch when your husband was murdered. Is that true?"

"Yes."

"But you told me, the prosecutor Mr. Bates, and Mr. Hewitt, and you swore under oath at your son's trial before judge and jury, that you were in Victoria at the time."

"Yes."

"Was that true?"

"No."

"You lied under oath?"

"Yes."

"You do realize that perjury is a criminal offence."

"I do. It was morally wrong. I shall have to live with that for the rest of my life."

The sergeant turned to a table behind him, picked up a rifle and showed it to Belle.

"Do you recognize this rifle? It's the rifle that was used to shoot your husband and your son."

She looked at it with disgust.

"I've never seen this gun. Whoever used this gun is evil and has done me a great wrong. They have killed the man I used to love and wounded my son."

The sergeant continued to press. "Didn't you bring this gun with you on Thanksgiving last year, and after you quarrelled with Bordy and he threatened you, didn't you go to your car, get the gun and return with the intent of shooting him? And didn't you see Bordy and your son fight over his gun in the great hall? And when your son was leaving the room and Bordy moved towards his gun, thinking he would shoot your son, didn't you then fire this rifle and kill your husband?"

With tears in her eyes she said, "If I had had a gun and had seen what you describe I would have."

"You lied about not being there, why should anyone believe you now when you say you didn't kill Bordy?"

"Maybe no one will believe me. If I go to jail for Bordy's death, it would be a fitting punishment for what I have done to my son. But I'm through lying and I'm thankful that Stan persevered and made me tell the truth."

"Did anyone else know about your lie?"

Belle's pause was hardly noticeable to the sergeant but to Stan it was a lifetime. This was a test of the statement she had just made about being through with lying. Would she now reveal that someone? Stan knew that there was only one person she would have confided in, and saying the name would mark the end of a relationship.

She replied to her interrogator, "Jack Parmenter."

"What did he say when you told him?"

"He said not to tell anyone, as my son's guilty verdict would be set aside, and he suggested that I fire Stan as his lawyer and get a Victoria lawyer, which I did."

"And is this the only reason he didn't want you to tell someone?"

"No. He believed that if the government knew that I was involved in any way with the death of Bordy, who was opposing the flooding of Tatlayoko Valley, they would not grant Vancouver Island Power Company the water licence that he so desperately needed."

She tried to soften the disclosure of the major's involvement by adding, "But he cared about my being involved. He is a very sensitive man."

The major hadn't interrupted while the sergeant questioned Belle. He watched and heard her answer the questions in an open manner, and now it was his turn as the sergeant turned to him. "Do you believe Mrs. Hanlon when she says that she did not kill her husband?"

The major was having difficulty balancing his affection for Belle and his loyalty to the company, and like a good soldier he did not shirk his duty.

"No, I don't."

"Did you believe her when she first told you of her trip to the ranch to see her husband?"

"I had my doubts."

"Did you do anything to protect her after the conversation?"

"She told me that she believed that Noah had seen the person who had shot Bordy and that she thought it might have been Ta Chi, whom she described as a nomad who haunts the ranch. Noah escaped to find his father's killer. If he found that Belle was there he may well have named her, and I believed that she had probably shot Bordy even though she denied it. She wanted me to find Noah. I sent Charlie to the Chilcotin to find Noah and to see if he could get him to reveal who he saw. He contacted Noah and spoke to him."

The major went further. He motioned towards Charlie, but directed his words to the sergeant. "Charlie told me that Noah would not identify that person, and that made me suspect it was Belle he saw. Charlie decided to let him go rather than bring him to me."

Stan was getting concerned with the shift of this enquiry towards Belle and said, "Surely you aren't going to charge Belle with Bordy's murder."

"She lied once denying any involvement. She may be lying again about not knowing about the gun."

Stan was trying hard not to let his emotions get in the way of his reason. He was in love with Belle and wanted to believe in her innocence even though she had directly lied to him in the past.

But the sergeant wasn't finished. He turned to Ralph, who was still standing by the door. "Tell them what you saw and heard this morning," he said, motioning to those sitting in the great hall.

Ralph had been following the investigation with increasing interest. He was able to fit his small role into the larger play, and it seemed to him that his observations and actions were factors that the major and Charlie had not considered in their schemes. He had no hesitation in telling them what happened.

"Charlie spoke to Snellgrove before he left camp this morning. I didn't hear what he said, but he spent some time with him. I don't know how the rifle could have been taken without Charlie noticing at the time. And when he discovered the gun was missing, he wanted to go alone to fetch it back and was annoyed that I went with him. He tried to lose me. Then after the shooting, with Snellgrove lying dead at my feet, Aaron said, 'We were set up.'"

Ralph continued. "I didn't see Aaron run. I was with Justine and Noah. There was no place for him to go. He was unarmed, and when Charlie said he had had an accident, I didn't understand until I went over the ridge and found Aaron. He was badly beaten and appeared to be in shock or scared witless. He refused to say anything."

When Ralph had finished, the sergeant arched his eyebrow at the major, who responded by smiling and shaking his head. "Now, sergeant! As a man of the law you can't believe that these suppositions and innuendos have any weight."

"Your 'man Friday,' Charlie Rainbow, had access to your guns."

"Are you seriously suggesting that Charlie had anything to do with the murder of Bordy Hanlon?"

"Yes, and with the attempted murder of Noah Hanlon."

Charlie, who had been sitting expressionless to this point, now shifted his position slightly. The major persevered. "I thought Snellgrove shot Noah." And the major shook his head while looking at Belle, who was becoming alarmed.

The sergeant continued, "Yes, he did, but I believe Charlie set Snellgrove up to do the job. He knew when Noah would be turning himself in. He knew that Snellgrove was determined to kill Noah if he saw him again. He told Snellgrove where he could find him, and he put the gun in his hands."

The major threw up his hands. "That's preposterous. You're making this all up. Charlie is the best guide in the country, but he couldn't possibly have dreamed up this fantasy; and for what purpose?"

The major's main audience member was not so much the sergeant as it was Belle, whose emotions were plainly affected by each new revelation and accusation. The sergeant persisted in his attack.

"Charlie was up at the Potato Mountain camp on Friday and was told by Alec Paul that Noah would be heading down the mountain to give himself up at the ranch on Saturday morning before noon. Charlie ran the camp outside of the survey. He arranged to have Snellgrove and Aaron booted out Saturday morning, and told Snellgrove when and where Noah would be coming down the mountain."

Belle spoke up. "Is there any other explanation? You were so wrong when you charged my son with murder."

The sergeant couldn't resist saying, "Of course there is another explanation. You could have taken the gun, as the major suggests, and shot your husband. Perhaps we wouldn't have charged your son if you had come forward sooner. But what you say about Charlie being of help is correct. The question is, who was he helping? He could have been helping you. Today when Charlie rode here for medical help at full gallop, Stan noticed that his horse was not breathing hard or lathered and asked me to time the ride back at full gallop to the scene of the shooting. It took twenty minutes, but Charlie took forty minutes to make the same ride. One explanation is that Charlie was in no hurry to get medical aid for Noah, and the longer Noah was unattended the greater became the risk he would die from his wound. Also, it was Charlie who noticed that the gun was missing and volunteered to get it. He was in no hurry to get there, expecting Snellgrove to have shot Noah. The purpose was to silence Noah, who you believed saw his mother shoot Bordy."

The sergeant looked at the major and at Charlie in turn. "It seems that you have some explaining to do. Will you come with me to our station in Williams Lake for questioning?"

"Are we under arrest, Sergeant?"

"No. I want to get a statement from you."

"I would prefer to have my lawyer present, and I am sure Mr. Rainbow will want the same."

Before the major and Charlie left for the Williams Lake RCMP station in the squad car, the major approached Belle. "Don't worry about me, my dear. I've been in worse scraps. I'll be back tomorrow, and we will carry on with our lives and our dream of damming the Homathko."

Belle, whose emotions were exhausted by the day's events, had enough Scottish pride and Chilcotin grit to tell her lover, "You know, Jack? The last time I said goodbye to one of the loves of my life was in this room when Bordy and I separated. I agonized over leaving that unfaithful bastard and the Chilcotin. You've made my decision to leave you much easier. Goodbye."

DEYEN

Stan represented Noah in the Court of Appeal while Noah convalesced in Williams Lake hospital. The Crown didn't put up an argument. Stan explained that Noah had escaped in order to find his father's killer and that he voluntarily turned himself in. The Court of Appeal was headed by the chief justice, who set aside the guilty verdict and ordered a new trial. He commented on Belle's actions and silence and said that had she come forward sooner the jury may well not have convicted. With all the evidence now pointing away from Noah, the Crown dropped the charges against him and he was a free man.

Noah's release raised the question as to who the Crown would charge for the murder of Bordy Hanlon, Belle, the major, or Charlie Rainbow—all of whom had access to the major's Lee Enfield. In the end, the Crown prosecutor didn't have enough evidence to charge any one of them.

Between Belle and the major lay a wasteland of distrust which could never be bridged. The major couldn't understand why Belle had put the company in jeopardy by confronting Bordy and then betrayed it by admitting she was there at the ranch. Belle believed that the major and Charlie had used Snellgrove in a plan that—had it been successful—would have cost Noah his life. The seeds of doubt having been sown, the harvest was the abandoning of the Waddington dam project. Belle was now in the ironic position of having taken over Bordy's adamant opposition to the dam. Within months the government expropriated the company and abandoned the plan to dam the Homathko. By the end of the year Belle had retreated from Victoria to the ranch—which she now owned outright—and brought her Bechstein with her.

Although Noah had killed Snellgrove, the Crown didn't lay charges. It was evident that he had thrown the axe in self-defence. As for Aaron, he was charged and convicted as an accessory to the attempted murder of Noah. Acton Bates represented him. Aaron refused to take the stand. He appeared in the courtroom a beaten man. Bates confided in Stan after the trial that he had wanted to put Aaron on the stand, but Aaron refused to even tell his lawyer what happened. He seemed afraid of his own shadow. Without Aaron's cooperation, the Crown did not have enough evidence to charge Charlie Rainbow as a co-conspirator. Aaron wouldn't repeat or explain what he had said to Ralph even when offered a reduced sentence.

Noah had no interest in managing the ranch. He and Justine moved to Vancouver in a basement suite off the Blanca loop, where he was painting his grand mural. Justine enrolled in her first year of nursing at the University of British Columbia.

The men in Belle's life—Bordy and the major—had been

attracted to her for what she could do for them while they kept to their main chance: Empire Ranch for Bordy and the Vancouver Island Power Company for the major. Belle—lively, talented and independently wealthy—wanted to share her life with a man, but the men she had chosen couldn't share; they were devoted to external causes. They were complete within themselves. Stan, on the other hand, although deeply flawed, had discovered after his boat accident how much Belle had become part of his life, and had changed to accept Belle and the Chilcotin on their terms. Belle realized that Stan had always been there for her, and wanted him to be there to the end of her days. Stan was out at Tatlayoko Lake every weekend. His cancer was in remission now that he had found a reason to look after himself. Belle discovered that he was good company, while his pleasure in life was to be with her. They came to the happy decision after consulting Noah that Stan would move out to the ranch and they would live together.

Stan did go into Williams Lake to represent a few old clients, but most of his time was spent amusing Belle, reading biographies of great men, studying the philosopher-anthropologist Claude Levi-Strauss, writing his memoirs and, of course, fishing. Belle sold off much of the land and changed the name of the ranch from "Empire" back to "Bar 5." Alec Paul became foreman and Belle looked after the business end of a much-reduced acreage.

Antoine disappeared into the mountains with Noah on Noah's frequent visits. Satisfied that Noah had survived all the tests, including jail, Antoine began preparing Noah for the role of deyen after he was gone.

In the summer following, Noah had finished the centrepiece in his mural, which would show the Chilcotin in its living, breathing and heart-beating glory. Belle insisted that there be an unveiling in the great hall and invited a host of people. An invitation was sent to all the denizens of the plateau for an unveiling on August 7, 1959. Everyone had an opportunity to speak. Justine paid tribute to Noah.

"My husband Wawant'x, who is also known as Noah Hanlon, lived his childhood in the Chilcotin. He moved to Victoria, and thanks to his mother, Belle, received a liberal education. He wanted to be an artist. He studied hard and showed talent. He returned to the Chilcotin and through sufferings and trials, Ta Chi introduced him to our land. I wish I could say that it was I who inspired his mural, but I have taken second place to the Chilcotin. Today he will unveil the first panel of the mural. The centrepiece is Mount Ts'yl-os. My thanks to Belle for commissioning the work, which she has named the 'Chilcotin Portrait.'"

When the curtain fell from the painting, the hushed room came alive with "ahhs" of appreciation, followed by hand-clapping from the whites and shouts from the Natives. The dignitaries from Williams Lake and Victoria, the Natives from the reserves, and the Stonys were overcome by the illumination of Noah's creation.

Belle had tried to come to terms with her betrayal of Noah. Most important to her was that her son had forgiven her. But she couldn't forgive herself, for she realized that she had been worse than Bordy when it came to exploiting the land. He had remained in the Chilcotin to run their ranch and had included the Natives in the running. She had intended to use the land by building a dam that would not only destroy the ranch but also interrupt the sacred circle that was the Chilcotin, and for what? Not for the benefit of the Chilcotins.

She could only say, "Noah's mural in this room means as much to us as it means to the people of the plateau." She paused to wipe away a tear. "I would like to pay tribute to my son by playing one of his favourite pieces, which he enjoyed listening to when he was a young, beautiful boy."

Noah blushed and said, "Play, mother, play."

She sat at her Bechstein and played Rachmaninoff's Prelude Opus 23 no. 95. When she played the last note, there were no dry eyes in the room. Stan was moved by Belle's performance. He could picture her playing for the King at Holyrood, but this audience was much more appreciative, and certainly he was more proud of her than was the King of England.

Before the artist spoke, the native drums beat a long tattoo.

"Justine urged me to finish this great mural, which was conceived when I was in the wilderness and so is part of me, part of Ta Chi and part of the Chilcotin. This is my gift to the Chilcotin people. I have attempted to reveal the secret life of the land, and while I was painting I felt the Creator's hand guiding mine. I hope that this mural will encourage Native art and culture on the plateau."

Standing beside Justine on the spot where Bordy had died, Stan looked out the open double doors onto the lawn and thought he saw, shielded by the trembling wind-rustled lilac, a small person—it could have been a child—looking towards the house. He nudged Justine and whispered so as not to interrupt the elders who were accepting the gift.

"Look outside at the lilac. Do you see that?"

She turned away from Noah's painting to look at the lilac.

"That's Ta Chi. I'm glad she came."

After the ceremonies, Stan went outside to the lilac where he had found the spent cartridge. As he approached the tree, a sparrow flew off towards Tatlayoko Lake. He wondered if Ta Chi, whom he had never laid eyes on, was real or another Chilcotin myth.

Studying the mural over time, Stan noticed that it appeared to be in constant movement; nothing was still. With Ts'yl-os in the background, the Chilcotin world seemed to circle Potato Mountain as Ta Chi circled it on her constant migrations, and as the stars circled the heavens. He had been up on the mountain's flat ridges and had seen the water on the east slope drain into Chilko Lake and then to the Chilcotin River, the Fraser River and into the sea, and on the west slope into Tatlayoko Lake and through the Homathko River to the sea again. He was beginning to understand the significance of this site to the Chilcotins.

Noah understood the oval and the circle. It was a leitmotif that he wove into his painting. He borrowed from the West Coast native art ovoid form, the U-form, the split U-form and the S-form. Stan remembered Noah explaining to him in Victoria that these lines and forms differed from Western linear art forms. Noah mentioned the Bayeux Tapestry that he had seen when his mother had taken him on a trip to Europe. The artists there showed the conquering of England by the Normans in a linear form. Noah reminded him of the Gothic cathedrals, which he said demonstrated Western society's way of creating a direct—and in their eyes, only—link to God. He preferred the Native way: nature's circle.

*****

That fall, Antoine—who was in his eighties—took to his bed in his lean-to. Belle wanted to move him to the main house. He refused. Stan spent a lot of time with him, as did Noah and Justine. She was eight months pregnant with their child and Antoine could feel the baby kicking. The old man was getting weaker. Dr. Hay told them that he might not last the week.

Stan and Noah were with Antoine one morning. The room was crowded with the three men in it. Antoine was on the bed, Stan sat on the only chair at the head of the bed and Noah sat cross-legged at the foot. Antoine seemed more alert that morning. Stan mentioned the failed project at Waddington Canyon. Without opening his eyes Antoine said, "Yes, Klatsassin, warrior chief, made sure no road."

Stan shook his head and Noah looked closely at his mentor, trying to hear and understand the old man's message. Stan said, "I am talking about the dam project two years ago."

"Yes, we stop it like Klatsassin, I guess."

Again Stan gently brought Antoine around to Stan's reality. "No, the Vancouver Island Power Company abandoned the project."

Then Antoine became the questioner. "Oh, why abandon?"

Stan fell into the rhythm of the old deyen, and Noah watched and half-listened as the two sparred over the past.

"Because Belle and the major lost faith in the plan and each other when I discovered the .30-06 cartridge on the lawn," Stan said.

"How did cartridge get on lawn?"

Stan humoured the old man, who seemed to have lost his memory.

"Bordy's killer left it there."

Antoine opened one questioning eye, but said nothing. Stan continued musing about his discovery. "I don't know whether it was by fate or chance that I found that damning piece of evidence which helped clear Noah and created such conflict in the power company that they had to abandon the project."

Antoine opened his other eye. Stan knew Antoine was pondering whether to say anything or to let Stan's musings float in the vapour. Antoine spoke.

"Not fate."

"Then it must have been chance."

"Not chance."

Stan looked at Noah, who shrugged his shoulders. Thinking Antoine must have some other metaphysical reason connected to the Creator, Stan asked him, "Then how was it I was able to find the shell that connected the power company to the murder?"

Antoine was ready. He said haltingly and with some effort, "When you come to Tatlayoko looking to find clue, I think to help. Alec find cartridge shell at power camp where they kill pregnant doe. He give it me. I place on lawn where you find it."

What could Stan say? He had played a part in a frame-up by an eighty-year-old deyen. There was plenty enough deceit and covering-up in this affair to spread across the whole of the Chilcotin, and he had unwittingly been involved. He looked at Antoine's face, cross-hatched with lines below the eyes and around the mouth, high unlined cheek bones and his unblinking clouded brown eyes, which were searching his and asking him a question to which Stan knew he had no answer.

Antoine put it into words. "Do you know who kilt Bordy?"

"I don't know. I had my suspicions that it was the major or Rainbow, but no proof. Now that I know that the cartridge was planted, I'm wondering if even my suspicions were correct."

There was another long silence before Stan asked Antoine, "Do you?"

Antoine was prepared for the lawyer's question, which was as inevitable as death. "Antoine watches Bordy and Noah argue in great hall. They struggle for gun. It fire and bullet whistle. Noah throw down gun, walk to door. Bordy bends down to pick up gun. She screams like eagle and gun snaps and Bordy falls."

Stan asked, "You saw this person?"

He leaned over Antoine and heard the whispered answer. "Mother of Noah shoot his real father."

Noah, at the foot of the bed and only able to pick up the odd word, heard the answer to Stan's question regarding the shooter as "Noah's real father."

Stan was alarmed by Antoine's deathbed declaration that the shooter was the "mother of Noah." Stan thought that Antoine was implicating Belle, Noah's adoptive mother, who would have had a good defence around protecting her son from being shot by Bordy. He spoke softly in Antoine's ear, "Was it Belle who shot Bordy?"

Antoine shook his head. "No."

Stan was relieved, but Antoine was speaking in riddles, so he persisted: "Then, old friend, who was this person?"

"Was spirit of Chilcotin."

"Is that a person?"

"Maybe."

At the foot of the bed, sitting cross-legged, Noah took a quick intake of breath and slowly exhaled. He had longed to know his real father since Bordy had started treating him like a hired hand. He dreamed that if his real father had been there he would have helped him. He had embraced Ta Chi's answer that his father was the Chilcotin, an ethereal being rather than an identifiable person. This thought had given him strength to fight on, to survive in the wilderness, and make the Chilcotin proud of him. Noah took Antoine's revelation as confirmation of his belief, for he had heard Antoine say that the killer was "Noah's real father," and that he was the "spirit of Chilcotin." Antoine was telling

Noah that his real father was a piece of the fabric of the land. The old man's final lesson was that there was a shadow line between reality and spirituality which was discovered by artists and deyens in each generation. Noah rose and went to the head of the bed. He knelt on the floor to the right of the dying man. Grasping Antoine's hand, he said, "I now understand the connection between the land and our people, between Ts'yl-os the mountain and Lendix'tcux the spirit, and between Ta Chi and nature.

Antoine could only smile, nod his head and faintly squeeze Noah's hand.

Stan the fact finder, lawyer and realist had heard Antoine, the old deyen, say that the mother of Noah—who had to have been Ta Chi—shot Bordy, who was Noah's biological father. Antoine had known this since the shooting, but like Belle had remained silent while Noah was on trial. Antoine for his own reasons hadn't come forward until he was on his deathbed. What those reasons were Stan could only surmise. Was Antoine protecting Ta Chi, or did he have faith in Hewitt's professional ability to successfully defend Noah, or was jail but another one of Antoine's tests for Noah? Reluctantly, Stan also thought that Antoine could be implicated in the shooting.

Antoine, the trickster, had protected the land by planting a false clue and had humbled Stan by telling him the truth about that. There was no reason to disbelieve him about who had shot Bordy and why. Antoine wasn't finished. His last words were barely audible.

"Spirit save Noah's life."

Antoine felt a lightness of being when he died, having spoken the whole truth to Noah, the deyen, and knowing that their sacred land would be watched over by Wawant'x, the new guardian.

Antoine's death barred the lawyer from asking Antoine how Ta Chi had obtained the rifle and where exactly Antoine had been in relation to Ta Chi at the time of the shooting.

Stan didn't tell Noah or anyone what he believed: that Bordy was Noah's biological father and that it was Ta Chi who shot Bordy and saved Noah's life. Perhaps Noah and Noah's children would read about it in Stan's memoirs, if they were ever published. There they would also read Stan's thoughts on how the younger generation survived the pressures and expectations that the older generations, both white and Native, placed on them.

Bruce F. Fraser, QC is a retired trial lawyer living in Vancouver who has practised law in the interior of BC representing Native clients. He is Chairman of the Board of Access Pro Bono Society of BC, which offers free legal advice and representation to persons of limited means. Bruce was on a survey team that surveyed the Homathko River in the 1950s. He is the winner of the Advocate's 2009 short story contest for "The Partner." Bruce and his wife, Gail, spend winters in Vancouver and summers on their ranch at Lac La Hache in the Cariboo Chilcotin.